Praise for MATCH

"There is nothing better than a murder mystery that keeps you guessing right up until the very end, and *Match* does exactly that. I loved the way Peele accurately captured the complexity and beauty of paired-exchange transplantation while keeping the reader thoroughly entertained."
—CAROLYN LIGHT, MPA, Executive Director of Transplant, UCSF and an altruistic paired exchange living-kidney-donor

"It is so refreshing and entertaining to read a mystery that accurately portrays kidney transplantation and the nuances of the paired-exchange process. A great read!"
—GARET HIL, founder of the National Kidney Registry

"When I first read *Cut*, I was hooked. Now, with her second book in this series, *Match*, I have renewed my Amy S. Peele fan club membership! *Match* will take you on a wild ride of friendship thrust into the world of donor transplants, politics, murder, and survival!"
—JANE UBELL-MEYER, founder of Bedside Reading

"In *Match* we are plunged back into the unshakable friendship of the characters we met in *Cut*. Peele offers a story that is straight from the heart and still manages to inform us about the world of organ transplantation. A warm and wonderful read."
—BETSY GRAZIANI FASBINDER, award-winning author of *Filling Her Shoes: A Memoir of an Inherited Family*

Praise for Amy S. Peele and her Award-Winning Medical Mystery *CUT*

"*CUT* follows an absorbing tale, through realistic and medically accurate transplant procedures, down a path of mystery, intrigue, and danger, from medical rounds to organ procurement organizations to surgical operating rooms; from San Francisco, to Miami, to Chicago. And what otherwise seemed to be a coincidence, turns out to be a murderous conspiracy. A page turner to the end!"

—KENNETH MORITSUGU, MD, MPH, FACPM,
former Surgeon General of the United States,
First International Transplantation Ambassador

"*CUT* is a suspenseful mystery whose story is an engaging way to shed light on the enormously challenging and complicated system of organ donation and distribution in our country."

—SUSAN HILDRETH, former Director of the Institute of
Museum and Library Services Currently Professor of
Practice, University of Washington Information School

"With *CUT*, Amy Peele has entered the medical mystery arena with a home run. When a couple of amateur sleuths delve into the world of organ transplantation, the result is a breath-taking race against time to ensure the integrity of the national system. Travel with these two daring ladies as they seek justice in a gripping nonstop ride that you can't put down. A realistic medical thriller!"

—MARK AEDER, MD, Transplant Surgeon, University
Hospitals, Cleveland Medical Center Cleveland, Ohio

"A terrific read. True to life in terms of the medical descriptions. Fortunately, the theme is pure fantasy but great entertainment."

—DR. NANCY ASCHER, professor of Surgery, UCSF

"A patient awaiting organ transplantation faces death if an organ isn't available in time. Ms. Peele's plot of her exciting novel is based upon a nefarious approach by a desperate patient to get an organ. While enjoying the ride, the reader should keep in mind how desperate the real-world situation is for these patients in need."

—JOHN PAUL ROBERTS, professor of Surgery, UCSF

"Amy Peele combines her vast medical knowledge with a love of writing to create something new: a murder mystery with a purpose. The diabolical characters will keep you guessing, and the message about the importance of organ donation may save lives."

—DEBRA ENGLE, best-selling author of *The Only Little Prayer You Need*

"*CUT* is the kind of murder mystery that can be eaten like candy. A little suspense, a little humor, a little romance, and a double scoop of friendship between the two sassy main characters. A fun read and a great escape."

—BETSY GRAZIANI FASBINDER, author of *Fire & Water* and *Filling Her Shoes*

Match

A Medical

Murder Mystery

Amy S. Peele

SHE WRITES PRESS

Published 2021
Printed in the United States of America
Print ISBN: 978-1-64742-018-5
E-ISBN: 978-1-64742-019-2

Library of Congress Control Number: 2020914023

For information, address:
She Writes Press
1569 Solano Ave #546
Berkeley, CA 94707

Interior design by Tabitha Lahr

She Writes Press is a division of SparkPoint Studio, LLC.

Chapter 1

Tightly squeezing Kayla's nostrils closed, the hooded figure poured the last of the second glass of opioid-laced milk down her throat and threw the cup across the floor of the abandoned basement. Kayla slumped forward, hands tied behind the chair, her body colliding with the cement floor. Blood oozed from her head. Ignoring the non-stop buzzing of her cell phone, the assailant shuffled up the basement stairs and outside.

Driving far away from the scene, Kayla's captor ripped off latex gloves and tossed them out the window.

• • •

Sarah Golden slammed her fist down on her desk. This was the tenth time she had left a message for Kayla in the past hour. She checked the time: 10:30 p.m. "Another exciting Saturday night for me," she muttered. It was far too late to be at her office on a weekend, but it was the only time she could get her desk work done at the transplant center without countless interruptions and meetings.

She shut down her computer and left her office in an angry huff. When she got home, Sarah poured herself a glass of merlot and soaked in her hot tub. *At least I have Sunday dinner with Jackie and Laura to look forward to,* she thought.

. . .

Early Sunday night, Sarah was heading out of her San Francisco apartment when her cell phone rang. She glanced at the caller ID and saw that it was her boss, Dr. Bower, the chief of the San Francisco Global Organ Transplant Institute. "Hi, Dr. Bower. What's up?"

"Hi, Sarah. I just received a disturbing call from Dr. Santos, at the Miami International Transplant Institute, about Kayla, our living-donor coordinator." Dr. Bower seemed to be struggling to get the words out; Sarah rarely heard him sound so shaken.

"What happened? I know she was checking on her grandmother in Miami. She's been ill for a long time."

Dr. Bower continued, "She was brought into the Miami ER yesterday with an opioid overdose and was declared brain-dead. Santos just transplanted her liver and both of her kidneys into recipients."

Sarah's knees buckled under her, and she collapsed onto the couch in her living room. "Oh my God, I can't believe this! I knew we were getting more organs from the opioid crisis, but I never thought it would be from one of our own."

"Dr. Santos told me the local police are investigating the case as a possible homicide and will contact us as soon as they know anything more. I never pegged Kayla as someone who'd be into drugs. Did you?" Dr. Bower asked.

"Not in a million years. It doesn't mix with how I experienced her, but I only knew her over the last year."

Sarah also couldn't help remembering that when she had met Kayla a year earlier, Kayla had made it clear that she thought of Sarah as just another manager who'd quit in a couple of years, and that it would be best if Sarah just left her alone to do her job. And she wasn't all that charming about it either. "I worked with her for over fifteen years and never saw any signs of drug addiction. I guess you just never know. Anyway, I gave Santos your contact info for the Miami PD, so you'll be hearing from a detective. You'll need to call an all-staff meeting first thing in the morning. Just tell them she died—no other details until we hear from the Miami PD. And you'll need to reassign her caseload so her patients don't get lost in the shuffle," Dr. Bower directed.

Miami. Couldn't it be anywhere but there? Sarah thought.

"Shit!" she said aloud, before she could stop herself.

"What is it?" Dr. Bower asked.

"I'm sorry, Dr. Bower." *Get it together, Golden*, she commanded herself. "Yes, I'll call a staff meeting and reassign her cases first thing. Keep me posted."

Dr. Bower went on, "Kayla was a real workhorse, and very clinically astute; she got our living-kidney-donor program off the ground. I know the coordinators never got along with her, but the docs will miss her. This is a huge loss for our program and our patients. I'm sorry to have to give you such bad news. You okay?"

"I've never encountered this type of situation before, but I'm okay. I'll see you tomorrow and let you know how the staff meeting goes. Good night, Dr. Bower."

"Good night, Sarah."

When Sarah felt as if she could finally stand again, she grabbed her car keys, locked her apartment door, and headed downstairs. She hopped into her beaten-up Toyota sedan and started driving in a daze toward the Golden Gate Bridge.

Sarah hadn't been to Jackie's house for dinner in over a year. A stay-at-home mom, Jackie usually preferred to spend her free time taking getaways to the city and they'd usually go out to eat and sometimes to a local comedy show. But tonight, Jackie had invited her to come for a Sunday supper in Marin with her wife, Laura, while their eight-year-old son, Wyatt, was at his friends' house. Based on her last conversation with Jackie, Sarah knew something was up with Wyatt's health, but Jackie insisted they discuss all the details in person. *I hope nothing is seriously wrong with him. I don't think I could take it if something happens with Wyatt,* Sarah thought as she drove.

When she pulled into Jackie and Laura's San Rafael driveway and got out of her car, the yelling coming from inside the house stopped her in her tracks. She recognized Jackie's voice immediately: "You're never home! You have no idea what it's like to run this household and take care of Wyatt now that he's sick."

"You're the one who wanted to be the stay-at-home mom, Jackie. I would never have agreed if I had known you would turn into a raging bitch!" Laura yelled.

Sarah waited for a moment, then knocked and walked into the cozy two-story bungalow.

"Hi, guys. I'm here, and I have fancy wine." She had been planning to share the news about Kayla, but now clearly wasn't a good time.

Jackie hugged her and said, "That wine won't touch what we've got going on here. I have rum for me and gin for you, my friend."

Laura peeked out of the kitchen and said, "Hey, Sarah, we're just having one of our usual Sunday 'swear and it's not fair' fests. What can I get you?"

"A martini sounds wonderful. Something smells good." Sarah handed Jackie the wine.

"I'll make the drinks. Laura, what would you like?" Jackie asked coldly.

"I'll be fine with some of Sarah's wine. Hey, is that the wine you and Handsome bought from Cline?"

"Gee, Laura, thanks for bringing that up as soon as I walk in the door."

"I didn't know you were still sensitive. You've never been one for happily ever after; I just figured this was one more for the road," Laura said, as she walked back into the kitchen.

Sarah raised her eyebrows at Jackie. Sarah had fallen for the guy they called Officer Handsome, a Miami detective, a year earlier. They had tried to make their long-distance relationship work, but it had ended six months ago, over the phone.

"I think we should have a cocktail out in the backyard and forget my wife just said that." Jackie prepared the drinks and motioned for Sarah to follow her. Once they were seated at the patio table, Jackie raised her glass. "Sorry Laura is so mean. I'm still paying for our escapades from last year, even though she said she forgave me. Not!"

Sarah took a large sip of her martini, "I wish it could have worked out, really. I have bad karma when it comes to relationships. What tanker crawled up her ass, anyway?"

Jackie laughed, "Going big, Golden. A tanker? Wow, did you see one under the Golden Gate Bridge on your way over?"

"Matter of fact, I saw three—two coming in and one heading out to sea. I bet if we really wanted to disappear, we could get on one of those babies as ship nurses and get the hell out of here forever." Sarah took another long sip of her cocktail and felt her shoulders begin to drop from around her ears. Then she looked more closely at her best friend's eyes and noticed the dark circles under them. "What's going on, Jack? Is Wyatt all right?"

"Not really. We had an appointment with a pediatric nephrologist, and it looks like his kidney disease is accelerating.

Laura and I need your advice and help. It seems highly likely he'll have to go on dialysis and eventually need a kidney transplant. Finally, your friendship will pay off after I met you all those years ago in nursing school."

Sarah knew Jackie was trying to lighten the exchange between them, but all she could see was the sadness in her friend's eyes. "Holy shit. Have you gotten a second opinion?"

"That was what yesterday was about. So, yes—and it was the same prognosis."

Laura opened the sliding glass doors that connected the patio to the dining area and said, "Dinner's ready. I can see Jackie is bringing you up to speed about Wyatt. Let's eat, I made my famous chicken cacciatore."

The rich, garlicky aroma emanating from the kitchen made Sarah's mouth water. Even in times of crisis, her appetite never failed her. Laura placed the chicken and a basket of garlic bread on the table and after they had all served themselves, asked, "How much do you know, Sarah?" She paused and took a bite of her chicken. "This may be my best yet."

"I know that Wyatt may have to go on dialysis and possibly get a transplant. Which, by the way, doesn't need to be the order of things. Wyatt can avoid the whole dialysis thing if we manage his care well." Sarah sampled her chicken. "Wow, this *is* delicious." Then she added, "Have you guys heard of a pre-emptive transplant?"

Laura cleared her throat. "I went to medical school, Sarah. I know what it is, and I don't mean to be rude, but I'm a doctor and you're a nurse, as is my wife."

Sarah saw a vein in Jackie's neck began to bulge. Trying to resist the urge to yell herself, Sarah spoke slowly: "Laura, you haven't practiced medicine or surgery since you graduated. No assistant medical examiner has a clue about how a transplant program works, so I think I may know just a little more than you do about the specifics here."

She took a deep breath, then continued, "I think, for the sake of Wyatt, we should all try to work together. But I need to tell you both that I'm pretty freaked out right now. Before I left my apartment, I got a call from Bower. One of our coordinators overdosed on opioids and was declared brain-dead. They donated her organs in Miami."

"That's horrible!" Laura said. "No wonder you're freaked out. Are you okay to stay to talk about Wyatt's case? We can pick this up another time if you're distracted."

"No, no, I want to stay. And I want to help any way I can. We definitely need to discuss Wyatt's case. The news just took me aback."

Laura continued, "I want to take his completed workup to the transplant institute in Miami. I'm sure you're aware they're the best pediatric kidney program in the country. Your team came in second."

Sarah just shook her head and looked over at Jackie, who was finishing her cocktail. "Our results are the same as Miami's, Laura. Their lead pediatric kidney transplant surgeon trained with us. I think I'd know who has the best results. I don't know why you'd want to make Wyatt leave his hometown and fly across the country for practically the same care."

Jackie stood up. "Just for the record, I am not in support of Wyatt going anywhere else but your place, but my wife is insisting we have two different programs evaluate him," she said, as she poured herself a second drink.

"I can have our pediatric nurse practitioner, Mary, call you first thing tomorrow so we can get you both typed and cross-matched to see if either one of you is a good match. I'm assuming you'd both want to be considered as possible living kidney donors," Sarah offered.

"Of course we would. Since Laura carried Wyatt, I'm guessing she'd be the best match, but if I am, you know I'm there, Sarah," Jackie said.

"Have either of you heard of a paired exchange?" Sarah asked.

Laura answered, "Let's say I am a healthy donor but don't match Wyatt, then I would give my kidney to a different person who matched my kidney and their living donor would give their kidney to Wyatt."

"I couldn't have explained it better myself. We do those types of transplants all the time. I think we'll want you both to come to the transplant institute to get your and Wyatt's blood drawn, and then we can go from there. I'll have Mary call Jackie, as I'm guessing she'll be doing the daily management."

"Well, one of us has to work to pay the bills, so, yes, Jackie will be the primary point person." Sarah watched Jackie wince with her wife's nasty barb. "However, we'll be making all of Wyatt's decisions together. I'm guessing Jackie's weight will prohibit her from being considered as a donor, so we won't need to get her cross-matched."

Sarah glanced at Jackie and saw her turned-down mouth. *I can't believe how condescending Laura is to Jackie*, she thought. *How long has this been going on?* Jackie might have been over-weight, but her BMI was likely borderline, which meant she could still be a donor candidate. Sarah knew that Jackie was healthy; she just didn't favor exercise. But this wasn't the time or place for Sarah to address this issue. Mary would work with the entire family.

The front door slammed, and Wyatt walked into the kitchen, "Aunt Sarah!" He ran into Sarah's arms and gave her a big hug. "Are you spending the night?"

"Not this time, you have school in the morning and I have to work."

As Sarah brushed Wyatt's brown hair back from his forehead, she could see that his color was pale and his eight-year-old-body was thinner than she remembered. "You're getting so tall, buddy. I bet you're making all the baskets on your basketball team."

"Nope, my moms made me quit, I'm bruising too easy." Wyatt's sweet face melted Sarah's heart.

When Jackie went over to give Wyatt a hug an open bag of Reese's Pieces fell out of his pocket and spilled all over the floor. "Wyatt! You know you can't eat peanut butter and chocolate. We've gone over this with you before." Jackie firmly stated.

"How much did you eat?" Laura took him by his shoulders, looking him directly in his eyes.

"I ate a couple handfuls, like the rest of my friends. You're making a big deal over nothing." Wyatt snapped back.

Sarah's eyes widened, she hadn't seen this side of Wyatt before.

"That candy is high in phosphorus and potassium, and your kidneys can't get rid of it. It builds up in your blood." Laura declared.

"Whatever." Wyatt replied flippantly looking away from Laura.

"No, not whatever. That candy can make your heart beat really fast, and we might not be able to slow it down. Then we'd have to take you to the emergency room."

"Why can't I be like a regular kid? This sucks." He started up the stairs. Sarah watched Wyatt, his head hanging low. "Bye, Aunt Sarah," he mumbled.

Laura followed him.

Sarah turned to Jackie, "Looks like our sweet boy is disappearing fast."

"He's still sweet sometimes. Our house is not a fun place to be right now. Laura is gone before he wakes up and gets home after he's in bed. It's been a constant battle watching what he eats and drinks."

"I'm sure it's no fun being the police mom all the time." Sarah said as she stood up and walked toward the front door, Jackie followed her.

"I'm so sorry for Laura's behavior. She's been impossible since this whole thing with Wyatt started and she got her promotion. It's just too much. She's taking out her anger on me." Jackie sighed.

"I'm always here for you, Jack." Sarah gave her friend a long hug. "We'll get through this together. We've survived worse things and lived to tell the tale. Not everyone can talk their way out of a Mexican jail, right?"

Jackie laughed. "We were much younger and prettier back then, but, yes, we survived."

Sarah reached over and hugged Jackie again. "I love you."

"I love you too my friend. Drive safe." Jackie walked back into the house.

As Sarah drove back over the bridge, she started to tear up thinking about Wyatt. He was the closest thing she would ever have to a son. She'd help Jackie get him back to his healthy, fun-kid self.

She knew Jackie and Laura had a solid relationship; she'd been in their lives since they'd met, nine years earlier. There were times when Sarah and Jackie's annual escapades had pushed Laura to her limit. It was nice that Jackie had a family to come home to—something Sarah had allowed herself to hope for when things had been going well with her and Handsome, but that now seemed like a distant dream.

She thought about when Handsome had come out to see her the first time and booked a hotel room. Courteously, he had not assumed he would stay with her, but he'd said, "I'll wait as long as I need to, Sarah Golden. I haven't met anyone I felt this strongly about in a long time."

"Me neither," Sarah had responded. "It's been a very long time for me too."

When Handsome kissed her that night, her whole body had tingled, and before long they were staying regularly at each other's places, hers in San Francisco and his in Miami.

She met his sister and her sons, whose dad had left them when the boys were very young. Handsome was their surrogate father, and that was eventually the deal breaker between them. Sarah was with Handsome in San Francisco when his sister called in hysterics. She watched his face, and when he hung up, his sad eyes met Sarah's. "I have to leave tonight. My nephew ran away yesterday; they found him, but my sister can't work full-time and parent both those boys alone without my help. I'm so sorry, honey."

When he said that, something shifted inside Sarah. "I thought you had that interview with the SF police department this week."

Handsome held Sarah's face with both hands and gazed into her eyes. "I'll have to reschedule it. I need to get home and settle things down and then come back out. You know I love you—just give me a little more time."

She drove him to the airport that night and, after their long embrace, watched him walk through the doors. She loved him too, and her gut told her to be patient, but her brain said this wasn't going to work out. He would never be able to relocate to San Francisco under these circumstances, and she wasn't willing to move to Miami. Jackie, Laura, and Wyatt were family. She couldn't leave them.

There were many San Francisco/Miami phone calls after that last departure. The final time, she called him to invite him to a transplant gala. "Hello, boyfriend. I just bought a very sexy dress, and all I need is a date. You busy next Saturday? I'll make it worth your while," she said, picturing how good he would look in a tuxedo.

"That's the best offer I've gotten in a long time, but I promised the boys I'd take them away for a three-day fishing trip so my sister can get some time off. I'm so sorry. How about I fly out the weekend after and take you to a nice restaurant to make it up to you?"

Sarah's stomach sank. *This is how it's always going to be, isn't it? I'm always going to be competing with his nephews,* she thought.

"Hello, Sarah, are you there?" Handsome asked.

"I'm here. Of course, I understand—you can't bail on them and your sister. You have responsibilities that will keep you in Miami for a long time. I think we need to take a break until the boys graduate from high school in three years and then see if we still have something. I guess our timing was off." Tears welled up in her eyes.

"Come on, Sarah—you know we have something here. I'm just asking you to be patient. I love you," Handsome pleaded.

"You know I care deeply for you, but your nephews really need you now, and it's not a job you can do long-distance. Let's be honest. Better we end things amicably before resentment takes over and it gets ugly. You're doing the right thing. I need a break, so let's agree not to talk for a while. I have to go now."

Sarah hung up, cupped her hands over her face, and started to sob. She could see Handsome calling her back as she turned off her phone.

• • •

The morning after her dinner at Jackie and Laura's, Sarah called the entire kidney staff together in the transplant auditorium. Her heart beat rapidly and her throat felt dry as she approached the lectern and said, "Good morning team." She took a drink of water, cleared her throat, and continued, "I know you're all busy, but I needed to share that, sadly, one of our team members, Kayla Newman, passed away. Dr. Bower was notified yesterday."

Sarah took another drink of water and scanned the group, many of whom were scrolling through their phones, not even glancing up toward the front of the room. A few were talking in the back row and seemed to be chuckling. Sarah knew Kayla hadn't been close to many staff, including her—but still, she would have thought the death of a teammate would upset some of them. She had taken Dr. Bower's words to heart and decided not to tell everyone just yet about how Kayla had died or that she was an organ donor.

"I will be meeting with the living-donor-kidney team after this to reassign her cases so that our patients and their families continue to get the best care we can provide. Any questions?"

One of the younger coordinators stood up. "Where can we send a condolence card? Kayla was very kind to me; she just finished training me before she went to visit her grandmother."

"I don't have a next-of-kin contact yet, but I'll let you know when I find out. Thanks for coming everyone. If anyone has any other questions, please come see me in my office."

As Sarah walked past some of the staff, she overheard a few coordinators talking: "Kayla was so mean to everyone. She got that one nurse fired. I hope they have the funeral in Miami; at least her grandmother will be there."

The other responded, "If it's here, they'll probably make us go. Remember what she did to that poor IT guy, Ned? He was in tears after she humiliated him in front of the whole team. She always seemed mad at someone."

Sarah slowed down, pretending to check her phone as they walked past her. Before they were out of earshot, one of them said, "Let's go get a cup of coffee before we go back to the coal mine." They all laughed and disappeared from sight. Sarah paused. She had no idea just how much Kayla was disliked. *People can sure hold a grudge. But still, the death of a teammate should have stirred at least a look up from a Twitter scroll.*

She stopped in the cafeteria for a cup of coffee and returned to her office, where she paged Mary to get her going on Wyatt's case. The voicemail light on her desk phone was blinking, and she listened as woman's voice came through: "Hello, this is Detective Lupe Campos from the Miami Police Department. I need you to call me as soon as possible regarding the death of Kayla Newman." The detective left Sarah her phone number, then hung up.

It's only Monday morning, and I have a dead coordinator, a Miami detective is calling me, my best friend's marriage is on the rocks, and a sick kid on my hands. Let's hope it gets better from here.

Chapter 2

Jackie replayed parts of the prior evening in her head. After Sarah left, Jackie screamed at Laura about how she'd treated Sarah, and about the Handsome comments. Laura barked back at Jackie that she needed to step up to the plate and not complain about handling the home front. There was some door slamming, after which Jackie spent a rough night on the couch in the den and didn't hear Laura when she left early for work. After Laura had gotten her promotion several months earlier, they had agreed it was probably safer for her not to drive home late, just to turn around and drive back five or six hours later. Several of their friends in the city offered Laura a place to stay.

After Jackie took Wyatt to school, she went home and called Sarah.

Sarah answered right away. "Is Laura still alive?"

"Who gives a shit, really? I told her to stay in the city for the next couple nights. We had a whopper of a fight last night, worst ever." Jackie remarked.

"Did it top the one you had after Laura's mom met you for the first time?" Sarah asked.

"Oh, that was pleasant, when her mom declared in front of me that if Laura had to be gay why didn't she at least pick a woman with class and a nice body? In hindsight, it may have been better if Laura came out first and then introduced me into the picture later. We were both so smitten with each other back then we got over that fight quickly. Her mother on the other hand, has made it crystal clear she only tolerates me so she can have access to Wyatt and Laura. Thankfully, she only comes to visit when you and I go on our annual funfests."

"At least she can watch Wyatt so Laura can still work, otherwise I don't think we get to go away for a week." Sarah said.

"That's true. Listen, I'm so sorry for the way she spoke to you last night. She's never acted like that before. I think she needs to take a few days off, but she refuses. I slept on the couch last night, and I'm moving all my stuff into the den today. I need a little distance right now."

Sarah jumped in: "She's clearly under a lot of stress, and who knows what else is going on with her at work? I have to say, the low blow about your weight was really uncalled for. I'm sorry you have to go through this right now. By the way, I did page Mary, so she may come by while we're talking."

"I need to understand the whole living donor thing." Jackie put her phone on speaker, placed it on the kitchen table, and pulled out leftovers to pick at while they talked.

"I can't believe Laura is insisting on going to Miami. I thought I was done with that place. The only fond memories I have are of Biker Bob and that rum speakeasy he took me to last year. He was an unexpected gift."

"Who would have thunk you and a huge biker dude would have bonded on a Harley in search of a gang member? That guy could just as easily have taken you out on a dark road and shot your ass." Sarah started to laugh.

Jackie smiled as she recounted the first time she'd ever seen him, when he'd entered the scummy Miami biker bar and sat at her booth, tattooed biceps the size of melons. If it hadn't been for him, they would never have cracked the case.

"Laura told me last night that she already made some preliminary arrangements at the Miami International Transplant Institute for all three of us, and—get this—she demanded I tell you to get Wyatt worked up immediately so we can move his case as quickly as possible. I need to change the subject before I explode. How did your staff meeting go this morning? Lots of Kleenex?"

"It was weird. The staff barely reacted. I overheard a few of the seasoned coordinators say some harsh things about Kayla. She didn't seem to have any close friends at work, which is odd, since she was here for fifteen years. I think she had maybe one friend."

"Did she have a boyfriend?" Jackie asked.

"She brought a few different gals to our annual holiday party over the years, but I have no idea about her social life. As much as she worked, I'm impressed she had one at all."

"Doesn't sound like too many folks will miss her." Jackie finished her leftovers and put the plate in the dishwasher.

"Actually, it will be hard to replace Kayla; she knew how to get things done. I received a voice mail from a Miami detective named Lupe Campos asking me to call her about Kayla's death. I have no idea what I can and can't say; after we talk to Mary, I have to go to the medical center attorney's office. Here's Mary. I emailed her a little background on you, Laura, and Wyatt last night when I got home. Mind if I put you on speakerphone, Jackie?"

"No problem. I have a pen and paper so I can take notes." Jackie sat down at her kitchen table. "I'm ready. Hi, Mary."

"Hi, Jackie. Nice to meet you over the phone. Sarah sent me an email about you and your wife. I understand you have an eight-year-old son, Wyatt, who may need a preemptive kidney transplant. I don't know much more than that, so will you bring me up to speed?"

Jackie began, "Wyatt's usually an easy-going kid, but he's acting out a little with the food and fluid restrictions."

"That's pretty normal." Mary interjected.

"About five months ago, he started to get tired after school, which wasn't normal for him. He always seemed to have to go to the bathroom, but peed only small amounts. I took him to our pediatrician, who, after running a few tests, informed me that his blood pressure was high and that he had a urinary tract infection again. He's had several over the past few months. Sadly, both of these things have damaged Wyatt's kidneys and he doesn't have much reserve left in either of them."

Mary chimed in, "I'm sorry to hear this, Jackie. Our team has experienced this clinical scenario before, and I know we can help you and your family get Wyatt the care he needs."

"Mary. You sound way too nice to be working for Sarah. Where has she been hiding you?"

Mary laughed. "We're so lucky to have Sarah here; she's whipping this place into shape. It's long overdue." She continued, "We take care of the entire family, so it's important for us to have an introductory meeting with your family and our team. Sarah said you want Wyatt to get a preemptive kidney transplant, and that you and your wife are possible living donors—that's great."

Jackie recalled Laura's comment about her weight. "I'd like to be considered as a possible donor, Mary. I'm a full-figured gal, very healthy. I do chair yoga twice a week, so I'm flexible and mostly muscle. My BMI may be on the high side, though—would that preclude me from being tested?"

Mary responded, "I wish I could do yoga twice a week. We've had a lot of great donors who are very healthy and on the high end of their BMI. We'll figure it all out when you come visit. When do you think you can bring Wyatt?"

Smiling from Mary's reply, Jackie said, "Wyatt and I can come anytime this week. Laura is a bit more difficult to pin down, as she's an assistant medical examiner. Do you need all three of us there at the same time?"

"Our first meeting needs to be with all three of you, but we can arrange an early-morning meeting so that Laura can get to work afterward. Tomorrow is Tuesday; if you think you can all come in that soon, I'll arrange for our team to be here around eight a.m."

"Perfect. We'll see you tomorrow bright and early." *We'll get this workup done in no time*, Jackie thought, and took a long, deep breath for the first time in quite a while.

"I look forward to meeting you, Laura, and Wyatt." Mary replied.

After Jackie hung up, she did some chair yoga, which helped calm her down and stretch. She decided to go to Wyatt's school a little early so she could let the principal and teacher know that he'd be missing some school and give them some information about his condition. He had enough kidney function left that his lifestyle wasn't completely changed, but they did need to watch how much fluid he drank and limit his salt intake. He was starting to get tired, so sports were out for a little while, until he got more energy.

Jackie picked up a framed photo of the three of them, unable to reconcile the smiling image with the fact that she and Laura were now at such odds. One thing she knew for sure, though, was that they both loved Wyatt and would do whatever it took to get him well again.

Chapter 3

Sarah dialed the number to the Miami precinct from memory, then realized it was because she had called Handsome there so many times. Another tug at her heart, a reminder of what was no more.

"Miami Police Department, Officer Mullens speaking."

"May I speak with Detective Campos?"

"We have two Detective Camposes here. Which one do you want?"

"Lupe Campos, please."

"Who's calling?"

Hoping Mullens wouldn't remember her, she lowered her voice and blurted out, "Sarah Bower," thinking, *Who gives a shit? I hate this end-of-relationship stuff.* The call was transferred.

"Lupe Campos speaking."

"This is Sarah Golden, from the San Francisco Global Transplant Institute. You left me a message to contact you regarding one of our employees, Kayla Newman."

Campos said, "Yes. I called about our active homicide investigation on Kayla. Until we're able to gather all the information, we need to investigate this as a possible murder," Campos responded.

"I'm no detective, but I think if someone gave her the drugs, they're likely on the loose in Miami, not San Francisco," Sarah said.

Campos continued, "These situations can be very difficult to understand. There are a few things I'd like to ask you, Sarah. I'll need some background on Kayla. I hope that with your cooperation and that of your staff, we can close this investigation quickly. What can you tell me about Kayla? How long did she work with your program, and what type of employee was she?"

"I've been advised by Legal here at the medical center that I can tell you how long Kayla worked for us, which was fifteen years. You'll need to file a formal request with Legal to obtain any other specific information about her employment records."

"That won't be a problem. An Inspector Davidson from SFPD is preparing some documents and will be contacting you and your legal office today. She'll need to interview your entire staff regarding anything they know about Kayla both inside and outside work. Once we review the interviews, we'll go from there. Why do you think someone would want to kill Kayla?"

Sarah thought for a moment. "I honestly have no idea, Detective. I joined this team over a year ago, and I didn't know her all that well. I will say that the few dealings I had with her were negative and that she was not well loved by the staff, as far as I can tell. But I'm not even supposed to tell you this. Also, did I hear you right? You're sending Inspector Davidson over here to interview all our staff? We're one of the biggest kidney transplant programs in the country, so our day-to-day job is to get folks transplanted. Is there any other way you can expedite your investigation?" Sarah let out a sigh.

"Procedure is procedure, Sarah. It might help if you could share anything else you know. We're up to our asses in deaths from the opioid epidemic, if you haven't heard about it in your part of the world."

"Detective, we get almost thirty percent of our organs from opioid overdoses so, yes, we're well aware of the epidemic. I just never thought it would happen to one of our own. Thankfully, they were able to use her organs after she was declared brain-dead. Anyway, it sounds like we're both busy. I hope you and your team can get this case solved, and I'll do what I can to help on my end."

"If you could give your team, which will include anyone and everyone who works with kidney transplant—the doctors, nurses, support staff, and IT—a heads-up about the interviews, that would help. The faster Davidson can get in and out of your program, the faster we'll get to the bottom of this."

"I can tell you that the doctors won't have time for any interviews; they're either with patients or in surgery." *Not to mention there's no way they'll talk to any detective in general,* Sarah added silently.

"If they don't comply with our requests, we'll have to summon them so, either way, they'll meet with Davidson. One last question: Have you ever heard of someone by the name of Zuzu?"

"I've never heard that name except in that Christmas movie. Why?"

"Seems Kayla had a Cuban girlfriend who went by Zuzu in Miami, and we think she was the last person to see Kayla alive. Short spitfire of a gal, rides a motorcycle."

"I told you, I didn't know Kayla well at all. If I hear Zuzu's name bandied about, I'll let you know." Sarah let out a chuckle.

"Thanks. Anything will help."

"I really need to go now, but I do have one last question for you, Detective: Do you know a Detective Rodney Strong?" Sarah asked. It was Handsome's proper name.

"I don't just know him—he's my partner. Why?"

"Oops, my beeper's going off. I'm sure we'll be in touch." Sarah hung up the phone and huffed, "Oh, shit!"

Chapter 4

The night before, Jackie had sat down with Wyatt to explain why they would be meeting with Sarah and her team to talk about a possible kidney transplant. After Jackie showed Wyatt what his kidneys looked like in a simple anatomical book for children, he understood what the kidneys did and why it was important for him to have a healthy one. Laura and Jackie had decided not to teach him about dialysis unless it was necessary.

The next morning, they met Laura in the lobby of the transplant institute and took the elevator up to the fourth floor. Mary greeted them in front of the clinic, then knelt down to Wyatt's eye level and said, "Hello, Wyatt. I'm Mary. I'm a nurse practitioner, and I'm going to be with you and your moms today. Do you know why you're here?"

Wyatt looked up toward Jackie and Laura and said, "I think so: My kidneys are sick, and I need a new one."

Mary, still kneeling, smiled. "Ten points for Gryffindor!"

Wyatt started to laugh. "How did you know I was a Gryffindor?"

Mary glanced up at Jackie, then continued, in her gentle voice, "Your mom told me you love Harry Potter. I do too. You're going to meet our team now and ask them any questions you have, and then I'm going to show you our playroom and where our kids go when they get their transplants. We even have some cool Harry Potter toys and *Star Trek* games. Do you like *Star Trek*?"

"I have a video game of it."

Jackie smiled, thinking, *Who wouldn't be comfortable with Mary? She looks like a tiny version of Glinda, the good witch from* The Wizard of Oz.

Everyone moved into the conference room, where Dr. Bower and Sarah were sitting with the rest of the team: a social worker, a financial counselor, and another nurse. When Wyatt saw Sarah, he ran into her arms and jumped onto her lap, then looked around the room as he said, "Hi, Aunt Sarah. Is that guy your boss?"

Before Sarah could answer, Dr. Bower smiled. "No, I think Sarah is *my* boss. You must be Wyatt." Dr. Bower extended his hand to shake Wyatt's.

"Hi, Dr. Bower, my mom is a doctor too." Wyatt pointed at Laura.

Dr. Bower stood up and shook Laura's hand, then Jackie's. "I know both your moms."

"Cool," Wyatt responded.

Mary redirected everyone to the front of the room and took charge of the meeting.

"Wyatt understands that his kidneys aren't working like they should and that he will need a new, healthy one. I'm going to review the living-donor options briefly, then take Wyatt on a tour of our pediatric playroom and show him where we take care of children when they get a kidney transplant."

Laura spoke up: "We discussed the possibility of either Jackie or me being a donor and that we need to get our blood drawn today to see if one of us is a match. Just to be clear, I'm the one who carried Wyatt, not Jackie, so I'm not sure if she'll be anywhere close to a match. I think we should limit our discussion to that, and when you take him on the tour, we can discuss the other living-donor options."

"Sounds reasonable, Laura." Mary played a short video geared specifically to kids, about a little boy who needed a kidney transplant. After the video, she asked if Wyatt had any questions.

"Nope. My moms already showed me lots of the pictures that were in the video. I'd like to go to the playroom."

Mary walked over to Wyatt. "Let's go, young man. We'll be back in about an hour. Does Wyatt have a fluid restriction? We may stop for a drink if it's okay, Moms."

Jackie responded, "Yes, he gets four cups of fluid a day, and he's only had half a cup of milk in his oatmeal, so he can certainly have half a cup of something to drink."

"Good. Then we'll see you all soon. Please feel free to page me if you need me. Ready to go, Wyatt?"

Wyatt nodded and took Mary's hand. "Will Aunt Sarah be coming, too?"

"No, buddy, I'm going to stay here with your moms," Sarah said, "but I'll see you soon. Have fun."

After Mary and Wyatt left, Dr. Bower addressed Laura and Jackie. "I have a case, so I thought I'd see if you have any questions for me before I leave."

Laura jumped in: "Thanks for taking my call this morning about introducing me to Dr. Santos at the Miami International Transplant Institute. I know you understand we want to see two programs and then make the best decision for Wyatt. Just how fast can you expedite his work-up?"

She didn't tell me she called Bower, Jackie thought. *I can see she's using her "I'm a doctor" card again.*

Jackie exhaled loudly through her nose and glared at Laura.

Sarah responded, "We can do most of the tests today while he's here. We were also planning to draw blood from both of you and run the tissue typing to see if either one of you is a match. If neither of you is a match, are you open to a paired exchange?"

Jackie looked at the other folks at the table and back at Sarah, who paused. "I'm sorry—I neglected to introduce the other two people. This is Janet, our living-donor nurse, who works up the donors for the pediatric cases; Roger, our pediatric social worker; and Nancy, our financial counselor, who will make sure everything is authorized—"

Laura interrupted, "My insurance will cover everything and then some; I work for the city of San Francisco. I will need to get my blood drawn and then head to work. Jackie can stay with Wyatt, meet with you folks, and fill out any forms. I would consider a paired exchange as long as it can be done in a timely manner. I believe everyone knows that we absolutely do *not* want Wyatt going on dialysis or getting a dialysis access placed in his arm."

Jackie knew she had to keep her frustration about Laura's blunt, condescending approach in check in front of the team, but doing that was getting more challenging by the minute. *Take a deep breath*, she told herself.

Janet began, "We use an online living-donor-history assessment so be sure that you input all your medical information accurately. The sooner you can get that done, the more quickly we can move to get your blood tested for suitability with Wyatt's. All our living donors see our independent living-donor advocate, who's a social worker. She makes sure that each donor is doing it of their own free will and understands the complications. If she has any cause for concern, she'll recommend that the donor be interviewed by Dr. Fowler, our consulting psychiatrist. Once we have all your blood results, either Mary or I will call you and let you know, and we can proceed from there. Who should we call, you or Jackie?"

Jackie chimed in, "Laura is usually doing an autopsy or in a meeting, so I'll be the main contact. I'll make sure you have all my information." Jackie looked at Laura and added, "I'm sure you have to get to work, honey, I'll let you go with Janet."

Sarah stood up as Laura was leaving. "If neither one of you are a good match for Wyatt, I plan to get tissue typed."

Laura locked eyes with Sarah. "I appreciate your generosity, Sarah, but I'm not comfortable with that option right now. I think it best if we keep all this on a professional level. Dr. Bower, may I see you out in the hall?"

Chapter 5

Detective Davidson sat across from Sarah in her office. Sarah had seen Jackie and Wyatt out after all the tests had been completed. Jackie had promised to come to the city on Wednesday for dinner so that they could hash out the insanity that Jackie was currently calling her life.

"Sarah, are you listening to me? We need to get moving on this investigation." Detective Davidson, a short, athletically built woman, was leaning in toward her.

"Detective Campos did tell me you would have to interview all our staff. That's concerning. I'll do everything I can to support you; I just know the staff will be irritated about time away from their work. We're lucky to have such a dedicated team. I apologize in advance if they seem rude."

Davidson continued, "I'll keep the interviews brief unless I pick up something that seems odd. If you can have your assistant arrange a small conference room and schedule back-to-back, thirty-minute interviews starting tomorrow, that would help. All the interviews with your team need to be completed by end of business Friday. Detective Campos will be coming out on the red-eye Sunday and will be here bright and early Monday morning to meet with me and then you."

"I did share with Detective Campos how busy we are. I'd appreciate anything you can do to complete this investigation in a timely manner."

Davidson stood up. "I apologize for all the inconvenience as well, but this is the way it has to be done. I'll be here tomorrow at eight to start the inquiries. Where should I come?"

Sarah said, "I'll have my assistant find a room close to our clinic, and then he'll call you."

"I'll need a list of all your employees; an organizational chart would be helpful. Just so you know, I did clear all my requests through your legal department."

Sarah stood to usher Davidson to the program assistant's desk. As they walked, she replied, "Thanks for doing that. Sorry I'm so curt, but this whole process is a little scary and new to me. Plus, I had a long morning, and this news just put me over the edge. I'm sure you can appreciate the pressure cooker this place can be. We're dealing with people's lives every day, and we can't make any mistakes."

"Did Kayla make mistakes, Sarah?"

Sarah stopped and studied Davidson's face. "What exactly does that mean? We're all human."

"It was just a question—don't get defensive. It's this type of work environment that can cause some people to go off the deep end after their workday is done. In my experience, they can be calm, cool, and collected all day long, and then— bam—they snap."

Sarah chuckled. "Then that should eliminate me, since I'm anything but cool and calm right now, eh, Detective?"

Sarah briefly introduced Davidson to the young man behind the desk and asked if he'd give her an organizational chart, block off the small conference room, and arrange meetings over the next couple of days.

When she returned to her desk, Sarah emailed the entire staff and faculty about the upcoming interviews, apologizing for the inconvenience but asking that everyone be prompt. Then she called Dr. Bower on his cell.

"What's up?" he answered.

"Just giving you a heads-up that SFPD plans to interview our entire staff, including IT and faculty, over the next three days. I already sent out an email to everyone, but I'm sure we'll both get some whining. It's not optional."

"I've got a packed surgery schedule, plus meetings, and I'm in the middle of a high-profile case that requires most of my attention, so I won't be able to meet with them."

"High-profile?"

"A politician and his nephew from out of town are being worked up for the paired exchange. No media, no real names. Guy is running out of places to put his dialysis access; his transplant has to happen fast."

Thinking of a few politicians she hoped the patient might be, she said, "Apparently, we're all suspects, so good luck with not being interviewed."

"Thanks for letting me know. Some of the faculty are out of town at a transplant conference and won't be back until next week. Gotta go." Dr. Bower ended the call.

Nice talking to you, Bower. I know you appreciate me handling all the bullshit—I'm really feeling the love.

Chapter 6

Wednesday at five, Jackie picked up Sarah in front of the hospital and took her first deep breath of the day when she looked at Sarah's face. After Sarah got in the SUV, Jackie began, "Before you say one thing, I need to tell you that I just heard on NPR that people with high IQs swear more than others, so you and I are fucking geniuses!"

"Fuck yeah!" Sarah yelled.

"I made reservations at Tadich Grill on California. They have valet parking right next door, plus cocktails. What else do we need?"

"Perfect. How're you doing, my friend? That scene with Laura and Bower was insane. Have you talked to her?"

"Oh, yeah—we had it out several times on the phone. She's been staying in the city so, thankfully, I'm keeping the home front calm, but she's out of her mind. I can't reason with her. She's turned into someone I don't recognize, but I have to pretend in front of Wyatt. I can't believe the way she spoke to you in front of your team. I am so sorry, Sarah." Jackie shook her head.

"It's not your fault, Jack. I don't blame you. I'm sure you know how embarrassed I was, but, as usual, Bower said nothing and Nancy, Roger, and Janet just went about their business. I'm guessing they're wondering what the deal is. It's been a shit storm at work; the SFPD is about to start interviewing every staff member."

Jackie smirked. "I just want you to know that I've done a little undercover work on Kayla's murder that I want to tell you about over dinner."

"You've got to be kidding. Laura will kill me if you get anywhere near this case. We'd have to change our identity and move to another part of world, not to mention kidnap Wyatt, 'cause I'm not leaving him with that bitch."

At that, Sarah burst out laughing and Jackie joined in.

"Don't worry—it's no big deal. Anyway, what's going on with the SFPD? Can't you stay away from cops, Golden?" Jackie asked, as she pulled up to the valet stand.

Once they were seated inside, they ordered cocktails. When Sarah's gin martini and Jackie's rum and soda with lime arrived, Jackie raised her glass. "Here's to surviving the next couple months it takes to get Wyatt on the healthy train, my friend."

"Hear, hear—and you wonder why I don't want a committed relationship. It always looks so good when you're on the ground, but when it starts getting up to the higher floors, strap on your seat belt. I'm proud of you for holding on, Jack. You have a kid, after all. I just don't have what it takes." Sarah said, as their server approached again.

"I'm starving," Jackie said. "I've been eating carefully when Wyatt's home, so I'm getting a steak and mashed potatoes." After they ordered, she asked, "What's going on at work?"

"They're investigating everyone on our entire team. This detective, Lupe Campos, is coming out from Miami on Monday to review all the interviews the SFPD does and do some final questioning. They want to rule out any possible suspects from our team, and—are you ready for this?—guess who her partner is."

"Handsome?"

Sarah nodded.

"No shit! This is too good to be true. I know you tried your hand at a long-term relationship with him, and I'm sorry it didn't work out, but here he is, back in your world anyway. Maybe it's a sign from the universe that he's your guy. I mean, really, why else would a dead coordinator who overdosed and became an organ donor happen? Even *CSI* couldn't come up with this shit."

"You know I'm a failure at relationships. Handsome put the final nail in that coffin. Why did she have to be murdered in Miami? *Why?* Anyway, I'm not dealing with him, only with Campos, and she sounds very nice on the phone. I'm sure she'll be here and gone in a couple days."

After the waiter brought their salads, Jackie said, "I put in a call to my buddy Biker Bob in Miami. Boy, was he glad to hear from me. He had no idea I got run over by a car in Chicago when we were chasing that asshole Sergio Torres. I had to bring him up to speed on how that case ended. He's good, living the wild life. I told him I'd likely be in his neighborhood when we bring Wyatt for his evaluation, so we'll get together. I told him what little I know about Kayla, the drug overdose, and her being an organ donor in Miami, and he said to keep him posted. He was born and raised there, so he may be able to find out stuff the local PD can't. He said there are drug overdoses happening on practically every corner in the sketchy neighborhoods. I have to say, it was a breath of fresh air talking to him. He's really a good guy. Looks like a murderer on the outside—who knew he'd be a sweetheart on the inside?"

"You sure didn't know how nice he was when you got on the back of his Harley, did you?"

"Well, to be fair, I did have quite a few cocktails under my belt, but fortunately my trust barometer was working on some level that night. What else can you tell me about the Kayla investigation?" Jackie asked, salting her steak.

"I'm not telling you anything, because I can't be responsible for you getting killed or in harm's way. You and Wyatt are all I've got, besides my transplant career, so *nada colada*. Tell me how Wyatt's feeling. What did he think of his time with Mary?" Sarah took a bite of her salmon.

"First of all, he loves Mary. Once she told him how much she loves Harry Potter, they were best buddies. While they were on the tour, he quizzed her about all the characters and Hogwarts, and she passed with flying colors. I can't see him getting transplanted anywhere else, but at this point I'm picking my battles with Laura. We're going there next week if all his tests are completed. Wyatt's barely able to finish a round of his video game right now, gets tired fast and he has no appetite. I'm working with a pediatric dietician the nephrology office referred me to, but you can't control the kid when he's at school, no matter what I tell him not to eat. His labs aren't horrible." As Jackie dug into her mashed potatoes, Sarah reached her fork across to Jackie's plate and took a big scoop for herself, then ate it in one bite. "Oh my God. This is so good," she said.

"Hey, get your own, Golden." Jackie moved it out of arm's reach.

"How much time does he have before they insist he get a shunt put in his arm for dialysis? Is he still peeing a lot?"

"Thankfully, he's still passing a fair amount of water, but his kidney blood levels have been going up, so they're thinking we may have only a couple months before we need to have a serious discussion about dialysis. As you know, they can always do emergency dialysis if we get into trouble. I think that's why Laura's freaking out about getting this done quickly."

"I know our outcomes are the same as Miami's, but I'm not going to get in the middle of this. I'll do what I can to support my staff to get everything completed."

The waiter cleared the table, and Jackie ordered coffee and dessert. "Can't you tell me *anything* about Kayla? I'm not going to try to solve the case. Please."

"Campos asked me if I ever heard the name Zuzu mentioned in relation to Kayla. Seems Kayla had her a short Cuban motorcycle mama when she visited her grandmother in Miami. They think she was the last one to see Kayla alive, so they're looking for her. Maybe she's in Biker Bob's motorcycle gang. But I've never heard of her."

"I don't think Biker Bob rolls with the lesbian biker gals," Jackie said. "Anyway, let's get you home. I have to get back in time to say good night to Wyatt."

"I have an early morning tomorrow. Our biggest insurance-contract bigwigs are coming in for the annual dog-and-pony show, and I have to give them a tour and play nicey-nicey. I have no time for this shit, but they send us all their members exclusively, so it's a necessary evil."

• • •

Jackie dropped Sarah off at her apartment and headed back over the Golden Gate bridge. She was deep in thought as she pulled into the driveway. *I can't even recall the last time Laura kissed or touched me. Life is too short to be this angry and unhappy. Maybe Sarah has the right idea about long-term relationships after all.*

Chapter 7

Campos watched the sun rising over the San Francisco skyline as her plane descended. *What a beautiful city,* she thought. This was her first visit, but she'd have no time for sightseeing. She was under strict orders to get the down-low from Inspector Davidson, interview any questionable suspects, and get back home to attack the growing caseload she and Strong had. When she had asked him if he knew Sarah, he'd said, "It's a long story" and left it at that.

Campos hopped a cab to her Airbnb, showered, and headed over to the SFPD to meet with Davidson. After conducting a two-hour review of the interviews Davidson had completed, she was ready to head over to the transplant institute. "You're sure there are only three people for me to interview again?" Campos asked Davidson.

"All the interviews I did indicated that no one liked Kayla—almost all the staff, to a person. Dr. Spencer's name came up as someone who always complained about her unprofessional behavior and pushed her to work harder. Sarah Golden was her manager, and she shared with me that Kayla didn't care for managers in general and told Sarah to leave her alone. Apparently, Kayla also publicly tortured the hell out of

Ned, the IT guy, but he seemed pleasant enough—you know how nerdy those guys are. That gives you three to interrogate. Oh, and several of the surgeons were out of town at a transplant meeting until this week. I circled their names in red, if you want to try to catch them. Here are the files, the org chart, my notes, and a thumb drive with all the computer notes from my interviews. Don't forget to check in with legal before you head on over to the transplant institute. The place is a maze, so give yourself plenty of time to get lost."

"Thanks so much. Why don't you come down to Miami and work for us? We're up to our eyeballs in opioid deaths."

"No, thanks. I was born here in SF and still have family here. Plus, I don't like the humidity in Florida. And we have plenty of those cases, too; it's a sad state we're in nationwide. Too bad you're not staying longer—I could show you the town." Davidson escorted Campos outside to hail her a cab.

Campos had been to all the major medical centers in Miami and wasn't intimidated by the size of the San Francisco Global Transplant Institute and its hundreds of people running from place to place. She found her way to Legal and then called Sarah Golden to alert her that she'd be over soon.

"Good morning. I'm here to see Sarah Golden," Campos announced to the assistant at the counter. The tall glass windows behind him gave onto a sweeping view of Golden Gate Park.

"I'll call her and let her know you're here." He called Sarah and let Campos know she'd be right out.

Campos sized up Sarah as she approached. *She doesn't look like a murderer, and I can see Strong and her together for sure. She's a beautiful brunette, and what a figure!*

"You must be Detective Campos." Sarah extended her hand.

"I am, and you're Sarah Golden?" Campos smiled.

"Bingo. What do you know—a detective with dimples. Why don't we go into the conference room so we can talk?"

As they walked, Sarah asked, "So, you're Officer Handsome's partner? Lucky you."

Campos chuckled. "Yes, I am—although I call him Detective Strong, his real name. And I really enjoy working with him." Campos followed Sarah inside and closed the door.

Once they sat, Sarah began, "I hope you don't think me rude, but I have a full schedule today, so I won't be able to spend much time with you. I'm sure you'll conclude your business as quickly as possible."

"I will be as efficient as you and your staff can be cooperative. I do need to conduct additional interviews with you, Dr. Spencer, and Ned."

"Are you for real? The three of us are suspects? That's a joke."

Campos moved forward in her chair. "I can assure you, Ms. Golden, this not a joke. If you'd like to go first, that's fine with me; if not, I'm happy to meet with the other two and finish with you. I also need to know if the surgeons who were out of town last week are back." Campos saw Sarah's jaw tighten.

"I'm not sure. As far as interviewing me goes, how does two this afternoon sound?"

Campos stood up. "That works for me. Could you please assist me with finding Ned and Dr. Spencer? I don't want to take up any more of your time than I have to."

"I'll ask our front-desk assistant to contact Ned, and you're welcome to interview him here—or should I say *interrogate* him? Did you run this by Legal? I'm wondering if we need an attorney with us." Campos could hear the agitation in her voice.

"These are just informational interviews; if at any time I think we're heading toward a place that requires us to contact Legal, they're at the ready."

"This all sounds a little scary to me. And for the record I have an alibi. I'll double check with Legal, and after I'm assured that Ned is okay to speak with you, I'll let him know. Feel free to enjoy some of our delicious cafeteria coffee and then make yourself at home in our waiting room. Shouldn't take me too long." Sarah walked out of the room.

Campos glanced at the open door and decided to wait in the conference room for a while and review Davidson's interviews on her laptop. She hoped to overhear any staff conversations as they walked back and forth through the hall where the conference room was located. She pulled up the notes on Sarah and started to review them. Sarah had had a successful career. She had been in Miami just over a year earlier as a traveling transplant nurse working at the Miami International Transplant Institute. That was probably how Strong had met her. She had never married, had no children, and had a brother who lived on the East Coast.

Campos had heard about Sarah's involvement in the investigation and arrest of Sergio Torres and Amanda Stein, a wealthy tech executive who had gotten a liver transplant very quickly after being put on the list. From what Campos recalled, this Sergio fellow had been very clever. The story had hit the morning news shows and all the papers.

As Campos continued to read, she noted the number of times Davidson had cited hospital staff mentioning that Kayla usually defied every manager the hospital hired, including Golden. She was just finishing up reading the interview notes when a thin man with blondish, curly hair and thick glasses knocked on the door. He was wearing a gray T-shirt and jeans. "I'm Ned Bisone. I understand you'd like to interview me." He extended his hand. When Campos took it, it felt wimpy and cold. *Yuck*, she thought.

"I'm Detective Lupe Campos, from Miami, and I'm here to investigate the death of Kayla Newman. Please sit down."

Chapter 8

After leaving Detective Campos, Sarah went down to the transplant conference room, where Dr. Bower and several of the other transplant physicians were visiting with the folks from Reseak, one of the largest payers in California, as they were there for their annual visit. Sarah's job was to give the Reseak team a tour of the new pediatric transplant intensive care unit, floor, and dialysis unit and answer any operational questions.

Dr. Bower stood as Sarah walked into the room, "This is our new nurse manager, Sarah Golden, and she'll be showing you our new pediatric units."

"What's your institute's percentage of preemptive kidney transplants?" Reseak's chief medical director asked.

Dr. Bower responded, "It's relatively low, it requires a living kidney donor, and we rule out about eight out of ten possible donors."

"Dr. Bower, if you want to keep our exclusive contract your program has to increase that number, its best for the patient and our bottom line. What's your turnaround time from referral until transplant once you find a viable donor?"

Dr. Bower looked at Sarah, "You want to take this one?"

Sarah didn't have a clue. She had asked Kayla for that data several times, but Kayla had just ignored her. Now, here Sarah was, looking like an idiot.

"As Dr. Bower said, it's been a challenge to find a healthy donor. It's always our goal to get folks transplanted before dialysis whenever possible." Sarah addressed the Reseak's medical director.

"You didn't answer my question, Sarah. We ask all the transplant programs to keep a dashboard of all our members, from the time of referral to transplant, regardless of what type of donor kidney they receive. I believe Kayla, your lead living-donor coordinator, kept a very comprehensive report. Would you be so kind as to ask her for it and get it to us after the tour?"

Fucking Kayla. Sarah pursed her lips and looked toward Dr. Bower, who jumped in: "Sadly, Kayla is not with us anymore, she died."

The room went silent, and all the transplant doctors and visitors stared at Dr. Bower. The medical director finally managed to say, "I'm so sorry. What a loss for your program. She really knew how to get things done. Hard to replace those types. Well, Sarah, when you get a chance to get us that report, I'd appreciate it."

"Absolutely. How about we go on our tour now?"

The visitors moved toward the door where Sarah was standing and then followed her to the various units, oohing and aahing at the new facility and state-of-the-art technology in each pediatric room. With its brightly colored walls and spacious rooms, it didn't feel like a hospital at all, one of the doctors commented.

The last stop was the dialysis unit. Sarah paused as she escorted the group in. There were children sitting in the comfortable lounge chairs, feet up, connected to machines washing their blood of all the toxins that their own kidneys could no longer filter. She stopped speaking and just watched them.

"Excuse me, Sarah." Sarah realized that the head nurse was speaking to her and that the Reseak team was staring at her.

"Hi, Molly," she said, snapping herself back to the present. "Do you have a few minutes to show our guests from Reseak our new unit?"

"I'd be happy to. We love our new facility, and our kids and families love it even more." Molly gestured for everyone to follow her, but Sarah lingered, spotting one of the patients and families she had met on inpatient rounds with Mary several weeks earlier.

"Hi, Mrs. Boswell. Is that Jenny I see there?" Sarah had to work hard to keep her facial expressions pleasant. Jenny was eight—exactly Wyatt's age. "I don't know if you remember me, Jenny, but I met you and your mom briefly when you were in the hospital a couple weeks ago. How are you feeling, honey?"

Jenny's big brown eyes welled up with tears. "It didn't work."

"I'm so sorry, sweetheart." Sarah glanced at Mrs. Boswell, who was trying to keep it together. Sarah glanced away, as if she were looking toward the nurses' station; she didn't want them to see the tears welling up in her own eyes. There was no right question or response in a situation like this.

She quickly wiped her tears away, then turned back and took Mrs. Boswell's hand. "If you need to talk to me or need anything, please feel free to call me. I mean it." She took a card out of her pocket and handed it to Jenny's mother.

"Mary has been an angel—beyond supportive. She already put Jenny on the waitlist, and we're hoping to find another donor in our extended family who'd like to help us so we can do a paired exchange." Mrs. Boswell put her hand on her daughter's arm, where clear plastic tubes were moving blood back into Jenny's body, and said, "Don't worry, honey—we'll get you another kidney."

"I'm sure Mary told you that all pediatric patients get priority nationwide on the list," Sarah said. As Mrs. Boswell nodded, Sarah fought the urge to run out to her car, drive over to see Wyatt, and hold him close. Instead, she finished the tour with the Reseak team and walked them to the exit.

"It was lovely to meet you all, and I'll get you that report."

Once they left, her first thought was, *I have to get someplace where I can lose it.* She found the closest bathroom, locked herself in the stall, and began to sob. Her worst fear had just stared her in the face. What if Wyatt's transplant failed and he had to go on dialysis? She had to leave work. Campos could wait.

Chapter 9

A t the end of Sarah's workday, Jackie called her cell. "Hey, girl, sorry to bug you, but I wanted to run some Wyatt updates by you. We heard back from Mary."

"What did she say?"

"We got the preliminary tissue-typing results back, and, as you would expect, I'm nowhere near a match. I also got ruled out by that online living-donor screening process that Mary sent us a link to. Neither Laura nor I was a great match, but Laura could be considered as a paired-exchange donor. I'm not sure she'll go for that, though."

"How are you feeling about not being a donor, Jack?"

"Well, as a parent, you want to fix everything for your kid, so I'm a little disappointed, but Wyatt and I spend so much time together that I know he feels all my love and support."

"Good attitude, my friend. He's going to need you to be full of your usual playful monkey business. And you're very healthy in general, so don't beat yourself up. Have you talked to Laura?"

"Nope. I asked Mary to call her directly with the news and feel her out about the paired exchange. Listen, Wyatt needs to come in tomorrow for a few last tests, so I was hoping we could stay at your house overnight and have some fun, just the three of us. Laura's got some dinner thing."

"Absolutely! But do you really want to stay with a suspected murderer?" Sara laughed.

"What are you talking about? Detective Campos isn't saying you're a suspect, is she?"

"I would be a prime suspect if Kayla were alive now. I would have killed her tonight in her sleep for setting me up to look like a fool with the Reseak team I hosted today. Talk about embarrassment—but I won't waste your time with this petty shit."

Jackie couldn't help chuckling. "Wow. You're a suspect in an actual murder case. This is good. I have to call someone—Handsome, Biker Bob, anyone."

"Detective Campos arrived at my doorstep bright and early this morning and informed me, after SFPD did their first run-through, that she's re-interviewing three people: me; Ned, our nerdy IT guy; and Dr. Spencer. The staff apparently reported that I hated Kayla and had it out for her, although that's news to me."

"You, Ned the nerd, and Dr. Spencer—I think they're pulling suspects out of their asses. Did you have your interview with Campos yet?"

"Tomorrow. My plate was too full today. She's got a big, beautiful smile with dimples that can be disarming—that's probably how she gets her perps to talk. She has that fancy haircut where it's shaved on each side, with a bushy crop on top. I think you wanted to get your hair cut like that and Laura put the kibosh on it."

"Well, I'm gonna get that cut anyway. I am so done with her. Wait'll you hear what she tried to pull today."

"Tell me."

"Laura did call me today and left me a message about speeding up Wyatt's workup process so we can get that second opinion in Miami next week. She said Mary isn't moving fast enough, so she's going to call Bower directly." Jackie took a deep breath.

"What? Mary is moving this case at jet speed!"

"I know, Sarah. I texted Laura and told her I'd take care of it so she wouldn't call Dr. Bower. But I'm still concerned, because I know Mary called her later in the day about the paired-exchange idea; I'm just hoping they didn't connect— Laura usually does autopsies in the afternoons and turns her pager off. I wanted to warn you so you could check in with Mary. Wyatt and I love her, and I don't want Laura's bad vibes screwing things up." Jackie shook her head as she spoke.

"This is a whole new side of Laura. I know she's never been my best friend, but this type of behavior is concerning. Do you think she's having mental health problems or going through early menopause?"

"I have no idea. We did get an email from Wyatt's nephrologist last night, and he's not sure we have even two months before we have to start dialysis, so maybe she's just freaking out. She bought our plane tickets to Miami afterward. She got a text from Dr. Bower today saying that everything was good to go at the Miami Transplant Institute, he even gave her Santos's personal cell number."

"Nice of Dr. Bower to let me know anything, and your wife is just being an unreasonable bitch. Fuck her!"

"Not in a million years, Sarah. Anyway, Wyatt and I will see you tomorrow. We're looking forward to having some fun with you."

When Jackie hung up, she picked up a framed wedding photo of her and Laura, next to where she was sitting, and stared at it. *I can't believe we couldn't keep our hands off each other when we first met. I had never felt so loved by another person.* The passion between them had seemed to promise they would be together forever. They hadn't even made it out of their honeymoon suite for three days.

As tears rolled down her cheeks, she thought, *I never could have guessed things would get this bad between us.*

Chapter 10

Campos found Ned very cooperative, albeit on the quiet side. And his pager kept going off while he was sitting with her. "I apologize for the interruptions. I'm the only person here to support the transplant team today. The other folks are on vacation. We installed new software fixes, so we're dealing with a few glitches. When these people want you, they want you *now*, especially the surgeons."

No time for small talk, Campos thought. "Did you find Kayla impatient and demanding?"

Ned stared at the floor as he spoke. "No more than the other coordinators. She had a short fuse, so if I didn't quickly fix whatever she wanted, she would start yelling at me, no matter who was around."

"That must have been uncomfortable. Did you yell back or report her?" Campos watched his face.

"Working with medical people, you get used to being yelled at. So many of them hate computers and software, and they don't like to feel stupid. I understand that, but I'm not a yeller."

Campos didn't see much of a reason to detain Ned any longer; his pager just kept beeping. "Can you think of any reason anyone on the transplant team would want Kayla dead?"

"We all have bad days, and Kayla could be very mean in front of a crowd, but at the end of the day, transplant is a team sport, and we all work well together most of the time. So, no, I really can't see someone wanting to kill her. That seems so extreme to me." Ned stood up. "I am so sorry, but can I answer this one page? It's from the chief. I can come right back if you'd like."

Campos stood up as well and said, "No need, Ned. Here's my card. If you think of anything else you want to tell me, or if you hear anything, please call me. They're lucky to have a dedicated person like you here."

"Why, thanks, Detective Campos. I'm honored to be part of the team."

· · ·

After Ned left, Campos asked the front-desk assistant to page Dr. Spencer. He came strolling in, wearing his blue operating scrubs and starched white lab coat, his name and ATTENDING embroidered over the pocket. His black hair was disheveled. "I just finished a case and have twenty minutes." He sat across from Campos and immediately started looking at his phone.

"My name is Detective Campos, and I'm here from Miami to re-interview a few possible suspects regarding the death of Kayla Newman. Did you know Kayla well?"

Without looking up, he responded, "I knew her as well as I know all the coordinators. You ask them to get something done, and they usually get it done. We're a busy program so we're not hanging around singing and dancing all day long."

"Did you know her outside work? Did you socialize with her?"

Campos still couldn't get him to look at her, but he said, "I'm married and have children, so when I'm not operating or on call, I spend time with them."

Campos continued, "Several staff shared that you're unprofessional toward the coordinators, especially Kayla. Can you comment on that?"

Dr. Spencer finally glanced up. "The coordinators are here to work, and they *should* work, leave their drama at home. They're all overpaid for what they do and, honestly, I resent that they make more money than some of my research staff. I've been nothing but direct with all of them; if that's considered mean, that's their problem, not mine."

As Campos took notes, she thought, *I've heard about these types of surgeons, but this one might be the rudest, arrogant one I've ever met.* She looked up from her pad and pressed on: "Dr. Spencer, is there any specific reason why you would want Kayla dead?"

Spencer stood up and glared at Campos. "Yeah, that's what I want to do in my spare time: have transplant coordinators murdered. It appears that Miami sent their B team out here. Looks like we'll never find out who killed Kayla, if you're any indication of your department's level of expertise."

Campos glared back at him. "I'm not done with you, Dr. Spencer. I'd hate to have to get a summons."

"We *are* done, Detective. Do whatever you have to do, but right now you're wasting my time."

Dr. Spencer walked out, and Campos jotted some summarizing notes on her computer, until she noticed she was banging on the keyboard. She glanced at her watch—time for lunch. Just as she closed her laptop, she heard voices in the hall.

"Honestly, I'm so glad Kayla is gone; she always acted so entitled. I just wish she had quit, not gotten killed."

"She wasn't going to leave until she got her full retirement and all her benefits. I heard she had a girlfriend in Miami. Kayla probably paid her to go out with her."

"I could hardly stand being around her negative energy. I reported her several times, but nothing ever happened."

"I just hope they get her replacement soon. We're all drowning in cases."

The voices trailed down the hall and became too distant for Campos to hear them. She peered through the door and saw the backs of several women retreating.

• • •

After lunch, Campos called Strong while she took a short walk.

Strong answered right away. "How's the land of fruit and nuts?"

Campos chuckled. "Real funny. One more interview, with Sarah Golden; then I'm coming home. I think I found a new candidate for our asshole competition: Dr. Spencer. What a dick. Unless Sarah Golden is the murderer, I'm not sure anyone out this way is a real suspect. I'm hoping this case doesn't drag on only to get cold."

As Campos walked up the hill toward the transplant institute, she began panting. Strong interrupted, "What's with the heavy breathing? You're at sea level. I'll let you rest your lungs for a minute. I have some news for you: We found Zuzu—she's in southern Florida—so when you get back, we'll make a run and see what she has to say."

Campos stopped and took a breather. "What is with these steep hills? I could never live here. I'll send all the notes from Detective Davidson and my interviews so you can read them, and we can discuss them while we drive to see Zuzu. How's things on the home front?"

"I closed two cases and we got three more, so quit playing

around and get your ass home. I need a vacation. No autopsy report on Kayla yet; the bodies are piling up at the medical examiner's office. I called and gave them a friendly nudge. I'll give the chief an update on the Kayla case. Wait'll you hear this one: I found out Kayla's grandmother's been dead for over a year. We're still looking for a next of kin." Strong paused.

"That's odd—SFPD's preliminary interviews with Sarah indicated that Kayla was visiting her grandmother four times a year, including the visit when she was killed. Who signed for her to be a donor, then? Don't they have to ask the next of kin?"

"Kayla signed up with the national organ donor registry, so they didn't need a next of kin to consent. That's considered first-person consent," Strong said.

"I never knew that. Any suggestions when I talk to Sarah? She certainly is a looker—you two would have made such an attractive couple." Campos chuckled under her breath. She loved giving him a hard time.

"She's very smart and hardworking and will try to get you to tell her everything you know about this case, so just keep redirecting. She and her friend think they're professional sleuths, since they helped solve that case last year. Please give her my best and call me when you land in Miami." Strong ended the call abruptly.

I think I may have struck a little nerve there, Campos thought, as she walked back to the clinic and checked in with the front desk. The young attendant looked at Campos and said, "Sarah called and said she won't be able to meet with you until tomorrow."

"Did she say what time?"

"No, she said she'd call your cell and let you know."

"Thank you. Here's my card. I'd appreciate a call if you hear anything about Kayla that you think would be helpful regarding this investigation."

The assistant took the card. "Sure thing, Detective."

Campos decided she would take a red-eye home and conduct a phone interview with Sarah instead. At this point, Zuzu seemed a more likely suspect than Sarah did. Best to focus on interrogating her.

Chapter 11

Mary met Jackie and Wyatt at the pediatric clinic bright and early. Laura had stayed in the city overnight, and Jackie was hoping Mary hadn't heard from her yet so that she could run interference.

Mary knelt and said, "Hi, Wyatt. So good to see you again. You ready for a few more tests today?"

"As long as they don't hurt." Wyatt squeezed Jackie's hand a little harder.

"I'll explain everything to you, but nothing should hurt today. We're going to take some pictures of your body in a fancy room that looks like the Starship Enterprise."

"Wow." Wyatt smiled. "Can my mom come with me?"

"You bet. She can't go into the actual room, but she'll be right outside the door. You ready?"

"Will Aunt Sarah be there?" Wyatt asked Jackie.

"No, honey, Aunt Sarah's going to meet us at the Exploratorium after all your tests are done. Then we're having a slumber party at her house. Sound fun?"

"The Exploratorium? Yes!"

Mary led them to Radiology and made sure Wyatt changed his clothes. He chose a Starship Enterprise gown. Once he was settled in his room, Mary turned to Jackie. "Jackie, I need to speak with you. Laura called me late last night and left me a rather unprofessional voicemail. I turn my phone off after nine."

Jackie swallowed hard. "Laura has been under a lot of stress and isn't herself. What exactly did she say?"

"That I'd better get all the tests done, or she's going to report me to Dr. Bower, that she needs to be informed of every decision you try to make for Wyatt, and she'll give the final approval. I have to say, I'm a bit confused here. I thought you were going to be the primary caregiver."

Laura has to stop micromanaging this, I'm sure at some level she feels guilty not being here for Wyatt, Jackie thought. "I'm so sorry about these mixed messages, Mary. I *am* the primary caregiver. I'll call Laura right away and clear this up. Why don't I go outside and call her now? How long will the scan take?"

"About an hour until he's back in his clothes. You can meet us back here."

Jackie was about to leave, when she remembered one more question: "Mary, did Laura mention anything about the paired-exchange option in her message?"

"Yes, she understands that she is not a good match for Wyatt and said she is open to donating her kidney to another recipient and their donor would donate their kidney to Wyatt, so we're running some possible pairs now. I hope to have an update for you before you leave today. I did need to notify Roger, our pediatric social worker, about this hiccup between you and Laura. We need to be sure we're all acting in Wyatt's best interest. You and Laura will likely need to meet with him in person or over the phone."

"Thanks, Mary. We'll do whatever we have to. I'll see you in a little bit."

As soon as she was out of Mary's earshot, Jackie started talking to herself out loud. "This has *got to stop.*" She walked a few blocks away from the institute and then dialed Laura's cell, which went right to voice mail. "Call me now!" she barked. Then she called Laura's office. When the receptionist answered, she said, "Hi, Marjorie. I need to speak to Laura now. It's an emergency. I'll wait."

"Is everything all right, Jackie? Is Wyatt okay?"

"I'm at the hospital with Wyatt now, and I need to speak with Laura. Thanks." Jackie took some deep breaths.

When Laura came on the line, she said, "Jackie, I'm in the middle of a big meeting. Is Wyatt okay?"

"I can't believe you told Mary she has to run everything I decide by you. Not okay. And you're the one slowing things down! You have to stop this behavior, Laura. If you want to take a leave of absence and take over, I'll step aside, but you have to stop threatening people. For Christ's sake. What were you thinking?" Jackie paused.

"You know I can't take a leave of absence, especially now, in the midst of the opioid crisis. One of us has to work to pay our bills."

"Are you going to stop your inappropriate behavior or not? It's a simple yes or no. You have to stop second-guessing me, it's delaying the process. I'm really concerned about you; I have no idea where your head is. I think you may need to see someone for help. Come on, Laura."

There was silence on the other end; then Laura finally spoke. "I'm in over my head at work with this new promotion, I'm freaking out about Wyatt, and I know our marriage is in trouble. It's too much. I know, I know, I'm a control freak. I'm sorry, Jack. I'll stop micromanaging you about Wyatt's care."

"He's getting his scans now, so I need to get back before he comes out of the dressing room. I'll let Mary know I'm back on as his primary caregiver. Unfortunately, she had to share our recent insanity with the peds social worker, so we may have to go see him for a 'session.' I'll see if Mary can delay that for a while, at least until we're back from Miami."

"Thanks, honey. Sorry again. Did Mary tell you I was fine to be part of a paired exchange?"

"Yes, she did. We'll be finding out about possible pairs before I leave today. I'll keep you posted. Wyatt and I are staying at Sarah's tonight, so don't hurry home after your dinner meeting. I'll call you later tonight or tomorrow morning when I have the updates on his scans and the paired-exchange info." Jackie sighed, then added, "I'm worried about you, Laura. Are you sleeping at all?"

"Not too much. Four, maybe five hours a night. I'll stay in the city tonight and try to get some sleep. I really have to go now, Jack. We'll talk more later. I do love you."

"I love you, too; I just don't like you much right now. We'll talk later."

Jackie stepped a little more lightly as she walked back to see Wyatt and Mary. She shared parts of her conversation with Mary, and Mary said, "Your wife has an extremely stressful job, and then with all that's going on with Wyatt, I'm sure it's hard."

Just then, Wyatt came out of the dressing room with the scan guy, smiling from ear to ear. "It's just like the sick bay on the Enterprise, Mom, way cool. I even got to play a *Star Trek* video game while I was waiting. A nice guy named Ned helped me log in. He said now that I have a log-in, when I come for my transplant, I'll already be in the system." Wyatt motioned for Jackie to stoop so he could whisper in her ear, "I used the same password we use for our game at home."

Jackie hugged him. "Good thinking, buddy."

Mary smiled at Wyatt. "Ned is so great with our kids; I paged him to come down to help Wyatt after you left to call Laura. These are the types of pages he loves, although he doesn't get them very often."

Wyatt continued, "Ned shared some codes, too. And my test didn't hurt at all. I'm kinda hungry and thirsty."

"I figured you would be, so I have a special lunch in the courtyard just for you. Follow me." Mary extended her hand, and Wyatt took it, Jackie in tow.

After lunch, Wyatt met with Roger, the pediatric social worker, and Mary took Jackie to her office to debrief her on paired-exchange options. Once they were both settled, Mary read a few updates and turned to Jackie.

"We had a new possible donor for the paired exchange with Wyatt. I didn't want to say anything until we ran the pairs, but it looks like with this new possible donor we have as close to a perfect match with the other pair as you could hope to get."

"I thought Laura was going to get worked up. Who's the new donor?" Jackie asked.

"It's Sarah. She had herself tissue typed, and she's a better match than Laura with the other paired-exchange recipient. More important, their donor is a great match for Wyatt."

Chapter 12

After an intense day of showing the bigwig payer group around and then seeing her pediatric patient with the failed kidney transplant back on dialysis, Sarah decided to text Mo Platt and invite him over. He was an old boyfriend who did stand-up comedy and happened to be in San Francisco. It was the only night that worked as Jackie and Wyatt were coming over to her place tomorrow night for a sleep over.

Mo was waiting for Sarah when she got home, a little after six. They walked together up the stairs to her apartment, and as soon as she closed her front door, she turned to him and gave him a long, passionate kiss.

She waved her finger for him to follow her into her bedroom, taking her clothes off as she walked. By the time they were on her bed, they were both naked, hands touching each other's bodies.

Mo kissed and caressed her breasts and then found the warm spot between her legs. He rocked gently back and forth on top of her until they both climaxed.

Mo and Sarah had been madly in love when she was in nursing school, until he left her for a pharmaceutical rep.

Years later, after she forgave him and swore off relationships, they reconnected. Sarah felt safe sleeping with Mo, and she got an orgasm and a laugh all in one. She had stopped seeing him casually while she'd been serious with Handsome, and she hadn't been with anyone else since.

Mo took Sarah's head in his hands and said, "I've missed you. I'm sorry it didn't work out with the Miami guy, but not so much right now."

Sarah turned away from Mo and pushed down the deep heartache that emerged every time she thought about Handsome. "I guess I'm just better at this spontaneous thing with you," she let out a deep sigh. "You hungry?" Sarah went to sit up.

"Just for you." Mo pulled her back into bed, and they devoured each other again. After they cuddled for a while, Sarah got up, slipped on a silk robe, and went into the kitchen. Mo followed her, "How have you really been? I thought wedding bells were looming last we spoke. I called a few times and sent you a couple texts but never heard back."

Sarah pulled some frozen lasagna out of the freezer and popped it into the microwave, then poured two glasses of wine and handed one to Mo as he sat at the Formica kitchen table. "It's over is the short answer. He was a wonderful man. We really did click. We were doing the long-distance back-and-forth thing on weekends. When he was out here, his sister summoned him back home to help with her teenage sons. Her husband left years ago, so he's the fill-in. I needed to put all my energy into my work, and it was too much." Sarah watched Mo's sweet face as he listened.

"How are your wacky friend Jackie and her family doing?" Mo asked while Sarah prepared a salad, set the bowl on the table, and told him to help himself.

"Not good at all. Their son, Wyatt, needs a kidney transplant, and Laura is insane. I'm having Jackie and Wyatt over tomorrow night for a much-needed slumber party after we go to the Exploratorium."

"Sorry to hear their son is sick; that has to be scary for everyone. Sometimes I go to the Exploratorium before my first show, now that it's right down the street on the Embarcadero. Kids are loving all the new hands-on exhibits. Finally, a place where they can touch everything." Mo started on his salad.

"You're still a kid, Mo—I love that about you. Wyatt loves it there, but Jackie hasn't been able to come in to the city while she's been managing all his health care and running things at home." Sarah refilled Mo's wine, then sat down and took a bite of her salad.

"How's your boyfriend Dr. Bower?" Mo smirked.

"That's my stand-up comedian. He's never been my boyfriend—you know that. In fact, he's been ice cold since last year. He barely gives me the time of day now. He's working on some top-secret politician case, and he won't tell me anything. He just wants me to keep all the wheels on the bus at work. One of our coordinators was murdered and became a donor in Miami last week. Now I have a real disaster on my hands, in addition to dealing with the day-to-day chaos." Sarah stood up again to plate their lasagna.

"Holy shit! That's serious. No wonder you invited me over—you always loved great sex when you were stressed. Glad I could help you out tonight."

After dinner, Sarah and Mo lit up a joint and binge-watched *Comedians in Cars Getting Coffee* in Sarah's bed. Sarah loved laughing with Mo; she hadn't had a good, long laugh in quite a while.

Around nine, Sarah walked Mo to the door, where he gave Sarah a long kiss goodbye, as he had to go do a set at Cobb's Comedy Club. "I'll be in town for a while, so call when you need me. I love you, Sarah Golden."

"Back at you, Mo."

After he left, she hopped back into bed and checked her work email. Nothing that couldn't wait until tomorrow. She opened the one from Mary and saw that she was a great match for one of the paired exchanges for Wyatt. She'd have to let Jackie know that she had gotten herself typed. She didn't want to start World War Three with Laura, but she'd just felt compelled to do it after her day in the pediatric dialysis unit.

• • •

Sarah got to work early the next morning, called Campos's cell number, and got her voicemail. She left a short message saying she'd be at her office until three o'clock. She made rounds on the transplant floor and then went to see how Jackie and Wyatt were doing with his final tests. When Sarah walked into the conference room, she found Wyatt, Jackie, and Ned there.

"What's going on here? Looks like a lively game of *Star Trek* to me."

Wyatt and Jackie didn't even acknowledge her, but Ned got up. "I helped them log in and play while they were waiting for you; you probably know it's Wyatt's favorite game. There's not a meeting in here for another hour, so I figured it would be okay to use the monitor."

"Thanks, Ned. Very kind of you. Yes, he tells me all about it, but, to tell you the truth, I have no idea what he's talking about. I know Spock and Captain Kirk; that's it."

Ned smiled and said, "I have to run. Bye, Jackie! Bye, Wyatt!"

"Thanks, Ned!" they both yelled, without looking away from the screen.

After Ned left, Sarah watched the two of them, their controllers clicking away rapidly. "Hello! Earth to Wyatt and Jackie! Who wants to go to the Exploratorium? Slumber party? Jump on my bed all night? Anyone?"

Wyatt put down his controller and turned toward Sarah. "Me! Me! Mom, will you save the game? Let's go."

· · ·

After their trip to the Exploratorium, they had a light dinner and headed back to Sarah's. Wyatt was so tired, he jumped only a few times before he fell asleep on Sarah's bed. After she and Jackie watched him for a few minutes, Sarah closed her bedroom door and said, "Jackie, I need to tell you what I did. After the payer day from hell, I got myself tissue typed. Please know that I didn't do it to start another battle between you and Laura."

"I already know. Mary told me today, and I think you're amazing for even considering to be part of Wyatt's exchange. Laura and I had a productive talk yesterday after the Mary incident, and I think the train is back on the track for now. We're leaving for Miami in a few days, and I'll have a calm conversation with her when we're there. Mary said the recipient of the other pair has to have a small surgical procedure, so we have a little wiggle room."

Sarah grinned. "That's good news, my friend. Would you like a drink?"

"I thought you'd never ask."

Sarah and Jackie curled up on the couch with cocktails and watched TV. Before Jackie went in to sleep with Wyatt, she looked at her friend and said, "I'm starting to feel like everything might turn out all right after all."

"Me too, Jack, me too. See you in the morning."

Chapter 13

Campos slept the entire flight from San Francisco to Miami. When she landed, she stopped at the bathroom and threw some cold water on her face, then walked outside and found Strong waiting for her curbside.

Campos threw her carry-on in his backseat and climbed up into the passenger side of his pickup truck. "Jesus, I need a ladder to get into this thing. Why do you need such a big truck? You're a cop, not a farmer," she barked.

"Someone cranky from sleeping on the plane? The squad car got a little banged up and is in for repairs. Don't ask." Strong pulled out and started driving toward the freeway.

"Don't tell me you crashed it again. I know you didn't have any high-speed chases while I was gone; I would have heard from someone. Anyway, thanks for picking me up. Where to?"

"Zuzu lives about an hour from here, in Wilton Manors. One of our guys picked her up and she's waiting for us, although she's pissed—says she's got a business to run," Strong said, as he merged onto Route 1.

"Of course, she lives in Gay City. Where else would a Cuban lesbian call home? They do have some great local dives, so we should plan on stopping for lunch after we're done." Campos chuckled.

"Been there a few times, Campos? I know you're a closet biker babe at heart."

"My brother owned a bar there, so I'd go see him on my days off occasionally. It's got a hopping night life for lesbians. If I recall, there are only about twelve hundred people living there. Free booze and a place to stay—how could I say no? Thankfully, I was much younger and sleep wasn't as important to me. My brother sold the bar about a year ago and made a boatload of money. It's all about the career for me now." Campos opened her backpack and pulled out her interview notes from San Francisco.

"I know—no partying or dating for you. You'll be running the department someday. I sure hope you'll be nice to me when that happens," Strong said, keeping his eyes on the road.

Campos flipped through her spiral notebook. "*You're* the one who said you'll never fall in love again, not me. Did you get a chance to read all the notes I emailed you yesterday?"

"I did, and it sounds like the place is a pressure cooker to work at, but I already knew that. No solid suspects; even this Ned guy seems like a real stretch. And the one transplant surgeon you did get to interview was an arrogant asshole—no surprise there. Doesn't look like you were able to interview the big guy, Dr. Bower, or any of the other surgeons. I'm guessing they all gave you the same line: 'We're transplanting.' Right?" Strong glanced over at Campos.

"What a flimsy excuse. If Zuzu isn't our gal, I may have to go back and track those surgeons down myself—unless you want to go?"

Campos watched Strong's face and saw his jaw clench. "It's a little early in the morning to be giving me shit. I'm your partner, remember?" he asked.

"You are, and I'm sorry if I hit a sore spot. I did bring you a bar of Ghirardelli dark chocolate with almonds, though." She pulled it out of her bag, unwrapped it, and handed him a big chunk.

He put it in his mouth. "This is some good shit. Thanks. And I got you an espresso. It's there." He pointed to the cup holder close to Campos.

"Thanks." She took a long slurp. "Double shot—perfect." Campos finished looking at her handwritten notes and put them back into her bag. "What do we know about Zuzu?"

Strong put his hand out. "That will cost you another hunk of chocolate."

Campos handed him another big piece. He devoured it, then said, "I called Penny, one of the four detectives who work in Wilton Manors, and she gave me a quick rundown. Zuzu was born in Miami and went from one foster home to another; I think it was nine or ten total. She witnessed her father shoot her mother point blank, and he's been in prison since then. Typical story: kicked out of all the schools, seems to be known as a badass throughout the local community. More chocolate, please." He put out his hand again, and Campos gave him the rest.

"Tough life. Does she have a job?" Campos threw the empty wrapper on the floor of the truck.

Strong glared over at her. "I know you'll pick that up when we get out."

"Of course, Detective. I know how you like to keep this thing tidy." Campos chuckled.

"Just 'cause I'm not a slob like you . . . Anyway, Zuzu was able to get enough money to buy a small motorcycle-fix-it shop in Wilton Manors. She's a decent mechanic; the detective

said she knows her shit. Not bad for a twenty eight year old."
Strong turned off the highway.

"She's had quite a life for being so young. I wonder how the hell she met Kayla." Campos asked.

Strong pulled into the Wilton Manors police station and said, "Welcome to Gay Pleasantville. Did you see that movie?"

Campos laughed and followed him into the station.

A female officer greeted them at the front desk. "Can I help you?"

Strong pulled out his badge and showed it to her. "I'm Detective Strong from Miami, and this is Detective Campos. I called yesterday and spoke with a Detective Penny. I believe you're holding a possible murder suspect for us to interrogate, a Zuzu Perez."

The woman walked around to him. "So *you're* the one to blame for this one. She's been swearing up a storm and is demanding to be released. She has a line of customers waiting for their motorcycles. You'd better get in there and get this done. Don't expect a hug and a kiss. Follow me." The officer motioned to Campos and Strong.

She led them into the area where the interrogation rooms were and signaled Detective Penny to come over. "These are Detectives Strong and Campos, from the big city of Miami. I will leave them in your capable hands."

Penny, a tall, thin woman with a buzz cut, extended her hand and shook Campos's first, then Strong's. "Let's dispense with the formalities. You need to get her out of here as fast as you can, either in handcuffs or by releasing her. She's been a full-time job, swearing like a sailor, demanding fresh coffee and breakfast from our local diner. I picked her up early this morning." Penny walked them to the room and opened the door. Zuzu stood five feet, wearing a wife beater and tight-fitting jeans, her long black hair slicked back.

"Zuzu, these are Detectives Strong and Campos, from Miami." Penny let them pass her and quickly closed the door behind her.

"Who gives a fuck? What gives you the right to hold me without telling me what for? Are you fucking kidding me or what?" Zuzu blurted out.

They both sat down across from Zuzu. Campos took out a notebook to distract herself from staring. *There must have been a special at the tattoo-and-piercing parlor,* Campos thought. She had never seen so much ink and metal on one person in her life.

"Can we move this along? I need to get the fuck out of here. I have a business to run," Zuzu demanded. Campos couldn't help but notice the barbed-wire, prison-style tattoo around Zuzu's neck. Both arms, with biceps that would have put any boxer on notice, had full tattoo sleeves.

Strong began, "Do you know a Kayla Newman?"

"Yes." Zuzu sat back in her chair, put her feet on the table, and glared at Strong with her dark brown eyes.

Strong continued, "In what capacity did you know her, and how long did you know her? Since we're trying to move this along, why don't you also tell me when was the last time you saw Kayla."

As Zuzu spoke, Campos noticed that her tongue was pierced, as well as both her eyebrows and her nose. While she wrote down Zuzu's responses, she also started two columns on the border of her paper: one for the number of Zuzu's piercings, and one for her tattoos. She made a line for each one and added the five piercings she had already counted.

Zuzu continued to try to stare down Strong. "We dated casually over the past three years when she came down to see her grandmother. Last time I saw her was last week. She drove down to meet me here, and we went out. She was complaining about how much she hated her job and the surgeons, how her new boss was a bitch, and how she was only putting in the time to get her benefits. She spent the night with me and drove back to Miami. I need to go now!" Zuzu pushed back her chair and stood up.

"Not so fast, Perez," Strong said, as he rose from his own seat.

"Get the fuck out of my way. I had nothing to do with whatever happened to Kayla. You must be desperate if you're thinking I did." Zuzu remained standing.

Campos said, "Zuzu, we just have a few more questions; then you're free to go. Please."

Zuzu sneered at Campos. "Unless you're going to charge me with something, I'm leaving. I have pissed-off bikers waiting outside my shop, wanting their rides. I got nothing else to tell you."

Strong responded, "Did you meet Kayla's grandmother?"

"No. I don't get involved with anyone's family. Never ends well."

Strong continued, "Are you aware that Kayla died of a drug overdose?"

Campos watched Zuzu's face drop and her mouth turn downward. "What? I thought she was just missing." Her eyebrows furrowed and a long silence filled the room. Finally, Zuzu added, "Surely you don't think I had anything to do with that. I've seen enough of the insides of jails."

"You're a suspect, Zuzu. Do you have any idea why anyone in Miami would want Kayla dead?" Strong asked.

Zuzu shook her head. "I don't really know who else she knew down here, other than her grandmother, and I'm guessing her grandmother wouldn't have wanted her dead. We kept things simple when we were together. She never asked me about my life here, and I never asked her about her life back home. Worked just fine."

Strong continued, "Do you know if Kayla did drugs?"

Zuzu grinned. "Pretty sure her drug of choice was alcohol and a little weed every once in a while. She wasn't into pills, best I knew. What did she OD on?"

"We're not at liberty to share any details of the case right now," Strong replied. "I'm going to need you to write down anywhere you and Kayla went when she was here last week and give it to Detective Campos here before you leave. I also need you to notify us if you plan to travel anywhere. Until this case is resolved, you're considered a suspect."

Campos handed Zuzu a pen and paper. "I bet you set off the airport metal detectors when you travel."

Zuzu finished writing and tossed the paper at Campos. "I hate fucking airports. Never fly, never will." Strong opened the door and handed Zuzu his card as she walked out.

Campos looked over at Strong after Zuzu left the interrogation room. "Did you count them?" she asked.

"The tattoos or piercings?" he replied.

"Let's go for both and see if we both have the same number. I'll bet you lunch on the way home you're wrong." Campos smirked.

Strong hesitated. "We know there are some we didn't see, of course, but if you're just counting the visible ones, I'm going with eight tattoos and five piercings."

Campos looked at her tally. "We're both right. Let's go eat and figure out our next step. You think she did it?"

"Nope, but I think she knows more than she's telling us. What about you?" Strong opened the door to the room, and they walked outside, thanking the front-desk clerk on the way out.

"She's a real piece of work. I think we have some more digging to do here and back in San Francisco," Campos responded.

"I can tell you one thing: We won't be wrapping this case up anytime soon. Let's hope there's more information from the autopsy report. The chief is not going to be happy we're at a dead end. We need to talk again with the cops who found her and see if we missed any other clues." Strong got in his truck and started the engine.

"Oh, shit!" Campos was looking at her phone.

"What now?" Strong glanced over.

"I just opened my work email. Chief sent us the cover of the *Miami Herald*: 'San Francisco Transplant Nurse Overdoses on Opioids in Miami; Organs Donated.' Who the fuck leaked that story?" Campos barked.

"Where's this dive café? Let's eat and regroup. The last thing we need is the press breathing down our necks," Strong said, as he pulled out of the parking lot.

Chapter 14

As Jackie entered the Miami International Transplant Institute, where she and Sarah had followed Sergio and Amanda only a year earlier, all she could think was, *I can't believe I'm back here—let alone with my own kid.* She led the way to the elevators, and Laura and Wyatt followed. Laura was holding Wyatt's hand and looked at him. "I made us a special appointment with Dr. Santos. He's going to tell us all about their pediatric transplant program. Then Mom and I will decide which program will be the best for you, sweetheart."

Wyatt looked up her. "I like Mary. Why do I have to come here?"

Jackie glanced at Laura and responded, "We just want to be sure you go to the very best place. You don't have to get any more tests done; you're just going to meet the team, and then you'll let us know what you think."

Wyatt smiled. "This place looks fancier than where Aunt Sarah works; they have lots of palm trees here."

The elevator door opened, and they went to Dr. Santos's office, where his assistant escorted them in. A tall, dark-haired man wearing a lab coat was waiting for them. He stood up.

"Welcome. You must be Wyatt." He reached out his hand, and Wyatt shook it. "That's me. These are my moms."

Dr. Santos continued, "Please, sit down." He gestured toward the small, round conference table. "Dr. Bower speaks highly of both of you. His team sent me all Wyatt's medical records, and everything looks great."

Laura began, "I'm Dr. Laura Gallagher. We spoke last week. This is my wife, Jackie Larson. It's extremely important that we move as quickly as possible. I'm sure you're aware that we would like to hear about your paired-exchange program. If I'm correct, your outcomes are better than San Francisco's."

A knock on the door interrupted Dr. Santos before he could respond to Laura, and a young man in a lab coat entered. "Hi, Dr. Santos. I hear there's someone in here who might want to play some video games while you and his moms visit."

Dr. Santos stood up. "Hi, Scott. This is Wyatt, Laura, and Jackie."

"Nice to meet you all. I'm the nurse practitioner who works with the kids who receive transplants. Welcome to Miami. I hope your trip was good."

Jackie surveyed Scott. "No problem getting here. Thank you for sending us all that information about lodging nearby. Our room is perfect. And thanks for the welcome gifts for Wyatt. He loves the *Star Trek* action figures."

Wyatt looked up from the table where he was playing with the figures, "Yeah, they're really cool."

Scott took the empty seat next to Wyatt. "I spoke with your friend Mary in San Francisco, and she told me you're a pretty cool kid and that you like video games."

"You know Mary?" Wyatt asked.

"Mary and I have been friends for a long time. We go to the same meetings every year. Isn't she just the best?"

"I like her a lot," Wyatt said.

"Would you like to come with me for a little while so I can show you where the kids who get transplanted play after they have surgery?" Scott stood up and extended his hand.

Wyatt looked at Jackie, then Laura.

"It's okay to go with Scott. I bet he's a fun guy, and I think if he's a friend of Mary's, he's a friend of ours," Jackie replied.

Wyatt stood up, put his action figures in his pocket, and followed Scott out, looking over his shoulder.

As Scott closed the door behind him, Dr. Santos continued, "Scott is great with our pediatric patients. I did hear from Dr. Bower that you were being considered for a paired exchange, Laura. Have you had any updates on that?"

Jackie stepped in: "She's in the preliminary stages, and we may have a great match in San Francisco, but we wanted to also be considered for your paired-exchange program. I understand that you work closely with the SF team and that they can share tissue-typing results with your team here. Do I have that right?"

"Yes. If you want us to plug your results into our internal paired-exchange system, no problem. We have a different ethnic mix than San Francisco, but you never know what kind of match you'll get until you put in all the information. I do need to set the record straight with you regarding our pediatric kidney transplant outcomes. They're the same as San Francisco's—"

Laura interrupted, "That's not what I saw on your website, and I also checked the United Network of Organ Sharing's database. Did I miss something?" She raised her eyebrows.

"There is no statistical difference between our outcomes." Dr. Santos's beeper went off, and he looked down at his phone. "Looks like we'll need to cut our visit short; they're paging me from the operating room. I can have our new pediatric surgeon, Dr. Devaney, come meet with you later this afternoon. Would that be all right?" Dr. Santos asked.

"That would be wonderful. Thank you for offering," Jackie said, as Laura nodded her assent.

Dr. Santos stood and walked to his office door. "Great. I'll have my assistant direct you to the cafeteria for some lunch, and if you give her your cell number, she can call you after she confirms Dr. Devaney's schedule."

Laura and Jackie followed Dr. Santos out and stopped at his assistant's desk as he updated her. He looked back at Laura and Jackie and said, "Thank you for coming to see us. I hope we have the opportunity to work with you and Wyatt and get him transplanted here." Without waiting for a response, he headed out the door.

"If you'd like to follow me, I can point you in the right direction to the cafeteria. When Scott gets back with Wyatt, I'll give you a call on your cell. By that time, I should also have heard back from Dr. Devaney." The assistant walked out of the surgical office, and Jackie and Laura followed.

Jackie handed her a card with her name and cell number on it. "Thanks so much. We'll see you in a little while." Jackie said.

Once they went through the line and paid for their food, Laura led the way to a small table in the far corner of the cafeteria.

Jackie was about to take a bite of her salad, when she noticed that Laura was staring at her intently. "What's wrong? You have a weird look on your face."

"You and I both know things haven't been good between us for a long time, even before Wyatt was sick. I know that most of that has been on me, with my promotion and then the tension around Wyatt's health." Laura sighed.

As her stomach suddenly churned, Jackie put down her fork and watched Laura's eyes.

"Part of the reason I've been on edge is that I started seeing someone while I was staying in the city a couple of nights a week. I feel terrible about it, but it happened."

Jackie felt a wave of bile rising up into her throat and narrowly resisted the urge to throw her hot coffee in Laura's face. "What the fuck are you talking about? How could you? Why would you? Laura, we have a son together! Jesus! You think you could have at least waited until we had Wyatt healthy again if you had to go in that direction?"

Laura responded quietly, "I didn't plan it this way, Jack. It just happened. I know the timing sucks. I don't blame you for being angry."

"Angry? I'm heartbroken, Laura." Jackie gritted her teeth and closed her eyes tightly to stop herself from crying.

"I don't know what to say. We need to deal with our relationship." Laura responded.

"We need to deal with this. . . . Actually, fuck no—*you* need to deal with this, Laura. It's your mess, not mine." Jackie yelled, feeling her neck and face get hot. Several heads at a nearby table turned toward them.

"I *am* dealing with it the best way I know how. I've arranged for my mother to come stay with us until things settle down. I've also made flight arrangements for Wyatt and me to fly home this evening so that we can meet her at SFO." Laura's voice had turned cold.

"Your mother despises me Laura. Only inviting you and Wyatt for Thanksgiving every year, sending me weight loss magazines, addressing every holiday card to only you and Wyatt. I don't want her in our home. She's not staying with us. I can't believe you're telling me all this here in Miami, now. You're not thinking straight." Jackie clenched her jaw and couldn't even look at Laura.

"There is no right way to do this, Jack. It's too late."

"I will sue you for custody and fight you with everything I have—"

Jackie's cell phone ring interrupted her rant. It was Santos's assistant; Jackie told her they'd be right up, then picked up her tray and walked toward the exit. Laura hurried to catch up. "And exactly what are we going to tell Wyatt?" Jackie asked.

"I'll tell him Granny has a surprise planned for us and that we're heading home tonight. You know he loves her and she spoils him."

"This is all moving way too fast, Laura. I'll allow you to take Wyatt home, but don't think you're going to control this whole thing. I can't say what I need to say to you right now, but we *will* be having a serious conversation when I get home. Just because you declare things over doesn't mean they are. And this means Wyatt's getting his transplant in San Francisco, *where we live.* That decision is made, period."

Jackie pressed the elevator button and took it up to the surgical office, where they found Wyatt and Scott laughing. It took everything for Jackie to smile while Laura went up to Wyatt and hugged him. "Let's get going, buddy. I have a surprise to tell you when we get in the car."

Jackie looked at Scott. "Thanks for showing Wyatt around. How did it go?"

"He kicked my butt in the video game, and I think he liked the playroom." Scott smiled over at Wyatt.

"I had fun. Thanks, Scott." Wyatt fist-bumped him.

"We'll be in touch, Scott." Jackie looked over at the assistant and added, "We won't be able to meet with Dr. Devaney today. Laura needs to get back to work in San Francisco."

"Please tell Mary hello from me if you see her, Wyatt," Scott said.

"Okay, Scott." Wyatt took Laura's hand, and all three of them walked out of the office.

Once they were in the car, Laura explained to Wyatt the

plan to leave for home. "What about Mom?" He looked toward Jackie. "Why isn't she coming with us, too?"

"It was too much money to change my ticket, so I'll be coming home in a couple of days." They stopped at the hotel room to pick up Laura and Wyatt's belongings, and Jackie drove them to the airport while Wyatt told them all about his time with Scott.

When Jackie pulled up to the curb, she helped Wyatt out of the car. "You have a safe flight, there are tons of fun movies. Remember if you suck on the ice it will last longer and you won't get so thirsty. Please be careful about what you eat and drink, okay? I love you so much." She picked Wyatt up and whirled around with him in her arms.

"I will, Mom." He put his hands on her face and kissed her on both sides of her cheeks and the tip of her nose; it was their ritual. Jackie bade Laura a weak farewell and watched as the two of them walked through the airport's sliding doors.

Jackie fought back her tears until she was back inside the car, then covered her face and started to sob. Once she gained control of her emotions, she managed to drive back to the hotel room, where she tried to reach Sarah, but the call went straight to voicemail. "Sarah, call me. I need to talk to you. 'What the fuck' doesn't begin to explain it."

She dialed Biker Bob's number next, and he picked up right away. "Jackie Larson. How the hell are you?"

"In need of the best rum in Miami, and I'm here in town. Are you free tonight?" she asked.

"I am now. You name the time and place."

"You already know the place. Why don't you pick me up at my hotel, and we'll take it from there?"

"Done. Give me your address, and I'll see you at seven."

Jackie gave him the details, set the alarm on her cell, lay down in a fetal position and cried herself to sleep. The ringing of her cell phone startled her out of a deep sleep.

"Hello?"

"Jackie, it's Sarah. What's wrong? You sound drugged."

"I wish I was. The shit has really hit the fan. You're not going to believe what happened, not in a million years. And before you ask, I didn't do anything wrong. Nothing." Jackie threw her legs over the side of the bed and glanced at the clock on the end table. It read six forty-five.

"Is Wyatt okay?" Sarah asked.

"Wyatt is about the only thing that's okay. Laura is cheating on me, and she told me here." Jackie said, carrying her phone to the bathroom.

"Laura is cheating on you? That's the last thing I expected to hear. How are you doing?" Sarah asked.

"My heart is broken. I vacillate between shock and beyond pissed. She also arranged for her mother to fly out, and she and Wyatt are flying home right now to meet up with the wicked witch." Jackie put the phone on speaker while she bent over the sink and splashed cold water on her face.

"Jackie, what are you doing, taking a shower while we're on the phone?"

When Jackie didn't answer, Sarah said, "Hello, Jackie—are you there?"

Jackie wiped off her face and bent over the phone. "I'm here. I had to wake up, so I was splashing cold water on my face. I have a date."

"A date! With who? Boy, you don't waste any time."

"Biker Bob. He'll be here in a minute. We're going out." Jackie actually smiled in spite of herself.

"Biker Bob? Things didn't end too well last time you were with him. Trouble is brewing for sure now. Did you call Handsome in case he has to bail you both out?" Sarah asked.

"I haven't called him yet. I didn't know I'd have any time on my hands. I need something to distract me until I can figure out how I'm going to deal with Laura. I plan on calling him tomorrow to offer him my help with this Kayla case."

There was a knock on the door, and Jackie put her phone to her ear as she opened it. "Hey, Sarah, I have to go. My rum dealer is here. I'll call you tomorrow."

Jackie opened the door without hanging up, and there was Biker Bob in all his glory: thick beard and mustache covering most of his face, black hair pulled back in a ponytail, standing over six feet tall, in full leather. He walked in and picked Jackie up.

Sarah screamed into the phone, "Don't do anything stupid, call me in the morning. Please."

With that, Biker Bob grabbed Jackie's cell, said, "Hi, Sarah. Don't worry—I'll take care of her," and ended the call.

Chapter 15

Jackie grabbed Biker Bob's waist, her arms barely making it halfway around his thick torso, as he floored his Harley toward Homestead, thirty miles outside Miami.

"Woohoo!" *I feel just like I'm in the movie* Easy Rider, she thought, and howled at the top of her lungs, Steppenwolf's song "Born to Be Wild" playing in her head. She leaned into Biker Bob's back and held on tighter as he accelerated. She couldn't have asked for a better escape.

Biker Bob pulled up to the Rum Wreck Dive Bar, killed the motor, and hopped off the bike, then helped Jackie dismount.

She handed her helmet to him. "I don't remember driving here last time. That was one hell of a ride!"

"This is an old-fashioned speakeasy place, and I'm a member. This guy knows his rum. I think he has the biggest collection in the States. Do you remember that?" Biker Bob put both helmets on his bike and led the way across the gravel parking lot, where several other motorcycles and cars were parked.

"Can't say I remember much, except I know the rum tasted great and we talked the night away, which could happen again tonight." Jackie patted her hair back to rectify her helmet head.

"That's more than enough." Biker Bob laughed.

They walked in, and the proprietor recognized him immediately. "Hey, Bob. Great to see you. Been a while." The bartender squinted at Jackie. "Is that the wild woman you brought in here last year?"

"Sure is. My name is Jackie. Nice to see you." She put out her hand, and he shook it as he laughed.

Biker Bob and Jackie cozied up to the bamboo bar in side-by-side, high-backed barstools. "Wow, you have an amazing rum collection!" Jackie said, as she surveyed the rows of bottles, most of them four deep.

"Thank you. What can I get you two?"

"How about we start with the Real McCoy? Ten-year limited edition, neat." Biker Bob suggested.

"Better make mine a double. I've had one of the worst days of my life," Jackie added.

The bartender gave Jackie a generous pour and put it in front of her. He poured Biker Bob half as much. "Enjoy."

"This smells like banana. Yum!" With that, Jackie toasted Biker Bob. "Thanks for bailing my ass out today."

"Happy to help, Jackie, and sorry to hear about your accident last year. I'm not sure what happened today, but we'll get there. Cheers." Biker Bob clinked his snifter with hers.

Jackie took a big gulp and said, "Wow, that's some delicious rum. Tastes like vanilla."

"It's ninety-two percent alcohol, so take 'er easy. Goes down too smooth."

The bar was appointed with old-fashioned metal diving helmets sitting on shelves, and an array of tall, colorful ceramic drink glasses.

The rum warmed Jackie from the inside out. "I think this will get me exactly where I need to go. Good choice. And before you say anything, the drinks are on me. God, it's so great to see you."

Biker Bob smiled. "Good to see you, too. How did your son's visit to the transplant institute go?"

Jackie took another sip. "His visit went well. Unfortunately, my wife informed me in the cafeteria that she's cheating on me and has her devil mother flying into San Francisco tonight."

Biker Bob snapped his head toward her. "What? Did that come out of nowhere?"

"I was flabbergasted, didn't see it coming at all. Thankfully, Wyatt was on a tour with the transplant nurse. I can't believe she decided to tell me while we were here, of all places. It's totally fucked up. I'm still in shock."

•   •   •

Over the course of the evening, Jackie shared all the details about Wyatt, her passive aggressive mother-in-law and her wife. Biker Bob ordered a pupu platter to help soak up some of the rum. Jackie interspersed her cocktails with glasses of water, hoping to avoid a banging hangover. After she covered her home life and was feeling no pain, she changed topics.

"Do you remember what I told you on the phone when I called you from SF to let you know I would be in town?"

"That one of Sarah's coordinators OD'd and then became an organ donor here in Miami?" Biker Bob responded.

"Yup. The case is being considered a homicide, and our best buddy, Detective Handsome, and his partner, Lupe Campos, are on the case. I'm guessing I'll have to don my detective hat and give it a go again, since I have a couple more days before I fly home to whatever the hell. I'm gonna need your local expertise." Jackie ate another bite from the pupu platter and chased it down with a sip of rum.

"You said something about wanting to find a biker chick named Zuzu?" Biker Bob asked.

"That's exactly what I need. I plan on calling Handsome to see if I can get something out of him, but I'm not counting on him giving me much since the breakup. We may need to canvass a couple lesbian bars and see if we can find her." Jackie watched Biker Bob's face.

"You know I'd help you if I could, Jackie, but I'm about to head off on a cross-country motorcycle ride with some buddies. We're leaving the day after tomorrow, early in the morning. We've been planning this one for over a year. We'll be meeting up with other motorcycle clubs along the route."

"Don't you mean motorcycle gangs?" Jackie chuckled.

"I'm too old for gangs anymore; after thirty, we divide into smaller, less violent groups. It's nice because we don't have to look in our rearview mirrors for cops anymore. More fun that way." Biker Bob finished off his rum and waved to the bartender for the check. "Give the lady one more before we hit the road, if you would, and then we'll be out of your hair."

Jackie glanced at her watch. "It's only ten o'clock. I was hoping we could pull an all-nighter. This may be the last time I get to have fun, now that I'll be a single parent."

"Florida is three hours later than SF, Jack, and I need to check on my business early tomorrow to make sure everything is handled before I go on the road." Biker Bob reached for the check.

Jackie moved his hand away and grabbed it. "This is on me, remember? And I didn't know you owned a business." Jackie pulled out her credit card and handed it to the bartender.

"It's nothing big, just an old-fashioned burger place. I bought it from a close biker friend a year before he died. The money helped him pay his medical bills and funeral expenses. The place has been around for over fifty years. We just serve burgers, chips, beer, and pop. Turns out it's a gold mine. I have a small crew of dependable folks who've been there a long time."

"Boy, I sure could use a greasy cheeseburger right about now. Can we stop by on the way back?" The bartender put the credit card bill on the bar and Jackie signed it, adding a big tip.

"I'd love to, but my cook would kill me; he cleans the place up and closes down at seven sharp every night. I don't mess with him. But I'll take you there tomorrow if you'd like." Biker Bob stood up and tilted his head toward the bathroom.

Jackie sipped the rest of her rum and closed her eyes. *I could float out of here.* "Ah, the magic of rum. If I lived here, I'd move upstairs or right next door—of course, if I were single." She smiled at the nice bartender.

"It always warms my heart when I see folks like you enjoying our fine rums. And any friend of Bob's is a friend of ours," the bartender said.

As Biker Bob returned from the bathroom, he smiled at Jackie. "You are officially hooked up to the source of all that is superb rum. I guess you're in now."

"I guess I am. What do I need you for anymore?" Jackie stood up and shook the bartender's hand, laughing. She started to sway a little side to side, and Biker Bob put his hand on her back. "I think you'll at least need me to get home and score you the best cheeseburger you ever had tomorrow."

"That's right—the cheeseburger connection. Can't mess that up." As she walked toward the door, she turned and waved back at the bartender and then glanced at the empty metal diving helmet on the shelf by the door. "Bye, Diver Dan. Nice seeing you again."

Biker Bob secured the motorcycle helmet on her head, mounted the bike, and then helped Jackie get on.

Jackie leaned into him and hollered and hooted all the way home. "This is so much fun. I'm getting one of these with a sidecar for Wyatt when I get back to the Bay."

• • •

The next morning, loud knocking on her hotel room door jolted Jackie awake. She sat up in bed and then immediately lay down again. *Ouch. I drank water, I ate the pupu platter, so why do I feel like I'm gonna puke? Can't I have even a little fun without being punished?*

"Who is it?" she whispered. The knocking continued, "Jackie, are you okay? It's Bob."

Jackie cupped her hands on either side of her mouth, hoping it would help her speak more loudly without adding more pain to her head. "I'm okay. Wait a minute." She lay on her side and then slowly pushed herself toward the side of the bed. *I knew there was a reason I stopped drinking so much, but it's just so much fun when I'm in the moment,* she thought.

More knocking. "I'm up!" She snapped. "Just a minute."

"Take your time. You'll feel better after your cheeseburger," he shouted through the door.

Jackie avoided looking at herself in the mirror facing the beds and went straight to the bathroom. She turned the shower on and got in before the water heated up. "Good morning!" she yelped.

After a quick rinse, she brushed her teeth, washed her face, and threw on her jeans, a T-shirt, and a baseball hat. She grabbed her bag and put her sunglasses on, before opening the door. "Good morning, sunshine. What a treat to see you two days in a row. Ready for the best hangover food you'll ever have?" Biker Bob grinned.

"Yes, please," Jackie almost whimpered.

"I brought you a chocolate milk shake before we head out."

"You are a saint." Jackie took the milk shake and sipped it, allowing the sweet, velvety contents to begin to revive her.

He handed Jackie her motorcycle helmet. "Let's get you fed."

Jackie put on the helmet, took another slurp of her shake, and threw it in a nearby garbage can. "I don't want to get brain freeze, although that might help." She grabbed Biker Bob's waist, threw her leg over the bike, and leaned in as he took off.

Fifteen minutes later, they pulled up to what looked like a shack barely standing up. There was a line out the door, and it was only eleven in the morning. He led Jackie around the back and opened the creaky screen door. "Morning, Sol. Looks like your regulars are lined up for those tasty burgers. This is Jackie."

Sol was tending to at least twenty burgers frying on the grill but gave her a quick "Hi."

"Can you put a double cheeseburger together for her? She had a rough time last night."

"You got it."

"I'll meet you out back," Biker Bob said to Jackie, and gestured to a screen door.

She made her way out to a small, rusty table and two metal chairs. While she waited, she briefly checked her phone to see if she had heard from either Wyatt or Laura. No texts or voice mails. She figured Wyatt had gotten all excited about seeing Laura's mom and forgotten to text her—and she knew Laura didn't give a rat's ass about her right now. She felt her lower lip begin to tremble just as Biker Bob walked outside.

"Don't cry, Jack. Your hangover medicine has arrived." He was carrying a bag of chips, a large soda, and Jackie's burger, which Sol had placed on thin white tissue paper inside a red plastic basket. "Here's some ketchup and mustard."

"Thanks," Jackie said.

Biker Bob's cell phone rang, and he said, "I need to take this." He answered and said, "Thanks for calling me back so fast, Dover. Yup, yup. That's her name. Great. Okay." Biker Bob hung up and clipped his phone onto the holder on his thick black belt, then sat back down to watch Jackie eat.

She squirted a liberal amount of ketchup onto her burger and took a big bite, not caring that the juice was running down both sides of her mouth. "Mmm," she groaned. The burger was medium rare, with extra cheese melted perfectly. After she had devoured it and wiped off her face, she opened the chips and took a sip of her soda. Finally, she looked at Biker Bob and said, "That was the best burger I've ever tasted in my life. No wonder there's such a long line out front. You cured my hangover—or, I should say, Sol cured it!"

Biker Bob smiled. "Glad to hear it. And I have more good news for you: I know where your prime suspect, Zuzu, lives. We can drive up there when you're ready."

Jackie stood up. "Ready when you are. Where we going?"

"We're going to Wilton Manors, not far outside of Miami. It's a beautiful day, so it'll be a nice ride. Turns out Zuzu owns a motorcycle repair shop, and I need a few spare parts to take on my road trip, so this whole thing works out perfectly for me." He tossed her motorcycle helmet to her, and she caught it and put it on.

"You think you should call your pal Handsome before we leave?" Biker Bob asked.

"Nope. Let's do our own digging first; then I'll have something to bargain with when I do call him."

Jackie followed Biker Bob out front and got on the back of his bike. Just before they took off, she texted Sarah: "Closing in on the perp with Biker Bob. Stay tuned."

Chapter 16

Sarah had just gathered several files from her office to take with her to a morning of meetings, when her cell rang. She did a double take when she saw the name on her screen. "Hello, this is Sarah."

"Oh, hi, Sarah. I didn't expect you to pick up so early. I was going to leave you a voicemail."

Sarah played it cool—"What can I do for you, Laura?"—as she thought, *What the fuck is wrong with you, and how could you break my best friend's heart?*

"I wanted to let you know that Jackie and I have decided that the SF Global Transplant Institute is the best place for Wyatt, so I'm authorizing you to go full speed ahead on the paired exchange, with me as a donor."

Sarah was silent. *God, I hate Laura so much right now, it's really hard for me to be civil to her, but I have to act professional.*

"Hello, Sarah? Are you there?"

"I'm here. So glad you're keeping Wyatt local. I know he took to Mary, and you just can't do better than her. Did you and Jackie discuss all the paired-exchange donor matches?" Sarah asked.

"As far as I know, I'm the only one who matches, so there's not much to discuss. Do you know something I don't know?" Laura raised her voice.

"Just in case you can't get a hold of Jackie right away, I should let you know that I went and got tissue typed anyway, and it turns out that I'm a better match than you for the current pair you and Wyatt are considering," Sarah said.

"What? I told you in no uncertain terms you were not be involved in Wyatt's clinical care!" Laura screamed into the phone.

"No need to yell, Laura. I'm sure our staff can run other matches that might accommodate you as a possible donor, but that will take more time. Once you and Jackie confirm what you want for the paired exchange, then we'll do all we can to expedite Wyatt's case. Did you and Jackie have a good visit to Miami?" Sarah wanted to see if Laura would take the bait.

"I'm sure Jackie called you the minute Wyatt and I got on the plane, so you know the deal. Don't play games with me, Sarah." Laura's condescending tone made Sarah want to scream.

"Laura, let's please keep things professional when we're discussing Wyatt. I'm sure you still want the very best care for him, and I'm at the ready to be a donor, should you and Jackie decide that's the right option for him. I think it's best that you deal directly with Mary and her team from now on. They're doing all the work and will know every detail. Of course, if there's a problem with anything, you're welcome to escalate things up to me. I'll ask Mary to call you this morning after our team meeting. Sound reasonable?" Sarah was clenching her teeth.

"Sounds perfectly reasonable, Sarah. I was about to suggest that myself. I'll call Jackie now. Please give Dr. Bower my best." Laura hung up.

Sarah was not the violent type, but right now she wished she could punch Laura in the face. She quickly texted Jackie a warning that Laura knew about Sarah's being a possible donor and that Laura was on the warpath.

Jackie quickly texted back: "Oops, forgot to tell her. My bad. On caper. Will call later."

Sarah noticed the voicemail light blinking on her desk phone and hit the button to pick up her message. She hadn't heard the voice on the other end in over a year. "Hello, Sarah. This is Kristin Gerard, Dr. Bower's wife. I was hoping to catch you at your desk. I need you to call me as soon as you can. I've set up that national think tank to increase awareness around organ and tissue donation in the Latinx community, I'm sure you'll recall where the twenty million dollars to fund it came from. Please be a dear and give me a call on my cell; I have an important question to ask you." Kristin left her number.

"'Be a dear'—really? Gross," she said aloud. But Kristin was right—Sarah did know exactly where the funding for the think tank came from. After Kristin's best friend, Amanda Stein, and her boy toy, Sergio Torres, had been arrested, the court had ordered them to donate ten million dollars apiece to the cause.

I can't deal with two bitches before eight in the morning, Sarah thought, and left the message sitting in her voice mailbox. She skipped over the call from Dr. Bower's wife and listened to the next message.

"Hi, Sarah. This is Detective Campos from Miami PD. Will you please call me at your earliest convenience? I have a few questions." Campos left her cell and office numbers.

Sarah's heart sank. She knew Jackie was with Biker Bob and hoped she hadn't gotten herself in trouble with Campos or Handsome—that would be all Sarah needed. She dialed Campos's cell, thinking, *Please don't let it be about Jackie; please don't let it be about Jackie.*

"Detective Campos."

"Hi, Detective Campos. Sarah Golden here. I got your call. How can I help you?"

"Thanks for calling me back, Sarah. Detective Strong and I have been working Kayla's case, and we've hit a couple of road blocks. I'm hoping you can help us out. Just so you know, I've already called your legal department, and they've approved my requests and are sending us a few things as we speak."

"I'll help you any way I can. I hope you found her girlfriend, Zuzu. Sounds like she may be the key to solving this case. What do you need from me?" Sarah asked.

Campos continued, "I'll need you to keep what I tell you confidential. Don't even tell Jackie. Can you do that? Detective Strong told me it's highly unlikely, but I'm going out on limb here. If I do find out you shared information with anyone, you could be arrested for obstruction of justice. I'd hate to go there, but if I need to, I will."

"I'm sure Detective Strong told you Jackie and I are best friends—really more like sisters—so it'd probably be better for you not to tell me anything that I can't share with her. I'm just being honest here." Sarah knew she'd tell Jackie whatever she heard about the case; they just couldn't help themselves.

"I appreciate that, Sarah. However, we're at a point in the case where, if information is leaked to the wrong people, we may never find the suspect. What I need from you is information from Kayla's HR file. Do you have it?" Campos asked.

"I have a copy of everything current, and the originals are with the HR department. Let me get it out." Sarah took a key from her desk, unlocked the confidential file cabinet that held her staff's HR folders, and pulled out Kayla's. "Okay, I have her folder. What do you need?"

"I need her next of kin and the addresses where she's lived since she started working there. Also, who she put down to call in case of an emergency." Campos paused.

Sarah flipped through the file and asked, "Did you get a chance to talk to her grandmother? I hope she'd know something, although I'm probably the only one who tells my nana everything."

Campos chuckled. "You must be close to your nana. I couldn't tell mine anything."

Sarah smiled and said, "Yeah, we've been close since I was a teenager. I lived with her when my parents got divorced, and stayed until I left for nursing school. . . . Okay, here's the information on her grandmother although I'm thinking you already have that." Sarah read off the grandmother's address and phone number.

"Thanks. I do have her grandmother's info. Just wanted to confirm it was the same as what you have," Campos said. "How about any other addresses in her file, and the names and numbers of emergency contacts?"

"Looks like she's lived in the same place in San Francisco for the last fifteen years, since she's worked here. This city is big on rent control, so some people never move. As far as emergency contacts go, there's only her grandmother, and then there's a number here but no name attached to it. I think both her parents are dead and she was an only child; HR should be able to confirm that." Sarah read Campos the phone number with no name attached, as well as Kayla's apartment address.

"Thanks, Sarah. I'll be coming out one more time to meet with the surgeons I didn't get to interview. I sent the chair of the surgery department a formal request, and your legal department will be following up to let them know it's not optional. I'll also want to interview you, since we missed each other when I was there last time," Campos said.

It sure looks like you're not making any progress if you're coming back out here, Sarah thought, but said, "I'm not going anywhere, so I'd be glad to meet with you. When are you coming?"

"Probably in the next couple days, Strong can handle things on the home front."

Handsome, Sarah thought, allowing herself to drift there for a moment, and then said, "I know he can handle just about anything they throw at him; he's a hardworking detective. Please give him my best. Let me know as soon as you know when you'll be back, and I'll clear my schedule. Say, did you or Strong hear from Jackie? She's in Miami."

"Why would Jackie call us? And what's she doing in Miami?" Campos asked.

"Her son was evaluated for a possible kidney transplant at the Miami International Transplant Institute. She and Handsome—I mean, Strong—got along well when he visited here, so she mentioned she might give him a call if she had time." Of course, Sarah hoped Jackie was just relaxing with Biker Bob before she had to fly home and deal with Laura.

"Strong didn't mention anything to me, so I don't think Jackie's contacted him. You know you gals don't need to help us solve this case, right?" Campos said.

"I'm too busy running things here, and I'm not even doing a great job at that, so I don't need any more work right now. And Jackie's got her hands full at home," Sarah replied.

"I know we both want this case closed sooner, rather than later. One more thing: I asked Legal about the files on Kayla's computer, and they said you may have a guy there—I think I met him: Ned—who can download everything. Would you ask him to download the information and put it on a thumb drive? I'll need to see it when I'm there. I know there's a lot of confidential patient information on it, so someone from either HR or Legal will sit with me when I review it," Campos said.

"Sure, I'll get in touch with Ned when we hang up. See you soon and please say hello to Detective Strong for me."

Sarah finished the call, paused and thought about Handsome again. He'd called, emailed her, sent letters and flowers after their big breakup call, but she hadn't responded to any of them. Still, Sarah knew they could have made it if things had been different. *I wish we could be together. I wish I could feel his touch again*, she thought, then stopped herself. *But he probably hates me now. Maybe I'm not supposed to have a boyfriend anyway. Maybe my career, Jackie, and Wyatt are enough. I'm so lucky to have them.* Sarah let out a deep sigh, then paged Ned.

He called her right back. "Hi, Sarah. What can I do for you?" He was always so energetic and responsive whenever she needed something from him.

"I appreciate your calling back so fast. I need you to download all the information on Kayla's computer and save it to a thumb drive. The Miami detective will be coming out and needs to review it."

"No problem, Sarah. I'll get on it right away; shouldn't take me long. I'll drop the thumb drive off at your office if you're going to be around," Ned said.

"I'll be here all afternoon. If I have someone in my office, feel free to knock. Thanks, Ned."

Sarah hung up and exhaled. It was nice to deal with something easy for a change. She was responding to her emails when a ding from her cell phone informed her that she had a text.

It was from Jackie: "Met Zuzu. Going undercover tonight."

Chapter 17

"Do you have a minute?" Campos was at the precinct, standing at Strong's desk as Strong pecked away on his keyboard with his two pointer fingers.

Strong was looking intently at his computer screen. "Let me finish this email." After a minute, he said, "What's up?"

"I just got off the phone with Sarah Golden. I thought we could speak privately." Campos looked around and saw that several of the other detectives were glancing her way, pretending not to be listening. Campos knew they were hoping to get more information they could use to make fun of her and Strong, who had been the butt of office jokes recently because of their growing caseload and low solve rates.

Strong stood up from his computer, followed Campos to a small interrogation room, and closed the door. "How's things in SF?" he asked.

"I got some more information on Kayla and let Sarah know I'd be coming back for one last visit. She was very helpful and even said to give you her regards." Campos watched Strong's face; his mouth turned slightly downward, transitioning to a poker face. *Boy, she must have really hurt his feelings*, Campos thought.

"That's nice," Strong said. "Did you tell her about Kayla's grandmother being dead over the last year and half?"

"Nope. I decided the less I shared, the more likely Sarah and Jackie would be to stay out of our investigation. Have you heard from Jackie? Apparently, she's in Miami."

"That can't be good. Did she say why Jackie was here?" Strong asked.

"I guess her son is sick and needs a kidney transplant, so she and her wife took him to the transplant institute in Miami. Weird, huh, since they have a transplant program in their own backyard." Campos opened up Kayla's file and started laying papers on the desk.

"If Jackie is here with her kid and her wife, there's no way she'd have time to stick her nose into our investigation. I know her wife would have nothing to do with it after what happened to Jackie last year in Chicago. So, where are we with Kayla?" Strong looked over at Campos as she continued spreading papers from Kayla's file out on the table.

"The ME's office finished Kayla's autopsy and confirmed it was an overdose; her blood levels were five times higher than most of the other ODs they get, which confirms our suspicion that she didn't do it to herself. She's a nurse and would know how much to take to get high."

"Maybe she wanted to kill herself and that's why she took the drugs," Strong suggested.

"Doesn't fit her profile, from everything I learned from all the staff interviews at the SF Global Transplant Institute. I'm not saying it's impossible, but it just doesn't fit—"

Someone knocked on the door. An officer popped his head in and said, "You got a minute?" Campos motioned for him to come inside.

"What can we do for you, Officer Cox?" Strong asked.

"You asked me to check the owner of the house where we

found Kayla's body with the address you sent me this morning, Detective Campos. The house was her grandmother's. When she died, she left it to Kayla. The place has been empty since her grandmother died, but the on-site investigators strongly believe that there were at least two people inside at the time of Kayla's overdose. There were some signs of struggle, but whoever was there knew what they were doing, because the place is clean—no fingerprints besides Kayla's. They're sending out someone from Crime Scene Investigation to recheck for prints inside and outside the house. They're also checking Kayla's clothes again for anything, and we're waiting for possible DNA under her fingernails." Cox stopped talking and checked his notepad.

"When do they think the DNA results will be back? I'm guessing you already interviewed the neighbors. Anything there?" Campos asked.

"You know the neighborhood, Detective—it's turned into a slum over the years. I'm not sure how an old woman stayed there so long. No one's home when you start knocking on doors, so no neighbors to interview. DNA should be back in a couple of days." Cox closed his notebook.

Just as he was leaving, Lorna, the chief's crusty secretary, walked in and said, "Chief wants to see both of you in his office right away."

Campos and Strong both lowered their heads at the same time. "*Now*, Detectives, you know he doesn't like to wait." Lorna shuffled out and headed for the front door of the precinct.

Campos looked at Strong and rolled her eyes. "Must be time for her hourly Pall Mall." She gathered all the papers and put them back into Kayla's file.

"Nobody gets in the way of Lorna and her cigarette break," Strong said.

As they walked into the chief's office he slammed down the phone. "Close the door and tell me what the fuck you two are doing out there! The *Miami Herald* is up my ass about this dead nurse from San Francisco, and the transplant programs don't talk to the press about the organ donors or recipients. You'd better have something, or I'm giving this case to real detectives." The chief took a gulp of his coffee.

"We were just going over every detail of the case, and we think we may have something; we just need a little more time to confirm the facts. Can you give us a few more days?" Campos asked.

"I'll give you a day. One day! I don't have time to deal with this newspaper shit—you know that. Maybe I should assign you each to a different partner; then you could close a case or two. You two have the lowest solve rate of everyone." The chief stood up, signaling Strong and Campos to leave.

"Chief, Campos and I work well together. I promise we'll have something for you on the nurse case by tomorrow. I just finished closing out the paperwork on four of the opioid overdoses; they should cross your desk this afternoon," Strong said.

Campos had seen that distressed look on the chief's face before. She knew they had to ramp up the Kayla case and close at least five more, or they'd be looking at pushing paper in the traffic department.

As they walked back toward the interrogation room, Strong's cell phone rang. He looked at his caller ID and saw that it was Jackie Larson. "Detective Strong. Just a minute, please."

Strong closed the door to the interrogation room and put Jackie on speaker.

"Hi, Jackie. I'm putting you on speaker. I'm here with my partner, Detective Campos, so keep it clean." Strong smiled.

"Hi, Detective Campos. Sarah told me all about you. No swearing this time, but no promises on the next call. You guys any closer to figuring out what happened to Kayla?" Jackie asked.

"Hi, Jackie. Nice to meet you over the phone. I spoke with Sarah today. She shared that you're here with your family, I hope everything went well in Miami."

"Let's just say there were a few surprises and Wyatt will be getting his transplant closer to home," Jackie said.

"I hope everything goes well for him. Listen, it's really a bad time. I'm buried in cases, so, although I'd love to see you, I have to pass." Strong glanced at Campos.

"Wyatt's home with Laura right now. I'm only here until tomorrow night. How crazy that here we are, back in Miami. So, no new updates on this dead coordinator Sarah's dealing with?" Jackie persisted.

"I wish I could talk to you about the case, but you know these things are confidential. I thought after you got hit by a car last year, you'd be running the opposite direction of this kind of stuff," Strong said.

"That was not a good time, for sure. Thankfully, I'm healed from that—just can't cha-cha like I used to. I understand you're swamped. It's just that Biker Bob and I took a ride today, and you'll never guess who we ran into."

"I couldn't possibly guess. Who?" Strong asked.

"Biker Bob needed a few spare motorcycle parts for his cross-country bike trip, so we took a ride out to Wilton Manors. Turns out there's this crazy woman named Zuzu who owns the bike shop. We got to talking, and she mentioned some Miami cops. One thing led to another, and—bingo—we have a mutual friend."

Campos's eyebrows lifted as she looked at Strong and mouthed, *What the fuck?*

Strong said, "You met Zuzu? She sure is a character."

Jackie replied, "She's a one of kind. And there's more: She's meeting me for drinks. She says she knows the best places to eat and dance, and I need both before I head home.

Don't worry—she has no idea who I am or that I'm connected to Kayla's case."

"Jackie, you're not connected to Kayla's case—you know that. I need you to stay away from this. Seriously, you could get yourself killed this time. Whatever happened to Kayla, these are not nice people. Do you understand me?" Strong asked.

"Cool your jets, Handsome. Zuzu may be a little rough around the edges, but I don't think she had anything to do with Kayla's death. However, she may have information that she wouldn't share with a cop. I thought we'd have a few drinks so I can do a little undercover work for you and then hand off whatever intel I get, 'cause once I get home, I have a cheating wife and a sick son to tackle, so I'll be off the case." Jackie paused.

"Jackie, I'm sorry to hear about your home situation, but you're not 'on the case.' I'm asking you *not* to do anything. Please don't force me to arrest you for obstruction of justice," Strong responded.

"I'm not doing anything illegal, I swear. If I do learn anything, I'll leave you a message. Take care, Handsome. Sorry things didn't work out between you and Sarah. I thought you were the one, for what it's worth." Jackie ended the call.

Campos watched Strong stare downward and could tell Jackie's parting comment hit close to home. When he looked back up at her, they both shook their heads. As they walked out of the interrogation room, Strong turned to Campos and said, "The last thing we need is Jackie meddling in this case. If the chief got wind of this, we'd be dead."

Chapter 18

After Jackie hung up with Handsome, she took a long, hot shower and thought about her field trip with Biker Bob to Wilton Manors.

Initially, Jackie waited outside while Biker Bob went in and talked motorcycles with Zuzu. After several minutes passed, she went inside.

"You about ready to head out?" she asked Biker Bob. Zuzu was behind the oil-stained wood counter, grabbing something off the shelf, her back facing both of them.

"Yeah, I just need the carburetor repair kit, and then I'll have everything," Biker Bob told Jackie.

"Here's your repair kit, Bob." Zuzu placed it in front of him and looked over at Jackie. "You'll have to wait a minute—I'm helping him." Zuzu gave Jackie a once-over, eyeballing her from head to toe.

"She's with me." Biker Bob glanced sideways at Jackie.

"Doesn't look like your type, but okay." Zuzu started ringing up all the items for Biker Bob.

"Zuzu, this is my friend Jackie. She's in from out of town."

Jackie usually didn't go for short, butchy girls, but Zuzu had a sweet, tough energy that made her attractive. "Nice to meet you, Zuzu. Can't say I ever met a Zuzu before."

"Gee, I never heard that, don't even start the Christmas-movie shit with me—I'm not in the mood," Zuzu snapped.

Biker Bob piped up: "Seems our fine Miami police gave her a hard time yesterday. She's not happy about that."

"Those fucking pigs. Why can't they leave folks alone?" Jackie said.

"I thought you were from out of town. How do you know about Miami cops?" Zuzu asked. She looked at Biker Bob and added, "Your total is fifty-six dollars—cash, if you got it."

Biker Bob opened his wallet, pulled out some bills, and handed them to Zuzu.

"I had a few friends visiting down here last year who got harassed by Miami cops—not a good scene. Despite all the real crimes they should be solving and drug dealers they should be arresting, they pick on innocent folks. Probably got their certificates from one of those online police courses, dickwads," Jackie said.

Zuzu chuckled. "Seems they got you all riled up."

Jackie decided to change the subject. "Say, Zuzu, can you recommend a good bar in Miami? I prefer girls only, and it has to have a great sound system."

"There's some great bars here in Wilton Manors, but when I'm in Miami, I go to this place a couple miles outside South Beach, called Fagina's. It's on the corner of Grand and Clark—no name on the outside, but there's a blinking neon sign in the window: HOT FLASHES. Stiff drinks, spicy chicken wings, and a clean bathroom—what else does a girl need?" Zuzu took out a piece of paper, wrote down the details, and handed the note to Jackie. Jackie caught Zuzu's eye for a brief moment, and they both grinned.

"Thanks. Sounds like the perfect place. How's their music selection?" Jackie asked.

"They have a great collection of Donna Summer, Barry

White, and Sylvester, from the old disco days, on their jukebox—just takes quarters." Zuzu followed Jackie and Biker Bob as they walked outside toward his bike.

"This place has my name all over it. After a few rums, I'll be dancing by myself and singing at the top of my lungs." Jackie laughed.

"I've seen her do it. You should charge for that, Jackie. No one knows how to get down like that anymore." Biker Bob handed Jackie her helmet.

"Tends to be a middle-aged crowd in there, so they could use some entertainment. Who knows—I may drop by; I have a few stops I have to make in the neighborhood after I finish working today." Jackie mounted the bike and held on to Biker Bob.

"Have a great ride, Bob. Jackie, have fun tonight," Zuzu said.

Jackie waved goodbye as Biker Bob gave the bike some gas. Zuzu waved back. *She is so going to meet me at that bar. I can see it in her face*, Jackie thought.

• • •

Jackie got dressed and called Laura's cell, the call went to voicemail, she left a message. "Hi, Laura. I'll be heading back on the red-eye tomorrow night and taking the Airporter home. Sorry I didn't tell you about Sarah being a better donor than you for the paired exchange. I was going to tell you, but your surprise announcement in the cafeteria really stunned me. Anyway, give me a call when you can. I think if Sarah's the best match, we should go with her—if your ego can stand it. Give Wyatt my love."

Jackie hung up and called home, and the demon answered.

Jackie sighed. "Hi, it's Jackie. May I please speak with my son?"

"Why, hi, Jackie. Wyatt had a Boy Scouts meeting after school. I'll be picking him up in a little while." Demon's voice was obnoxiously sweet. *Did you drink a bottle of maple syrup?* Jackie wondered. She wanted to mimic the fake tone but elected not to—who knew whether, if there was a custody battle, Laura's mother would testify against Jackie. "Will you please let him know I called, and tell him I'll be flying home late tomorrow night and will pick him up from school?"

"Sure will. It's so nice to have some alone time with my grandson while Laura stays in the city. We've really bonded. Laura works so hard; I hope she can get a break soon."

A break from banging What's-Her-Name, you mean, Jackie thought. "She's a hard worker for sure. How's Wyatt feeling? Are you being careful with his fluid and dietary restrictions?" Jackie asked.

"Following everything to the letter. He's tired at the end of the day, so we watch a little TV and then read before he goes to bed. I know he misses you, so it will be good when you get home. I'm so glad you and Laura want me to stay until after his transplant," Laura's mother responded.

Fuck if that's going to happen. Jackie tasted acid rising up from her stomach. "I need to run. See you soon." Jackie didn't give her a chance to respond and ended the call, then grabbed a bottle of antacid from her suitcase and chewed a handful.

Jackie recalled what Laura's mother said privately to her when she visited after Wyatt's birth, "This gay thing won't last, Jackie, and when it ends, Laura can marry a man who can support her and Wyatt." Jackie took a few more antacids.

Her last call was to Sarah, who picked up right away, "Hey, Jackie, what the hell? You met Zuzu?"

"Sure did. Looks like we may meet at this lesbo bar tonight. Nothing firm, but I'd say it's gonna happen," Jackie said.

"I'm not sure if that's such a good idea. I spoke with Campos, and this case sounds dangerous. Why not let them solve it?" Sarah said.

"I know, I know. I spoke to them, too. I'm sure they'll solve it eventually—just thought I'd gather some intel for them before I head home to total chaos. Nothing dangerous, believe me. I have to tell you, I had the best time with Biker Bob; he owns a killer burger place down here. And we went to Zuzu's biker shop. She's quite a kick—a short and sassy butch, and smart." Jackie sat down on her hotel-room bed.

"Be careful, Jack. You've got enough on your plate already. Promise me you won't do anything stupid and get in any trouble acting like a PI. You know you're not one, right?" Sarah pleaded.

"I promise. I'm going to have a couple scoops of fun tonight, though. If I see Zuzu, great; if not, I don't care. They have rum, chicken wings, and disco music at the bar she recommended—a perfect trifecta. I left Laura a voicemail about you being a donor, so I hope she can see her way to agreeing with that move. Any update on when you might get full clearance?" Jackie asked.

"I'm getting a few more tests done, but I'm hoping to get the all-clear in a couple more days," Sarah said. "I'm going to see the psychiatrist who consults on complicated living-donor cases, just to have the evaluation on the record. I'm sure there won't be a problem. If you and Laura decide I'm not right for Wyatt's match, I may go ahead and be an altruistic donor on the waitlist after we get Wyatt all squared away."

"What's an altruistic donor?" Jackie asked.

"It's someone who donates their kidney but isn't part of any paired exchange. It's pretty cool. Usually they donate to someone who doesn't have a living donor, or they start a paired exchange. They do it out of the goodness of their heart and are healthy and want to help. We do about five or six of those a year. I figure, why not? I'm not going to have any kids, and while I would prefer to be part of Wyatt's paired exchange, if it doesn't work out, at least I can help out someone else," Sarah said.

"You're a mensch, Sarah. You warm my heart and soul. I can never repay you for what you're willing to do for Wyatt, whether it works out or not."

"You'd do the same if the tables were turned, my friend. Call me when you get home. And behave yourself tonight," Sarah added.

"I'll have to—you're not here to party with me, and Biker Bob is on the road. I've gotta be in good shape for my boy. We'll talk soon, buddy."

Jackie ended the call and thought, *I'm the luckiest girl to have Sarah as my best friend. There's no one better in the whole world.*

• • •

It was close to 9:00 p.m. when Jackie walked into Fagina's. An old-fashioned disco ball twirled around from the ceiling, casting rainbow lights on a dance floor packed with women. She muscled her way to the bar and waited her turn to order. "I'll have a double Bacardi coconut rum with a splash of club soda and a slice of lime."

Behind the bar, a large black woman with a four-inch-deep cleavage nodded and returned with a tall glass filled to the top. Jackie handed her $10. "Keep it." After she took a long drink, she turned around and cased the place, looking for Zuzu. It was a dense crowd, so she wasn't sure she'd be able to find her, even if she was here. Donna Summer's "Rumour Has It" was blasting, and the dance floor was going crazy.

Jackie finished her first drink, got another, and decided she would dance her way around. It was close to midnight when she looked at her watch—many drinks and a basket of wings long gone. Still no Zuzu, so Jackie decided to have one more cocktail and dance and then head back to the hotel, when she spotted Zuzu walking through the door. *She sure looks cute. If I wasn't married, I'd definitely ask her out,* Jackie thought. Cocktail in hand, Jackie danced up to Zuzu. "Howdy, stranger. This place is the best! Can I buy you a drink?"

Zuzu looked at Jackie and smiled. "Of course. Double Jack Daniel's and Coke." Jackie danced her way back to the bar, ordered up, and returned to a small table Zuzu had secured. "Here you go! Cheers." Jackie clinked her glass with Zuzu's, and they both took a long drink. Barry White's "You're the First, the Last, My Everything" came on, and Jackie put her glass down on the table, "I'll be right back; this is one of my favorites. Feel free to join me if you'd like." Jackie left Zuzu sitting at the booth as she went out and joined the rest of the girls on the dance floor, singing and smiling. When the song had ended, she rejoined Zuzu at the table, where there was another drink waiting for her and Zuzu was enjoying her second.

"I was just about to head out," Jackie said. "You made it in the nick of time."

Zuzu smiled. "I can't stay long, either. Work to do tomorrow. Thought I'd stop by, though. Always a good time in this place. I met my last girlfriend here about four years ago."

Jackie's mind slowed down for a minute; she was feeling no pain but wasn't bombed, as she had paced herself over the evening, knowing she needed to be careful if she was solo in Miami.

"This would be a great place to meet someone. Everyone is so friendly. The alcohol helps, of course. Is your girlfriend going to meet you here?" Jackie asked, hoping Zuzu would share something about Kayla.

"Nope. She's left the planet. But when I'm ready, I'm sure I'll meet my next gal here or in Wilton Manors." Zuzu took a drink.

"Sorry about your loss." Jackie left it at that.

"Crazy shit. She died of a drug overdose, and she didn't even do drugs, so I'm not sure how that happened. That's why the cops were giving me shit, thinking I know something, which I don't. Enough about me, though. What's your story? Why are you in Miami?" Zuzu finished her drink.

"My son is sick, and we took him to a specialist at the medical center. My wife took him home to San Francisco a couple days ago, and I'm heading back tomorrow." Jackie saw a brief look of disappointment flit across Zuzu's face when she mentioned Laura.

Zuzu lifted one eyebrow. "Married, huh? That's too bad. I'm getting another drink. Want one?" Zuzu stood up.

"I'm good. Still enjoying this one. Thanks." Jackie watched Zuzu walk toward the bar, thinking, *I'm not about to play the cheating game like Laura, but it sure is tempting.*

Zuzu returned and sat across from Jackie. "Sorry to hear your son is sick. I hope he'll be okay."

"He will be. We just want to make sure he gets the best care he can; my wife is a doctor, so we want to make sure we know all our options." As Jackie took a sip of her drink, several women walked by their table and said hi to Zuzu.

Jackie smiled. "You're a popular gal."

"This is my stomping ground." Zuzu finished her drink and stood up. "I'm heading out. You need a lift back to your hotel?"

"That would be great. Thanks." Jackie stood up and followed Zuzu outside, expecting to see her motorcycle parked nearby. Instead, Zuzu led her to a black van.

"Hop in. I had to pick up some big motorcycle parts, so I brought my van." Zuzu got behind the wheel and waited for Jackie to get in on the passenger side.

"I'm staying at the Best Western near the medical center," Jackie told her, and Zuzu turned her van in that direction.

Jackie thought she'd take a chance and ask a question about Kayla: "Do you have any idea why someone would have given your girlfriend an overdose?"

"Beats the hell out of me. I'm sure she didn't do it to herself. She was way too smart for that. All I remember is that she was really nervous when she left my place, and I asked her what was wrong. She said some guy from work wanted to meet her at her grandmother's house. I was confused because no one from her work ever came out here that I knew of, but then, we didn't always tell each other everything." Zuzu pulled into the Best Western parking lot.

"What'd the cops say when you told them about the work guy?" Jackie opened the van door.

Zuzu looked over at Jackie. "You know, I don't think I mentioned that; I was too pissed off that they had the gall to think I would kill her. Anyway, it's their case to solve, not mine."

"Got it. Well, it sure was nice to meet you, Zuzu. Keep an eye on my friend Biker Bob." Jackie said, as she got out of the van.

"Funny, that's what he told me to do with you. I have delivered you safe and sound, so I've fulfilled my promise to him. Take care, Jackie. Hope your son is better in no time." Zuzu put the van in gear and drove away.

Chapter 19

Sarah's first meeting of the day was with Ned. She met him in Kayla's office, where he was sitting in front of her computer. All of Kayla's belongings were in two cardboard boxes on the floor, the walls barren, as if no one had ever occupied the space. *Sad how quickly a fifteen-year employee can just be erased in a few minutes*, Sarah thought.

When Ned saw Sarah, he stood up immediately and offered her a seat next to the desk.

"Sit down, Ned. You okay?" Sarah noticed perspiration on his upper lip, and his cheeks were rosy against his typically pale complexion.

"I'm fine, I'm fine. Just trying to clear out all of Kayla's files; she collected a lot during her time here."

"Did you get a chance to look at the information in her personal files?" Sarah asked.

"I didn't feel comfortable reading any of them, but there was one entitled 'Grandmother,' and it was big. There were some files I wasn't sure what to do with, so I'm glad you're here." Ned glanced at Sarah.

His big aviator glasses looked like they needed a good cleaning, and he had some crumbs left over from his breakfast on the edges of his mouth. *Gross,* Sarah thought. "What are the titles of the files?" she asked.

Ned shifted uncomfortably in his chair. "I'll pull them up and show you."

Sarah moved her chair next to his in front of the computer and noticed Ned's body odor. "Ned, were you here all night?"

"Yeah, I had some system upgrades to install overnight, and then I wanted to get this done for you, so I caught a few winks in my office." Ned opened the files.

Sarah's mouth dropped when she read the file entitled "Manager Blackmail." Ned clicked it open, and there was folder with her name and a separate file for each of the previous managers. "That's concerning. Why don't you download that on a separate thumb drive?"

Ned pushed a new thumb drive into the side of her computer and transferred the file to the icon on her desktop. Ned clicked on the next file, and Sarah's eyes skimmed the title: "Surgeon Fuckups and Indiscretions." "Oh boy," she said. "Seems like Kayla was an inside detective collecting all kinds of information. I'm sure Dr. Bower will want a copy of this. Put one on my thumb drive, make a separate one for him, and bring it by his office, please." Sarah glanced at her watch and realized she was late for her appointment with the living-donor psychiatrist. "Ned, I have to go. Can you put all the questionable files on my thumb drive and drop it off at my office?"

Ned stood up. "Sure thing, Sarah. And sorry about this. I'm sure it has to be distressing, but I'm not surprised. Kayla didn't seem to like anyone here, so I guess she felt the need to document everyone's actions. Who knows if this stuff is true or not? She even had a file on me!"

"You?" Sarah responded. "You wouldn't hurt a church mouse, Ned. She wasn't a happy person, so don't worry—it's likely all made up. I know she was mean to you, and I'm betting you didn't like her, either."

Ned sighed. "I tried to stay out of her way. I saw how she treated people, including me, so I figured it was best to get her whatever she needed and move on."

As Sarah was walking out of the office, she noticed that Ned's cheeks and neck had turned a deep red. "It's okay, Ned; this is all temporary. Please don't mention these files to anyone, including Detective Campos, until I have time to talk to Legal and Dr. Bower."

"No problem, Sarah." Ned smiled at her and then turned back to the computer.

As Sarah made her way to the elevator, she thought about how lonely and disheveled Ned looked some days—but then, that was usually the life of a medical-center IT guy, in her experience. She wondered if Ned had anyone in his life but then thought, *Who am I to talk? I don't have anyone telling me I have spinach in my teeth or that I smell. I'll probably be single the rest of my life.*

Dr. Fowler was waiting in his well-appointed office when she walked in. "Welcome, Sarah. Nice to see you." He stood up and motioned her toward a leather chair across from the one he was sitting in, a small coffee table between them.

"Sorry I'm late. I'm dealing with all kinds of crazy things, as usual." Sarah sat down and collected herself.

"I was so sorry to hear about Kayla. As you know, she and I worked together on living donors. Dr. Bower shared the circumstances of her death. Quite disturbing. Have there been any updates?" Dr. Fowler asked, leaning forward in his chair.

"It's very sad indeed. There's an active murder investigation under way in Miami, but no suspects yet," Sarah responded.

"Please let me know if there's going to be a service in San Francisco. I'd want to attend."

"Did you know her outside work, Dr. Fowler?" Sarah asked, wondering if she should tell Campos about him.

"Not really—just an occasional cup of coffee on campus to discuss one case or another. She seemed like a great gal, and she sure was a super coordinator. What a loss to our program. But that's not why we're here. Tell me a little about this case you're considering being a donor for."

Sarah sat back in her chair and took in Dr. Fowler's presence, as he slowly crossed his legs, interlocked his fingers, rested his hands on his lap, and gave her his full attention. "My best friend, Jackie Larsen's, son, Wyatt, needs a living donor kidney. I've been very close to him since he was born, and it appears I'm the best match for a paired exchange he's being considered for." Sarah paused.

"Sarah, I reviewed your living-donor paperwork and noticed that you've been taking Ativan for anxiety over the last year. Can you tell me a little about why you were taking it?" Dr. Fowler asked.

"I was a traveling nurse, working at the Miami International Transplant Institute, last year, when I discovered that one of my liver transplant patients had a boyfriend who helped her obtain a liver illegally. Unfortunately, the local police didn't believe me or Jackie, so we ended up playing detective, and it got very serious and scary. I was shaken, and my best friend was almost killed, so I needed something to calm my nerves. It all turned out okay—they were able to convict the couple—but it was touch-and-go for a while." Sarah's mouth felt very dry, so she took a sip of water from the bottle Dr. Fowler had set by her chair.

"That does sound very scary. Are you still taking the Ativan?" he asked.

"Very rarely. Actually, I can't remember the last time I took it. Usually a martini or a glass of wine does the trick. I don't need to tell you how stressful this place can get."

"No, you don't. Our transplant program can be a very stressful place to work, and becoming a living kidney donor can add its own pressures," Dr. Fowler said.

"The living-donor advocate did a great job of reviewing the entire process, and I must say that it seems less stressful than most of my workdays. I do understand it's major surgery, though. If I'd known I'd have to take six weeks off afterward, I would have been a living donor a long time ago." Sarah chuckled.

"Who will be at home to help you recover?"

"I have an old boyfriend, Mo, who's a comedian and will be in town. He'll help me laugh my way to a quick recovery." Sarah answered, then added, "I fell in love with him when I was in nursing school. We were together for almost two years; then he married and divorced someone else. We've become good friends over the years." *If Handsome and I were still together, he would have taken exceptional care of me*, Sarah thought.

"It does sound like you have what you need and are ready to move forward. I want to mention that if there's a family in your future, there's evidence that women who get pregnant after they have donated a kidney have a higher risk of complications."

"I understand, and appreciate your reminding me of that. I don't think I'm the marrying type or much interested in having children. Please be assured that I have given this serious thought, and I must say, it feels like the right choice in my gut." Sarah noticed she was leaning in toward Dr. Fowler and sat back into the chair, stretching her legs out a little in front of her.

Dr. Fowler made a few notes and then looked up at Sarah. "I know that Jackie and Laura don't want Wyatt to go on dialysis or get an access, which means his transplant is being fast-tracked."

Sarah sat up. "It *is* happening fast, but you should know that even if the situation were moving at a slower pace, I'd still make the same decision to donate."

Dr. Fowler arched his eyebrows. "I hear you, Sarah, and it seems you have approached this with a level head. I also understand that Laura was being considered as a living donor as well; has she expressed any concern about your being the donor instead?" he asked.

"Given her recent promotion at the ME's office and Wyatt's health, I know she's been extremely busy, so we don't talk that often." *While you're at it, you may also want to ask the bitch why she's cheating on my best friend*, Sarah thought.

Dr. Fowler stood up, and Sarah followed him as he walked her to the door and opened it. "If you have any questions or thoughts about donating your kidney, feel free to pick up the phone and call me, Sarah, and please do let me know when Kayla's memorial is."

Sarah nodded. "Will do, Dr. Fowler. Take care."

As Sarah made her way toward her office, her cell phone started ringing. "Hey, Jackie, are you back?" Sarah put her phone to her ear as she continued walking, electing to take the stairs so she could talk to Jackie and get some exercise at the same time.

"I'm about to catch the Marin Airporter to the land of Grandmother Hell and Cheater Town. Thank God I had a couple scoops of crazy with Biker Bob, but don't worry, I didn't get too wild—no arrests, and a hangover I cured with his un-fucking-believable cheeseburgers. I just wanted to let you know I landed safe and sound, since you're the only adult in my life who truly cares about me. How's your world, my friend?"

Sarah talked as she walked up another flight of stairs. "I just finished meeting with Dr. Fowler, the psychiatrist. He interviews any questionable living donors who the social worker thinks need a closer look."

Jackie laughed. "Were you able to play it straight, or are you getting admitted to the nuthouse? Be sure to ask for two beds, because I may be right behind you."

Breathing rapidly, Sarah reached the floor where her office was located and opened the stairway door. She chuckled and said, "He's a great guy, but he did interrogate me about the fact that I've never had a long-term relationship and whether I want to get pregnant at some point. I assured him I'm not looking to get married or have a family. His line of questioning left me feeling like a total loser in that department, but oh well."

"You sound out of breath. Are you okay?" Jackie asked.

"Yeah, I just wanted to increase the blood flow to my brain before I tackle the rest of my day, so I took the stairs. Did you have a chance to talk to Laura about my being a donor?" Sarah left the stairwell and began to walk toward her office.

"I left her a message, but I haven't heard back from her, so I'm guessing we'll be having a festive family dinner tonight, and then I'll know more. Can't wait to hug my boy. I can tell you one thing: We're having the transplant at your place, so that's one question off the table," Jackie said.

"That sounds like it's in everyone's best interest. Call me tonight after everyone is in bed and give me the update. I know you hate Granny from Hell, but be nice—we may need her to watch Wyatt so you and I can take a few days away before the transplant and who-knows-what with your marriage. The only good thing about that is, you don't have to ask Laura if you can go anywhere now." Sarah arrived at her office, opened the door, and sat down at her desk. She saw the thumb drives from Kayla's computer that Ned had left for her next to her desk phone.

"I'm not asking her shit. Once we have the transplant date, we'll go up to Calistoga, take a mud bath, get a massage, have a nice dinner, and relax. I know it won't be our usual blowout 'cause you have to stay tip-top for the big donation day, but it will still be nice to get away. Gotta go—the Airporter bus is here. I haven't even told you about my night out with Zuzu; I may have some intel. I'll call you tonight," Jackie said, and hung up.

Sarah smiled. *Jackie always makes me feel better, even when nothing else in my life seems to be going well.* When she noticed the voicemail light flashing on her desk phone, she tapped in her code and put the phone on speaker so she could jot down the messages.

"Hi, Sarah. This is Kristin, Dr. Bower's wife. I'm not sure if you received my first message, but it is imperative that I speak with you today about a project. Believe me, I know how busy everyone is at that place, so I'll just take a minute. Be a doll and give me a call." As Sarah wrote down Kristin's cell number, she said aloud, "Doll? Yuck." But then she thought, *Still, I'd better just get back her so she'll leave me alone.*

Sarah dialed the number, and Kristin answered. "Hi, Kristin. Sarah Golden here. Sorry I wasn't able to call you back right away. What can I do for you?"

Kristin's breathy voice came through the speakerphone. "Oh, Sarah, thanks so much for the call back. I totally understand your hectic schedule—I'm married to a transplant surgeon, after all—so I'll get to the point. I spoke to the new board I formed about the need for someone who really knows the ins and outs of the transplant and organ-donation world to join us, and I recommended you. Everyone was unanimously in favor, so I'm calling to offer you a seat at the big

girls' table. What do you say? Of course, it's a paid position."
Kristin paused.

Sarah's stomach sank. The last thing she wanted was to
have any contact with Kristin after all she had learned about
her when she and Jackie had followed her last year. Jackie
and Sarah had followed Kristin and Amanda Stein when they
were in Miami for a fashion show and had discovered that
Kristin was publicly cheating on Dr. Bower. But all she said
was, "I am so very honored and grateful, I really am, but my
plate is more than full with my work here. I barely get home
to sleep."

Kristin interrupted, "My husband told me you'd decline,
so I have a counteroffer: How about you become a paid con-
sultant when we need someone to go do fieldwork, check out
how the grants are coming along? I'm sure you've heard how
well the project in Miami is going—big increase in Latino
organ donors, especially with this opioid crisis, sad to say. I
won't take no for an answer."

Sarah was gritting her teeth but paused. A side gig could
help offset the future travel costs she and Jackie might have
once Jackie and Laura's divorce was final. "How about you
send me a list of the dates and places I'd need to conduct
a site visit, and then I'll let you know? I really need to go
now, Kristin, but please let the board know I'm flattered to
be considered."

Sarah was about to end the call when Kristin piped up,
"I'll get that list off as soon as I hang up. I also want you to
know, Sarah, that I don't blame you for what happened with
Amanda and Sergio last year. I had no idea how he got her
liver. I'm just glad my name was cleared. Goodbye."

Sarah didn't want to even think about last year's chaos.
She looked at her cell and saw that Jackie had texted her: "On
the bus. The last thing Zuzu told me was that Kayla left her to

meet some guy from the office at her grandmother's house. Does that make any sense?"

Sarah read the text several times. *I have no idea who the guy could be*, she thought.

Chapter 20

Campos and Strong spent the entire day writing down all the facts of Kayla's case and listing all the outstanding suspects. Campos was taking a red-eye to San Francisco that night, and they were both hoping she'd uncover some clues that would lead them to the killer.

"The way I see it, there are several possible suspects." Strong walked up to the whiteboard in the empty precinct staff room and started to write down names.

"We have Zuzu, who I need to interview again while you're in San Francisco. She's still a prime suspect in my mind," Strong said.

"I only got to interview the one surgeon, and if the others are like him, I'll shoot myself. Write down SF surgeons as a group of possible suspects. It really is hard to pin them all down at once. I did get an update from the chair of the department of surgery that the best she could do was have them all in one room for a half hour before their kidney-selection meeting. Any idea how to question a group of distracted, arrogant doctors?" Campos chuckled.

"That's a new one for me," Strong said. "But Sarah once told me this crew loves to transplant as many patients as they can—it's like a contest to see who can do the most transplants when it's their turn for call—so my advice is to put them all on the defensive by threatening to shut down their transplant program until we find the killer. Then watch them squirm."

"They're smart surgeons; they know we can't shut them down. Great idea, though. I may do it just for fun and get them riled up," Campos said.

"I'd also ask who worked closely with her. Maybe go around the table and have them answer why they think someone would kill her and who they think it could be. You never know. How many surgeons are we talking about here?" Strong asked.

"There are ten surgeons, but I already interviewed one, who I may interview again. I just can't imagine that any one of them would take the time to fly to Miami to kill Kayla; it doesn't make any sense," Campos said.

"Was there any kind of transplant meeting in Miami during the time Kayla was murdered?" Strong asked.

"Turns out there was—the American Society of Transplant Surgeons was having some kind of organ-sharing symposium. Three SF Global Transplant Institute surgeons were in attendance. I had requested a separate meeting with them, but the chair said it was too disruptive to their surgical schedule. If a surgeon did kill her, it would have to be one of those three, don't you think?"

Strong was quiet, stroking his chin. "Hmm. That would make sense, but we know logic doesn't always apply when it comes to murder. I think you may have to escalate this request up to the CEO of the medical center and override the chair. You have to get a one-on-one with each of the three surgeons, if for no other reason than to eliminate them as suspects."

"I'm leaving in about four hours on the red-eye. I'm not sure I can get that done," Campos said.

"How about I work on the request after we list the rest of the suspects?" Campos nodded, and Strong wrote the rest of the names on the whiteboard.

Campos read them all aloud: "Zuzu; Sarah Golden; Ned Bisone; the three surgeons who were in Miami for the transplant conference—we'll call them the Miami Three; and then maybe there's someone we haven't even thought about yet, right?" She added "Unknown?" to the list.

Right after Campos had read all the possible suspects, a fellow detective walked into the room and glanced up at the whiteboard. "I see we have murder by committee—is that right? Wait'll the boys hear this." He walked out, laughing.

"Fuck you!" Strong shouted after him, as he erased the board before the rest of the peanut gallery came by. "He's such an asshole. Good thing you're going out of town so you don't have to be around this shit."

"I'm pretty sure it will be here for me when I get back." Campos grabbed her notes and started to walk back toward her desk to finish preparing for her trip, and Strong followed.

"I'll call the CEO and keep you posted. I'm heading back out to Wilton Manors tomorrow for another visit with Zuzu. I'll follow up on the DNA, too. You just bring me back a killer, Campos," Strong said.

"How about I bring you back two while I'm at it?"

Strong shrugged. "That's twice the paperwork, but why not?"

Campos left the precinct, rushed home to throw some clothes in a carry-on, and raced to the airport, barely making her plane. Her body ached from exhaustion, and she didn't even make it through the seat belt announcement before she passed out. Her eyes opened as the pilot announced their descent into San Francisco. She glanced out the window and took in the skyline, just as she had on her first flight. *Maybe someday I can come visit just for fun*, she thought. She stopped at the airport bathroom to freshen up, then headed out to the street to catch a cab. As the car headed to the transplant institute, she listened to a voicemail from Strong. "Hey, Campos, I got to the CEO through SFPD, and the three surgeons will make themselves available to you. Go to the chair's office, and they'll set up the meetings. I wasn't sure if any of the other surgeons would need a one-on-one, so I got SFPD to demand that you get what you ask for. I think they used the obstruction-of-justice line. Anyway, go get 'em! I'm on my way to see Zuzu. Maybe I'll see if I can tease anything about her encounter with Jackie in a roundabout way. Keep me posted. Call me with good or bad news."

After she listened to Strong's message, Campos reviewed the list of the names of all the surgeons, their photos, and their backgrounds, which she had printed from the surgery department's website. *Sounds like a friendly bunch, if you believe what's written here. Very accomplished lot.*

Campos stopped in the hospital bathroom to make sure she looked presentable. She ran her fingers through her short, curly hair to puff it up as she checked out her reflection in the mirror. Blue suit, button-down, collared white shirt, and a fresh complexion. *Not bad for sleeping on a plane all night*, she thought.

She took the elevator up to the fourth floor and showed the young man behind the desk her badge. "Detective Campos, Miami Police Department."

"Ah, yes, Detective Campos, we've been waiting for you. Please sit down. May I get you a cup of coffee? How was your flight?" He stood and walked around his desk toward the small kitchen.

"Slept the entire way. Black coffee would be great, thank you."

The young man returned with a paper cup and handed it to her. "Here you go. Dr. Bower will be here shortly and would like to speak with you before the surgeons' meeting. I'll page him and let him know you're here."

"Thanks." Campos sat down, pulled out her notebook, and reviewed the notes she and Strong had assembled. The desk phone rang, and the assistant answered and ended the conversation quickly. "Dr. Bower will be down in about thirty minutes. He was on call last night and is finishing a transplant."

Campos glanced up. "May I use a house phone to see if Sarah Golden is available while I wait?"

"I'll call her for you and see if she can come meet you." He paged Sarah, who returned his call immediately. "Hi, Sarah. Detective Campos is here and was hoping you might have a few minutes to talk while she waits for Dr. Bower to finish in the OR . . . Sure . . . Okay." He looked over at Campos. "She'll be right over."

"Thanks." Campos finished her coffee, reviewing her notes on Sarah, and was adding a few more questions just as Sarah walked into the office.

Sarah walked over to Campos's seat and said, "Welcome back, Detective. Have you eaten?"

Campos closed her folder and stood up. Sarah looked very professional in her white lab coat with her name embroidered over the chest pocket, her thin, strong figure, and long dark hair pulled back, highlighting her glowing complexion. *It really is a shame she and Strong didn't make it work—what a great-looking couple they would have made*, Campos thought. "I'd love to get some breakfast. May I leave my bag here?" Campos asked the assistant.

"Sure. I'll put it under my desk." After Campos handed him her bag, he added, "Sarah, I'll page you when Dr. Bower gets here."

"Sounds good. I'm taking her to the coffee shop on the first floor." Sarah led the way out. As she and Campos got off the elevator on the first floor, Sarah began, "So, how's the case coming along? Are you any closer to catching the killer?"

"I think we have some strong leads. I'm hoping you and your team can provide me with some more information. Were you able to get the files off Kayla's computer? I was hoping to look over what she had while I'm here, hopefully with Ned."

Sarah didn't respond right away but eventually answered, "Yes, Ned was able to get the files off her desktop. I have a thumb drive to share with you. I'm sure you know you can't take it with you, but you're welcome to review the contents while you're here. Once I know how long you'll be with the surgeons, I'll let Ned know when we'll need him."

They arrived at the coffee shop, where they waited in line with folks in blue hospital scrubs and lab coats, beepers going off periodically. When it was her turn, Campos ordered an egg sandwich and another cup of coffee. Sarah got a coffee and a scone. They sat at a small table across from each other, and before Campos started to eat, she asked Sarah, "Have you heard from your friend Jackie?"

Campos watched Sarah's face as she answered, "I sure did. She just got back from Miami yesterday. Why do you ask?"

"I'm sure she told you that she called Detective Strong and offered to help us out with the case, which is a bad idea, and we told her as much. These are bad people who did this to Kayla. We don't want Jackie meddling in our case, but she did mention that she might meet up with Zuzu. Then we never heard back from her about it. Did she happen to tell you what they discussed?" Campos asked.

Sarah said, "She didn't tell me too much about her visit; she's mostly concerned with her son's health, so she's focusing on getting him transplanted as soon as they confirm the living donor."

Campos kept eating, watching Sarah divert her eyes down toward the table while fiddling with her coffee cup. Finally, Sarah broke the silence: "She had a fun time with Zuzu at some bar. That Zuzu sure is a character, from what Jackie told me. I would never have known Kayla had a girlfriend in Miami, let alone one who owns a motorcycle repair shop. You don't have to worry about Jackie meddling. She's way too busy with her home life to waste any time on this case. Plus, I told her to stand down." Sarah looked up from the tabletop at Campos.

"That's great news. Did Jackie mention if Zuzu said anything specific about Kayla's death or who she thought might have killed her?" Campos finished her sandwich.

"She was sure it wasn't Zuzu; she's had a tough life and has no need to make it more complicated. Didn't you and Handsome go out and interrogate her?" Sarah asked.

Campos chuckled. "Oh, so your friend Jackie's not the only one who calls him Handsome. I call him Strong, and when I mention your name, he does get a little flustered." Campos watched Sarah turn red from her neck up to her cheeks.

Before she could respond, Sarah's beeper went off. She glanced down at the message and then said, "Dr. Bower is waiting for us upstairs." She stood up, and Campos followed. After they cleared their table, they took the elevator up to Dr. Bower's office.

He stood up from behind his desk when they entered his office, and put his hand out to shake Campos's. "Nice to meet you, Detective. Please come in and sit down. Thanks for bringing her by, Sarah. Will you close the door on your way out?" He motioned for Campos to sit in the chair across from him. Sarah walked toward the door and, before closing it, said, "Please have your assistant page me when the detective is finished questioning all the surgeons."

"Will do. Ned was just here and brought me a thumb drive of information from Kayla's computer; he said you told him to give it to me. I'm not sure what that's about." Campos turned to watch Sarah's face. She pursed her lips and rolled her eyes toward the ceiling.

"Oh, yes, there's some information about the donor cases she was working on, and we'll need to discuss which surgeons you want the coordinators to work with on each case. Maybe later today?"

Dr. Bower responded, "Won't happen today. I have a couple kidneys coming in and a living kidney transplant to do before that. Maybe tomorrow. I'll let you know. Why don't you just look over the cases and assign them? You know how to do that. If the surgeons complain, let me know."

Sarah gave him a thumbs-up and closed the door.

Dr. Bower redirected his attention to Campos. "You can see we run a very busy program here. I'm sorry you and your partner had to call our CEO and threaten her with the SFPD. It was never our intention to obstruct justice, Detective."

Campos took a deep breath and looked straight into Dr. Bower's brown eyes. He looked like a guy she had once dated in Miami—*handsome and not to be trusted*, she thought. "I am not here to cause trouble, and I will be as efficient as possible, Dr. Bower. I admire what you and your team do here, and my partner and I are just trying to solve this case. Anything they can share that might help us find the killer would be helpful; sometimes one small clue leads to another. I have a few questions to ask before I meet with your team. I will need to meet one-on-one with the surgeons who were in Miami at the meeting that happened at the same time as Kayla's death. I want to ascertain whether they had any contact with her while they were there, and, if so, how she seemed or whether she said anything unusual or concerning." Campos paused as she took out her notebook.

Dr. Bower was watching her intently, and she noticed her heart rate increase. "I understand that you worked closely with Kayla and considered her your best coordinator—is that correct?"

"She was our best coordinator by far; she got things done without complaining and was respected by our faculty. I am aware that she didn't get along with many of the transplant staff, but we're not running a social club here."

Campos was making notes. "Were you aware of any drug problems with Kayla? As you know, she died from an overdose of opioids."

Dr. Bower responded, "I was shocked to hear that. In the fifteen years I knew her, I never saw any behavior that would have led me to think she was any type of addict. It's a national epidemic, of course—115 people die every day from a drug overdose. The only good that comes of it is that these are young, healthy people who, after being declared brain-dead, are excellent donors. Kayla was well aware of these facts. I'd stake my reputation that she didn't take opioids; someone must have drugged her without her knowledge. Very sad indeed."

"I agree. We're still investigating this case. Tell me, do you or does anyone on your team prescribe opioids of any kind to your patient population?" Campos asked.

Dr. Bower frowned and sat back in his chair. "Rarely, if ever. Why do you ask?"

"We're trying to understand where Kayla could have gotten the drugs from if she did have them on her when whoever it was drugged her." Campos picked up her pen and made some notes, waiting for Dr. Bower to answer her.

"We never write prescriptions for our staff, Detective; they all have their own physicians, and their health matters are private, so I wouldn't know if anyone wrote Kayla a prescription for anything." Dr. Bower looked at his watch. "The other surgeons will be waiting in the conference room, so we should head out."

"A couple last questions: Who do you think would kill Kayla, if it was someone on your team? And why would they kill her?"

Dr. Bower stared at Campos. "Detective, we simply do not have the time to kill anyone, even if we hated them. I can assure you that our workload is such that we're barely able to eat and sleep most days and nights. Honestly, I find this line of questioning very offensive." He stood and opened his office door, glancing over his shoulder. "Our conference room is to the left. I'll meet you in there."

Campos stood up and gathered her things, walked to the end of a short hallway that led to a door marked CONFERENCE ROOM, and opened it. Inside the room was an oblong wooden table surrounded by surgeons, all on their phones. They didn't even glance up at her, so she quietly found a seat and put her notebook on top of the table. Dr. Bower walked in and sat down. "This is Detective Campos, from Miami. She's here to ask you a few questions. It seems we're all under suspicion for the murder of Kayla, so if you would be so kind as to answer her questions, she'll be on her way quickly."

The surgeons all glanced up, and one at the end of the table chimed in, "Kill my wife, maybe, but not Kayla. She was our golden girl when it came to getting people transplanted."

Everyone laughed, and Campos cleared her throat. "Let's get started."

Chapter 21

When Jackie got home from Miami, Wyatt was playing in the front yard with the kid next door. As soon as he saw Jackie get out of the cab, he made his way toward her slower than usual, put his arms around her neck, and kissed her on her cheek. "I missed you, Momma!"

Jackie's heart sank as she bent down and hugged him back, sensing he was getting weaker. "I missed you, too, buddy."

"Grandma's inside, cooking, I told her that her food tastes yucky with no salt, she said I was being fresh. Can I hang out with my friend longer?"

"You sure can, take it easy though. I'll come out and get you when dinner is ready." She rubbed his head, and Wyatt walked back to his friend.

Jackie took a long, deep breath as she opened the front door. *Stay cool*, she told herself.

The aroma of cinnamon and baked apples permeated the house before she caught sight of the evil one; a tall, red-headed woman emerged from the kitchen with an apron on. "Welcome home, Jackie. I decided I'd bake an apple pie for our family dinner tonight. Wyatt said it's his favorite, but you don't bake, so I decided, why not?"

And we're off, Jackie thought. This was exactly how Laura's mother made her nuts. She always started with little digs that escalated slowly, until Jackie wanted to stab her. "How nice of you. I'm sure he'll appreciate it, and I know Laura loves home-baked goods, too." *Maybe her new girlfriend is Betty fucking Crocker*, Jackie thought.

"Did Laura mention when she'd be home?" Jackie asked, as she started upstairs.

"She's hoping not to have to work late again, that poor girl. She said maybe six-ish. That new job sure has taken its toll on her. I wish you'd all have said something earlier; I would have come out to help in a minute," Grandma replied.

"Well, you're here now. I'm going upstairs to unpack and make a few calls. Then I'm taking Wyatt to the forest preserve for a little stroll."

Jackie didn't wait for a reply and went into the bedroom she and Laura shared. It was all tidied up, bed made, likely by Laura's mother. Laura was always running out in the morning for some work catastrophe or another, leaving Jackie to clean up after her in the bathroom and bedroom, in addition to caring for Wyatt.

The scent of Laura's mother's strong perfume greeted Jackie before she stepped into the study, where Jackie had moved her things following her big fight with Laura after Sarah's visit. All of Laura's mother's things were in the closet. Laura must have moved Jackie's stuff back into their room, wanting to make it look like everything was hunky-dory.

"Momma! Momma!" Wyatt yelled, as he walked up stairs.

"I'm in the study," Jackie replied.

Wyatt came in and gave her another hug. Then his nose wrinkled. "What's that funny smell in here?"

"That's Grandma's perfume. Kinda strong, eh?"

"Yeah, it makes the inside of my nose itch a little. It smells like rotten fruit." Wyatt followed Jackie into their bedroom and lay down on the bed.

"You tired, buddy?" Jackie asked.

"Only a little. Grandma let me sleep in this morning. I'm always thirsty, I don't like sucking on ice. Can't I have just a little more water?"

Jackie filled a small cup halfway with water from the bathroom sink. "You'll be able to drink as much as you want soon. How about we go to a matinee? I'll check to see what's playing. Sound good?"

Wyatt took the water and drank it down fast.

"The *Wild Life* movie is playing—you know, the one about the funny talking parrot and his friends who help the guy who gets stranded on the island, like Robinson Crusoe? How about it?" Jackie had quickly decided that a nature walk would need to wait. She had to adjust Wyatt's activity depending on his energy, which was consistently declining. She could tell it was time to have his kidney blood levels checked, to see how much they had declined; she already knew the answer.

"That sounds fun. Can I invite a friend?" Wyatt asked, sitting up on the end of the bed.

"Not today. I missed you so much, I just want to be with you."

Jackie's cell phone rang, and she saw Laura's name on the screen. "It's Mom. Why don't you go downstairs and let Grandma know we're going to the movies? Tell her I'll be down in a minute."

"Okay." Wyatt got off the bed and left the room.

"Hello," Jackie answered.

"Hi, Jack. I see you got home okay. Everything all right?" Laura asked.

"I think you know the real answer to that, Laura. Your mom has already started with her passive-aggressive comments. Such a nice thing to come home to." Jackie could feel the muscles in her neck tensing up as she spoke.

"I'm not going to get in a fight with you, Jackie, at least not over the phone. I wanted to let you know that I got your voicemail about Sarah being the living donor, and I'm going to give you this one. And, as we discussed, Wyatt will get his transplant in San Francisco."

Laura's condescending tone was just too much. "'Give me'?" Jackie snapped. "You're in no position to *give* me anything, Laura. It's in our son's best interest to get the best match, so don't make it sound like you're doing me this huge favor. Listen, I'm taking Wyatt to a movie now. Why don't you call your mental mother and let her know when her little girl is coming home from her hard job. Poor little Laura. Are you bringing your new girlfriend home to meet your mama? Maybe she'll actually accept that you're gay." Jackie hung up abruptly, turned her phone off, put it in her pocket, and went downstairs.

Wyatt looked up at Jackie as she walked into the living room. "Momma, your face is all red. Were you exercising?"

Jackie laughed. "Oh, buddy, you are something else. It must have gotten red from me running down the stairs."

The demon came out of the kitchen and said, "Wyatt told me you're taking him to the movies. I sure hope you'll both be home in time for dinner. You know I like to serve it at six o'clock sharp. It's important to keep Wyatt on a schedule. I've been feeding him dinner every night at six. Bed by eight." She smiled.

Just then, the house phone rang and she picked it up. "Hello," she said, in a fake-nice voice. "Oh, hi, Laura. How's your day going, honey?"

With that, Jackie motioned for Wyatt to follow her as she grabbed the car keys and headed out the front door, giving a short wave with her fingers.

"Just a minute, Laura." Demon put her hand over the phone mouthpiece. "Jackie, Laura wants to speak with you after I'm done talking to her."

"Tell her we'll be late for the movie, we can catch up when she gets home for work." Jackie closed the door. Once she and Wyatt were on their way to the movie, she put the car window all the way down and inhaled some fresh air.

Wyatt looked over and asked, "Can I get some candy at the show, Momma?"

"I say let's split something. You okay with that?"

"You're not always a good sharer, Momma. How about we each get our very own little treat bag?" Wyatt asked.

"Always the negotiator. Perfect idea." Jackie chuckled.

Inside the theater lobby, Jackie got a box of Good & Plenty and Wyatt chose a box of red licorice. The outside world disappeared as they enjoyed their treats and watched the movie. Jackie smiled as she listened to Wyatt laugh out loud at the disappearing lizard and crazy parrot. It was about five-thirty when they walked outside.

Wyatt entertained Jackie as she drove them home, telling her about a silly friend from school who made him laugh with knock-knock jokes.

Laura's car was parked in the driveway when Jackie pulled up. "Yea, Mom's home." Wyatt said, and hopped out of the passenger seat.

Jackie waited in the car for a minute. *You need to pretend it's all right. Hide your pain for Wyatt's sake,* she told herself. Yet, despite her pep talk, tears welled up in her eyes as she tried to imagine a life without Laura and what divorce would do to their son. She pulled down the vanity mirror and saw that her eyes were red. As she wiped them she thought, *Just pretend you're happy. Detach until you can vent with Sarah.*

Jackie watched as Laura came out the front door and Wyatt hugged her. She saw Laura glance at her and then turn around and walk into the house holding Wyatt's hand.

Laura, Jackie, and Wyatt all sat at the nicely set dinner table as the Laura's mom served each of them a plate with meat loaf, mashed potatoes, and gravy. "There's fresh cranberry sauce on the table. Wyatt, I know you love warm rolls with butter, so help yourself; they're in the basket under the blue napkin."

"Thanks, Grandma. Pass the butter, please."

"I know salt can cause water retention. That's the last thing Wyatt needs with his kidney failure, so I got him unsalted butter," Grandma mentioned.

"Thanks, Mom. I appreciate how careful you're being with Wyatt's dietary needs right now. It's all temporary," Laura said.

Jackie decided to keep her composure as she moved food around the plate, her silence would be best for everyone right now. She noticed Laura was watching her, likely noticing her red eyes.

As Grandma sat down, she looked around the table and said, "It's really my pleasure to be here and help out, and I must say, when Wyatt's at school, I get to catch up on all my soap operas. You won't believe what happened on *General Hospital* today. Anna was cheating on Bob with a doctor at work. I was shocked." She put her hand on her chest. Jackie looked toward Laura and raised her eyebrows, *you have got to be kidding, these are not real people,* she thought.

"Mom, we have no idea who these characters are. Jackie and I never got into soaps. No time." Laura turned her attention to Wyatt and asked, "How was the movie?"

Wyatt was scooping up his mashed potatoes and gravy with a spoon. After he finished his bite, he said, "Mom, you'd love it. There was a funny parrot and a lizard that disappeared when he got nervous. They're all stranded on an island with exotic animals. I wish we could live on an island with them. You can swim anytime you want to."

"Well, I'll have to go see it with you, too," Laura said. "How'd you like it, Jack?"

"It was beautifully animated, a takeoff on Robinson Crusoe. We should all go and see it again together," Jackie said, pushing the bland food around on her plate.

After the meal, they all cleared the table, and then Jackie motioned to Laura to follow her into the backyard while Wyatt helped Grandma clean-up.

Once they were outside, Jackie closed the sliding glass doors and said, "I think we should have your mom put Wyatt to bed so we can go out and talk."

"I was going to suggest the same thing," Laura said, and walked back inside.

Jackie stayed outside for a minute and watched Laura talk to her mom and Wyatt, until she noticed she was holding her breath. She inhaled deeply, then walked inside.

"Okay, you two, don't get into any trouble. Mom and I are going out for a little while. See you in the morning." Jackie gave Wyatt a hug and headed for the door. Laura followed after she kissed Wyatt goodbye.

They drove in silence until they got to a local Italian restaurant that had a bar area. Jackie pulled into a parking spot and started to get out.

"Wait, Jack. I think we need to talk before we go in there, so we don't make a scene. I really need us to do our best to be calm as we figure out what our next steps will be. Screaming and yelling won't get us anywhere." Laura paused.

Jackie turned toward Laura. "I hear what you're saying, and you need to know that I'm working hard to keep my emotions in check, at least in front of Wyatt, but we need to go see a therapist, someone who can help us navigate emotional landmines. Will you agree to that?"

"I agree, and yes, I will make the time."

"No canceling these appointments because of work, Laura. Our family, however it shakes out, is more important than your job," Jackie said.

Laura let out an audible sigh as they got out of the car and headed into the restaurant bar. "I don't need you preaching at me right now. Can we just have a drink without fighting? You think you can do that?"

"I'll do my best, but I'm not making any promises. Surely you have to understand how angry and deeply hurt I am right now, you cheated on me." Jackie said.

Italian music played in the background as they slipped into a maroon leather booth. The counter bar was filled with a variety of folks sipping martinis and beer and nibbling complimentary nuts. The waiter approached and asked, "How may I help you tonight?"

"I think we'll take a bottle of the house red and a couple glasses of water," Jackie ordered.

"Perfect. I'll be right back," the waiter replied.

After he walked away, Jackie looked over at Laura, her stomach churning, and said, "Listen, Laura, I know you don't want to talk about this, but I need to. I'm just so sad about where we are right now, and hurt by what you've done, and I'm not really sure how we're going to work it out, but the bottom line is, I want you to know that I love you. Is there any chance you want to reconcile?"

The waiter came to the table, opened the wine bottle he'd brought, and filled each glass, then left again.

Laura took a sip and looked over at Jackie. "I don't know. I'm confused. So many things are happening, and I have to admit I don't have my head screwed on straight. I think it's a good idea for us to see somebody and figure out the ground rules as we navigate Wyatt's care."

As Jackie took a sip of her wine, tears began to stream down her face.

Laura reached for her hand and said, "I'm so sorry, Jackie. I didn't mean for this to happen. I really didn't."

Jackie looked down at the table and slowly shook her head back and forth. "You act like you had no choice, but that's just bullshit."

"I wasn't out looking for a new relationship. You have to believe me."

"Don't play innocent with me, Laura—it takes two people to have a relationship. You have sent all our lives into a fucking tailspin." Jackie clenched her jaw. "And then you bring your mother out when you know she hates me and I cannot stand her—she blames me for you being a lesbian. My parents may have broken my heart when they disowned me for being gay, but at least they were straight-up about it. Your mother just tortures me; she has a PhD in passive-aggressive behavior."

"She drives me crazy, too. But we need her until we figure things out. Fair?"

"Fair, but I have to limit my exposure to her. I really do. I can't believe she still watches those mind-numbing soap operas. You'd think she'd watch the ones in Spanish; at least she could learn a new language. She really needs to get a life." Jackie leaned back in the booth.

"That's her life right now, and we're not going to change it." Laura shifted gears abruptly: "I want you to know that I'm fine with Sarah being the living donor for Wyatt's paired exchange if she's the best match. Why don't you connect with a living-donor team and just let me know what you need from me?" Laura paused. "Also, for now, I think it's important for us to be together at home, let my mom sleep in the den, and work to be civil with each other."

"I'll do my level best." Jackie replied as she poured more wine for herself. She took a sip and then looked at Laura. "Who is it?"

Laura stared at her wineglass. "No one you know. Someone from work."

Jackie asked again, a little more loudly, "Who is it, you fucking asshole? Who is worth breaking up our family?" Jackie saw a couple of heads at the bar turn in their direction.

Laura replied calmly, "Her name is Jennifer. She's doing her fellowship in pathology and plans to become a medical examiner."

Jackie shook her head and grunted. "And to think I always judged my friends who said they knew their husbands were working late and then found out they were sleeping with their secretary. It's so trite. I just can't believe you fell into this trap."

After a prolonged silence, Jackie had to ask, "You have risked everything we have built. We had a good life, or at least I thought we did. We both adore Wyatt. Have you totally given up on us?"

Laura responded, "Again, I don't know, Jack. We were in trouble way before Wyatt got sick. I'm willing to let Jennifer know we need a break while you and I go to therapy and put everything on hold until after Wyatt's surgery. That's the best I can do right now."

"*Willing?* That's the best you can do!" Jackie stood up. "Would you be *willing* to pay the fucking bill and meet me in the car?"

Aware of more people staring at her and then glancing over toward Laura, Jackie left the restaurant, got in the car, and started the engine. "I can't think straight I'm so angry," Jackie said out loud.

She sat behind the wheel and stared out the windshield while Laura slid into the passenger seat. Sadness coated the interior of the vehicle as the silence between them consumed all the energy. As Jackie pulled out of the parking lot she said, "I'll drop you at home. I need to call Sarah and talk to someone I can *actually trust.*"

After Jackie took Laura home, she headed to a nearby playground, where she sometimes took Wyatt to play, all the while thinking about her next steps: *I'm going to have to get a nursing job. I haven't practiced in eight years. And I'll probably need to buy Laura out of the house, which I don't have the money to do. It'll turn my life inside out.*

She parked the car and called Sarah. When she answered, "Hey, Jack. How you doing?" Jackie started to sob uncontrollably into the phone.

Chapter 22

There were a few cancellations in Sarah's schedule, so she closed her office door and decided to review everything she thought she knew about Kayla's case. She had watched Handsome analyze his cases when they were together, so she mimicked his approach.

She put an eight-by-eleven-inch piece of paper on her desk and listed the possible suspects, writing each name on a separate Post-it and lining them up across the top. There was Ned, Zuzu, surgeons from the Miami meeting and surgeons at home, and then a Post-it with a question mark for a different potential murderer, if it wasn't any of the people she'd just named. *I know I didn't do it*, she said to herself, *so that's one down.* Then she wrote "motive" under each name and stopped to think about why each suspect might have wanted to kill Kayla. Kayla had humiliated Ned in public, so how about revenge? As for Zuzu, maybe Kayla cheated on her, broken her heart; Sarah would ask Jackie for more on that when they talked. All the surgeons loved Kayla, so she wrote down a question mark both for the ones in Miami and for the ones at home.

Just then, Sarah remembered that Ned had left her a copy of the thumb drive with the file that Kayla had kept on all the surgeons. She uploaded that file, opened the one that Kayla had labeled "Surgeon Fuckups and Indiscretions," and started reading. Kayla had created a page for each surgeon, listing when he or she had started at the Institute and any case-related mistakes he or she had made. Kayla would have known this information, as she went to the weekly conference where each transplant case was discussed, along with what, if anything, the surgeon or team could do better next time. Since the San Francisco Global Transplant Institute had some of the best outcomes in the country, the comments Kayla had made were minor.

Sarah scanned each page, noticing that Kayla had listed personal information of note for each doctor. As Sarah read Kayla's comments, she couldn't help commenting out loud on some of them. "Oh, my, I can't believe he slept with that coordinator, Really?" She could feel her own mouth hanging open as she continued. "Wow, wow, and double wow!" *How did she know all this?* Sarah wondered. *Did she hire a private investigator to follow these people around?*

Sarah listed each surgeon's name, wrote a brief note about his or her trespasses, and then looked at the ones with the longest lists of indiscretions.

Three surgeons stood out: Dr. Wood, Dr. Edwards, and Dr. Lester. Sarah took out the call schedule and looked at the list of the surgeons who had been in Miami when Kayla had been killed. Two out of the three, Wood and Lester, fit the bill; Edwards had been at home and on call. Wood had the longest list of points against him; apparently, he wasn't getting any at home, so, according to Kayla's notes, he had banged several of the coordinators and a few assistants. Wood was also the best living-donor surgeon.

Lester had had many temper tantrums, screaming at anyone within earshot if something wasn't perfect, and throwing things. *I would never have guessed this stuff in a million years—if it's true*, Sarah thought.

She finished scanning all the pages and also noticed that Kayla had noted each surgeon's DEA number, which they used to write prescriptions for narcotics. *Why would she need to know that?* Sarah wondered. Kayla had been a nurse practitioner and had had her own DEA number.

A strong knock on her door jolted her out of her concentration. "Who is it?"

"It's Ned. I just wanted to make sure you could open those files on the thumb drive."

Sarah put her papers into a folder and quickly opened her door. "Yeah, Ned, no problem. I was just reviewing them. Thanks for checking."

"I just came from Dr. Bower's office, and he wanted me to ask you to meet with him after selection today about those files," Ned said, as he moved his fingers through his oily hair.

"Selection? What time is it?" Sarah stood up and looked at her watch. "Shit, I'm late. I'm glad you stopped by, Ned. I've got to go." Sarah checked her lab coat pockets to be sure she had her beeper and cell phone and then walked past him. "Do you need me for anything else?"

"No. I just needed to give you Dr. Bower's message."

Sarah took the stairs down to the second floor and quietly went into the conference room, where the kidney team was already reviewing cases. She scanned the room, full of surgeons, nephrologists, social workers, and coordinators, all the recent information she had just read fresh in her mind.

Dr. Bower was at the head of the table. "Nice of you to join us, Sarah."

All the heads turned toward her momentarily, and she felt her cheeks flush.

They continued discussing the cases until they got to Wyatt's name, whereupon the living-donor coordinator glanced at Sarah and said, "It might be better if you step outside until we're done with this case."

Sarah nodded and went into the adjoining conference room. Ten minutes later, the coordinator came to retrieve her. "You can come back in now."

Sarah studied the coordinator's poker face to see if she could tell how Wyatt's case had gone, and put her thumb up and then down. The coordinator just shrugged her shoulders.

When the selection meeting disbanded thirty minutes later, everyone got up to leave, including Sarah. As she made her way toward the door, Dr. Bower called to her. "Sarah, do you have a few minutes?"

"Sure." She glanced at her watch. It was after five. She had planned to go to her gym for a dance class that she hadn't been to in years and wanted to start taking again. *Not today, I guess.*

After everyone left, Dr. Bower looked at Sarah from across the conference table. "I think it's a bad idea for you to be part of Wyatt's paired exchange. It's too complicated, and I know you and Laura aren't on the best terms."

Sarah bit the side of her mouth, considering how to respond. It wouldn't be smart to argue with him. Then she said, "You may be right, Dr. Bower, but will you hear me out?"

"Sure."

"It's no secret that Laura and I aren't close and really never have been. However, I'm a much better match with the other paired-exchange recipient, and their donor seems to be the best match Wyatt could have, unless he had an identical twin. Is that correct?" Sarah asked.

"That is correct, but the other pair is a high-profile case, so you won't know who you're donating to—not now, not ever. In addition, if anything goes wrong, Laura and Jackie will blame you. Why would you jeopardize that friendship?"

"I don't care who the other pair is, as long as Wyatt gets the best match he can. Did you speak with Dr. Fowler?" Sarah started to fiddle with a pen on the table.

"Dr. Fowler did come to the selection meeting and shared his findings about his interview with you. He was in support of your being a donor. It's just that you can never be sure of what the future holds, Sarah, or what you'll be called on to do if you choose to have a family." Dr. Bower's face softened.

Sarah sat farther back in her chair and took a minute, before responding, "I believe that you truly have my best interests at heart, Dr. Bower. You need to know that Wyatt is like a son to me, likely the only child I will be this close to the rest of my life. You also know how passionate I am about my transplant career. It's extremely important to me, more important than finding a man or starting a family." Sarah was looking directly into his eyes as she spoke, and he held her gaze.

"I hear you, Sarah, I really do, but I felt we needed to have this discussion before we went forward with anything. Sounds like you've made up your mind, then." Dr. Bower stood up.

Sarah got up from her chair and said, "I have, and I hope you'll support me through this process. I'd like Dr. Wood to remove my kidney, if possible."

Dr. Bower chuckled. "If he's here, he's all yours. You know he's on some national committees, so be sure to tell the living-donor coordinator to check his calendar when she schedules the case."

As they walked toward the conference room door, Sarah looked at him. "I'd like you to do Wyatt's transplant, if that's at all possible."

They stopped at the elevator bank, and Dr. Bower said, "I was planning on it. Oh, and one other thing: I got the thumb drive from Ned. Have you opened it yet?"

Sarah felt her stomach tighten. "No, I haven't had much time, between the police investigation and trying to find a new coordinator to replace Kayla."

"Don't look at that file. I think it's better you get rid of the thumb drive. Kayla tended toward drama, so who knows if anything in that file is true or not? She was a hard worker but an odd duck for sure." The elevator doors opened, and Dr. Bower got on and motioned for Sarah to join him.

"I think I'll take the stairs. I need the exercise. Thanks for your concern and support," Sarah blurted out as the doors closed. While she made her way through the stairway, she realized she hadn't read all the surgeons' files yet. *I wonder if there's something about Bower in one of those files that he doesn't want me to know about.*

As Sarah approached her office, she saw Ned standing outside, waiting for her. "Ned, I hope you haven't been standing here the whole time I was at selection."

"Oh, no, I was fixing one of the coordinators' computers; then I got a text from Dr. Bower just a few minutes ago, telling me to stop by and get the thumb drive containing the doctors' information. He wants me to clear the info, for some reason." Ned was standing a little too close to Sarah.

"Excuse me, Ned. I need to unlock my door. Just a minute—I'll get that thumb drive for you." Sarah let herself in and closed the door. She pulled the thumb drive out of the side of her computer and then minimized the file on her computer desktop. She opened her office door and handed Ned the drive. "Here you go. Crazy place we work at, eh?"

"Sure is, but I quit asking questions a long time ago. Just come in and get my work done as best I can each day—that's all I can do." Ned was still standing right next to her.

"I really need to finish a few things before I go home. Do you need anything else?" Sarah asked.

"No, no. I was about to ask you if you needed anything else before I leave," Ned offered.

"No, I'm good. Have a nice evening."

Sarah closed her office door, then unlocked her file cabinet containing all the employee HR records and pulled out Ned's and Kayla's. She wanted to review them when it was quiet. She opened Kayla's first, skimming her date of employment and prior work history, taking a few notes for quick reference.

Prior to working at the transplant institute in San Francisco, Kayla had worked at a drug rehab clinic in Florida. Sarah made a note to call that clinic, if it was still operating, and see if she could get someone to give her more background on Kayla.

After Sarah read the trail of past managers' handwritten notes about Kayla's unprofessional behavior, she checked for the official write-up letters, and, sure enough, found none in Kayla's file. This confirmed what Sarah already knew: Hospital policy allowed employees to request that past negative write-ups be removed from their file once three years had passed since the incident.

There were also at least five letters from various surgeons, including Dr. Bower, about what a fabulous coordinator Kayla was. *I wonder if she blackmailed them to write these*, Sarah thought. She made another note, to call HR and try to learn more about the past disciplinary actions that were no longer in Kayla's file. She searched for a next of kin, and there was only Kayla's grandmother's phone number and another telephone number, that one with a question mark next to it. She wrote down both numbers on her follow-up list.

Sarah closed Kayla's file and opened Ned's, which was much thinner, probably because he had been with the medical center for only four years and had moved around between different departments. His evaluations were middle of the road, nothing outstanding in his file. Sarah jotted down his next of kin's name and number, in case she needed to follow up. *That guy barely has time to brush his teeth and bathe—the things nerds can tolerate*, she thought. *Killing someone just seems like a huge stretch for a person like that.*

While she wrapped up her notes, Sarah's cell phone came alive with Jackie's signature ring tone, "Born to be Wild," by Steppenwolf. It always gave Sarah a good laugh, because it forced her to picture Jackie on the back of Biker Bob's Harley. She glanced at her watch and noticed that it was after 7:00 p.m.

"Hey, Jack, how's my born-to-be-wild pal?" Sarah started to chuckle, then stopped. All she could hear was Jackie's guttural sobbing.

Chapter 23

Campos had gotten through only half of her questions with the group of surgeons, when Dr. Lester stood up. "I have a transplant to get to. Best of luck with your investigation, Detective."

"Thanks, Dr. Lester. I'll need to meet with you later after your case; I believe you were in Miami when Kayla was murdered," Campos said.

As Dr. Lester walked toward the door, he added, "I have many alibis for my time while I was there. I'll send the names to Dr. Bower so he can share them with you."

After he left the room, Campos continued to ask the remaining surgeons the rest of the questions she and Strong had prepared back in Miami. "Did any of you ever prescribe pain medication to Kayla?" Campos looked at the group seated around the conference room table, almost half lost in their cell phones, ignoring her, the others flipping through paperwork. She caught Dr. Bower's eye and raised an eyebrow.

He cleared his throat. "Uh, Detective Campos really needs your undivided attention. The sooner you can answer her questions, the sooner you can all leave." They all looked up and over at him almost in unison. Dr. Bower shifted his gaze back toward Campos, and they followed.

"Thank you, Dr. Bower." Campos repeated her previous question: "Once again, did any of you ever prescribe Kayla pain medication?" She had made a list of each of the surgeons, so when they responded, she noted their comments. One by one, they shook their heads, except when it came to Dr. Spencer, the arrogant doctor Campos had interviewed on her last visit. "I did write her a script for some Oxycontin after she had all four of her wisdom teeth removed. She tried to rough it out, but it was clear she needed something when she came to work and was visibly in pain. Later that day, she was able to process several living donors, so it was worth it." Campos noticed the other surgeons look briefly at Spencer and then toward Dr. Bower.

Dr. Bower stared at Spencer and asked, "Her dentist didn't give her any?"

"He offered, but she refused."

"Was Kayla a patient of yours, Dr. Spencer?" Campos asked.

"Matter of fact, I was seeing her for a private medical matter, so it was all kosher," Spencer said.

Campos watched as the other surgeons glanced sideways at Spencer again. "Other than Dr. Spencer, did any of you ever prescribe anything to Kayla?" They all shook their heads no. "Any reason you can think of why someone would want Kayla dead?" Campos addressed the group, whom she was losing to their phones again.

Dr. Edwards, a thin Indian woman, responded in a soft voice, "I must say that Kayla was very rude and unprofessional to most of the transplant staff, doctors included, but I hardly think anyone would have killed her. Regardless of her gruff manner, she was a key part of our team and catapulted our living kidney-donor program to the top ranking in the country."

All the surgeons mumbled in agreement, and Campos looked over at Dr. Bower, who was pointing at his watch, indicating that her time was up. She quickly skimmed the remaining questions. "Thank you for your time. I know how busy you all are. I will let Dr. Bower know which of you I'll need to speak with separately later today."

As the surgeons began talking to each other about various cases, Campos remained seated and finished writing her observations, until everyone but Dr. Bower had left.

"Dr. Bower, I would have expected better cooperation from your team. I'll need to interview you and the three Miami surgeons for sure. I'll let you know who else I need to meet with when I'm finished."

"Shoot," he said.

"I'll need to access your surgeons' narcotics prescription history over the last four years. Can one of your staff get me that information?" she asked.

"That will take some work, but I'll see if I can get our pharmacist on it."

"Do you routinely prescribe opioids to your patients posttransplant?" Campos inquired.

"There's a very small incision for the kidney recipients and four very small incisions for the kidney donors. They really shouldn't be in a lot of pain postoperatively. If they need something the first couple days in-house, then of course we give them the strong stuff. But once they go home, Tylenol usually does the trick."

"Do your nurse practitioners or physicians' assistants prescribe narcotics for your patients?"

"Not usually. We have protocols that everyone uses to manage our patient population, and opioids are not part of those protocols." Dr. Bower was tapping his finger on the table.

"I just have a few more questions for you, Dr. Bower. Everything I've heard from your team suggests that you're a real taskmaster. Did you drive Kayla as hard as you do the other coordinators?"

"I didn't have to, Detective. Kayla was harder on herself than the surgeons or I could ever have been. I actually had to tell her to slow down, she was so intense, which is why you hear everyone say she screamed at people all the time."

"What do you think drove her so hard?" Campos asked.

"I think she was just wired that way. Once we all agreed on a plan to efficiently process every living donor, she went full steam ahead, and anyone who didn't was a target for her."

"If you had to take a wild guess about why someone would have killed Kayla using opioids, what would it be?" Campos sat back and studied Dr. Bower's face.

He frowned slightly as he said, "Kayla was a very lonely person. She was married to her work. I got emails from her at all hours of the night. She also shared with me that she was supporting her grandmother, so she always volunteered for any on-call time she could get. Our on-call pay is extremely lucrative. My guess is that you may find she killed herself; she wasn't close to anyone at work, and she lived alone. Sometimes, all that loneliness makes people get in their head in a bad way, when they have no one to bounce ideas or dark thoughts off of. I'm sure that's why she went to see her grandmother anytime she could. And I'm guessing she didn't want to burden her grandmother with her problems. How is she, by the way? She must be devastated."

Campos ignored Dr. Bower's question and changed the subject. "It's unfortunate that Kayla didn't feel as if she could trust anyone at work, for as much time as she spent here. There wasn't one surgeon or physician you can think of who she confided in?" Campos was not about to share with the San Francisco folks that Kayla's grandmother had been dead for over a year and half, or tell them about Zuzu. If she did that, they'd just wonder why Kayla had continued to go to Miami four times a year. Plus, Sarah might want to start digging more deeply into the investigation, and that was the last thing Campos wanted.

Dr. Bower sighed. "The only thing the surgeons wanted from her or any of the coordinators was to do more transplants. That's our only agenda. We're not a touchy-feely kind of team. The only other team member I can think of who may have spent some time with Kayla is Dr. Fowler, our consulting psychiatrist."

Campos wrote his name down. "Can your assistant contact him so I can meet with him over the next couple days?"

"Sure. Detective, I'm late for a meeting. Is there anything else you need from me?" Dr. Bower asked, as he stood and made his way toward the door.

Campos stood as well, and said, "Dr. Bower, one thing we know for sure is that it wasn't a suicide; there were signs of a struggle at the scene. The only other thing I'll need is access to all the files on Kayla's computer. I did ask Sarah for them, so hopefully she or Ned Bisone will have them ready when I meet with them today. Is there anything in those files that you think may help solve this case?"

"I have no way of knowing that. Your guess is as good as mine."

"Okay. Well, thanks for corralling your team today— worst case of adult ADD I've ever witnessed. And I thought detectives were bad." Campos chuckled.

Dr. Bower grinned. "We're best when we're in the operating room, concentrating on one thing. I hope you solve your case, Detective. Feel free to use the small office next to my assistant's desk for the remainder of your stay. Let him know what you need, and he's ready to help any way he can. Good luck." Dr. Bower shook Campos's hand.

After he left, Campos went into the small office and closed the door. She reviewed all her notes and made a list of all the interviews she needed to complete before she could fly home. She added Dr. Fowler to the list, then called Strong.

"Hey, have you solved this case yet?" she joked.

"Well, we're getting closer. I just hung up with Forensics. They did find some hair strands at the scene, and they're not Kayla's. They've got the DNA results, but there's no match, which means our killer isn't in the system, so that rules out Zuzu. You got any prime suspects up your sleeve?" Strong asked.

"Just met with a group of knucklehead surgeons; they give 'distracted' a new meaning. I have one new possible suspect, a Dr. Fowler, who's the transplant institute's consulting psychiatrist. Kayla was evidently not a happy camper here, and nobody really gave a damn. I'm hoping to do some more digging with Sarah and Fowler. How did your visit with Zuzu go?"

"She was a little friendlier than the first time we met with her. She didn't bring up her visit with Jackie, so I didn't ask. And she didn't tell me anything new, except that she and Kayla deliberately didn't share anything with each other about their family or work lives. It was purely sex and a few laughs when Kayla was in town, which suited Zuzu just fine."

Campos felt her stomach start to growl and said, "I'm going to get a quick bite before I interview Ned and Sarah. You got anything positive before I hang up?"

"Oh, yeah, I forgot to tell you, we finally got a judge to grant us permission to open Kayla's bank account, since we still don't have a next of kin. I'll be calling the bank this afternoon to see what surprises await us there."

"You never know. I'm hoping to finish up with everyone by late afternoon tomorrow and head home on the red-eye. Call me after you talk to the bank. Say, has the chief been chasing after you?" Campos opened the office door and put her cell phone to her ear.

"I left him a message to let him know you were out there and that we're getting close. The media is chasing some other story, so the heat's off him for a while. Good luck this afternoon." Strong hung up.

Campos walked over to the assistant and handed him a piece of paper with the names of the people she needed to interview. "Dr. Bower said you'd be able to schedule some time with each of these doctors to meet with me, either after three o'clock today or anytime before four tomorrow."

The assistant reviewed the list and said, "This isn't going to be easy; several of these docs have cases tomorrow. But I'll do my best, Detective."

"I'm happy to meet with them as early as five or six in the morning, since I'm on East Coast time."

He looked up at her, his eyes glancing to either side, and whispered, "I can tell you they won't be thrilled, but that's not my problem. I'll let you know when I confirm them. Should I text or call you?"

"I put my cell number on the bottom of the paper. A text will suffice. Thanks."

She left the building and found a deli across the street. She wolfed down a turkey sub and chased it with a Coke. Glancing at her watch, she saw that she had only ten minutes to get to the transplant clinic, where she was meeting Ned.

He was waiting for her when she entered the small conference room.

"Hi, Ned. How are you today?" Campos sat down and opened up her file.

"I'm beat. All kinds of computer problems. I must say, I'm confused about why I'm here again." Ned took off his aviator glasses and rubbed his eyes. He looked exhausted.

"Ned, I wanted to ask you a few more questions about Kayla, and then I was hoping you could sit with me while I review the information that was on her computer."

Ned's eyes widened. "I wasn't expecting to review her computer files with you; maybe Sarah can help you with that." He began to fidget in his seat. Campos recalled that he had been more relaxed during their last visit.

"Are you okay, Ned? Is something wrong?" Campos asked calmly.

"I'm just tired. Lots going on and not enough time or people to get it all done. Sorry if I'm short." He lowered his head.

"When was your last vacation?"

"I don't really have anywhere I want to visit, and it's near impossible to take time off anyway."

"Sometimes things look different after you get away. Just something to think about," Campos offered. Ned stared downward, without responding to her comment, and she paused a beat before she began her questioning.

"I understand that Kayla was extremely mean to you in public multiple times. Last we spoke, you indicated that it was only once. Why didn't you tell me about the other times? Why do you think she attacked you so much?"

Ned started to tap his foot and slowly looked up at Campos. "I didn't think it would matter how many times she humiliated me publicly, and it's not something I enjoy remembering. I don't think she liked me, plain and simple. I could never fix things fast enough for her, and she expected me to be available around the clock. I wouldn't answer her calls after ten at night. She treated me as if I was her personal computer assistant, and I finally had to put a stop to it, which no one had ever done before."

Campos jotted down some notes. "Did you report her to your manager?"

Ned grumbled, "I did mention something in passing to Dr. Bower, and that really caused a huge blowup at an all-staff meeting. She called me an incompetent idiot and a waste of space. Said I should go work for the people in the morgue, since they were dead and wouldn't be revolted by my gross face and stinky body."

"Whoa, that's harsh. Did anyone step in and say something?" Campos sighed.

"Yes, Sarah demanded that Kayla leave immediately and then later brought us both into her office and made Kayla apologize to me."

"Did Kayla threaten Sarah after Sarah made her leave the staff meeting? She must have been so embarrassed by being called out in front of the entire staff," Campos pushed.

"I heard Kayla yell at Sarah after I left the office, but I couldn't hear everything she was saying—just lots of f-bombs and a very loud 'How dare you?' You'd have to ask Sarah about that exchange. I wanted to be long gone when Kayla walked out of Sarah's office."

"How was Kayla toward you after that?" Campos asked.

"Whenever she needed any computer support, she would call the other team members, and she ignored me, as if I was invisible, when we passed each other in the halls, which was fine by me," Ned said.

"Anything else happen after that incident?"

"Well, she also started some rumors that I was a loser and that I had some mental problems, which was why I didn't have any friends at work. I don't think anyone believed her, though."

"I don't know how you tolerated all that negativity, Ned. Did you have someone to talk to, either at home or at work?"

"I did talk to Sarah several times. That really helped. She's a great manager and the first person I ever saw stand up to Kayla. Sarah coached me to ignore Kayla and said that if

Kayla ever made any other inappropriate comments, I was to tell Sarah. I told Kayla as much, and she finally left me alone." Ned sat a little taller in his seat.

"I have to give it to you, Ned—it takes a lot of restraint not to react. Good for you for being the bigger person."

"I didn't want to stoop to Kayla's level; other than her, I really like the transplant team, especially Sarah—she's very dedicated and professional. The staff really likes her a lot." Ned was about to go on, when someone knocked on the door.

Sarah peeked her head inside. "Detective Campos, I just wanted to let you know I'm in the waiting area whenever you're ready."

"I'll be right with you, Sarah," Campos responded, and then looked back at Ned, who was staring at Sarah with puppy-dog eyes and a grin. *Someone has a crush*, she thought.

Chapter 24

The night before, Jackie waited until she knew everyone in the house was fast asleep before she went inside. After she'd stopped sobbing, Jackie had recounted to Sarah the conversation between her and Laura at the restaurant, including the part where Laura had finally owned up to who she was sleeping with. Sarah had mostly listened and let Jackie know that she was there for her no matter what Jackie decided to do. Jackie had been so upset that she now realized that she had forgotten to ask Sarah about her being cleared as a living donor for the paired exchange.

Jackie awoke the next morning and glanced over at the other side of her and Laura's king-size bed. It was empty. She hadn't even heard Laura leave for work.

Just then, Wyatt opened the bedroom door and got into bed next to Jackie. "Hi, Momma." He gave her a long hug and kiss on the cheek and then laid his head on her shoulder.

Jackie's heart melted. "Hey, buddy. How you doing? I was going to take you to school this morning."

"I'm tired, Momma. Can I stay home with you today?"

Jackie could tell his energy was low; otherwise, he would have been jumping on the bed by now, yelling for pancakes.

"Everything else okay?" she asked, as she put her hand on the side of his face that wasn't next to her shoulder.

"I just went to the bathroom, and no water came out when I tried to pee," Wyatt said.

Jackie kept her voice calm as she asked, "Is this the first time this has happened, honey? You were making some water when we were in Florida."

"I couldn't pee last night before bed, either, Momma. Where's the water I'm drinking going?"

"Well, when your kidneys don't work, the water stays in your body, but they can give you a pill that will help you pee. I think we'll go in to see your kidney doctor today to see if he can give you something to get that water out." Jackie rubbed his head.

"Okay. Can Grandma come, too?" he asked.

"No, she needs to stay home; it'll just be you and me. How about we have some breakfast, then get on the road?"

"I'm not real hungry, and my head hurts a little." Wyatt sat up.

"Okay, then why don't you just go get dressed while I take a quick shower, and then we'll go?" Jackie gave Wyatt a hug, and they both got out of bed.

After Wyatt left, she noted that this was the first time since Wyatt had been diagnosed with kidney failure that he hadn't made any urine, and she knew his headache was due to his kidneys' inability to clear out the toxins from his blood. *We're going to have to move faster on this transplant*, she realized.

Wyatt came back in, and Laura's mom poked her head into the bedroom a moment later. "Good morning, family. Coffee's on. Wyatt, I have your cereal ready before I take you to school. Jackie, I can tell you've put on some weight, so I made you some fat-free muffins. I found a recipe in *Good Housekeeping* and have been dying to try it."

"Hi, Grandma." Wyatt went over and gave her hug. "I'm not going to school today."

She looked at Wyatt, then over toward Jackie. "Is everything all right?"

"I'll need to take him to the doctor today. He stopped peeing, so it's time to give him some help in that department. I'm going to shower and make some calls, and then we'll be heading into the city. And, for the record, I'm about the same weight as I was when Laura and I got married," Jackie said. *And you can take your fat-free muffins and shove them up your ass*, she added silently.

"Well, I'm happy to tag along," Grandma responded in her syrupy voice. "I can pack up the muffins and be ready to go in a couple minutes."

Sure, and I'll just throw you and your fucking muffins out of the car while we're driving over the Golden Gate Bridge. How'd you like that?

"Thanks for offering, but I think it will be just Wyatt and me today," Jackie said, as politely as she could.

"Okay. Wyatt, let's go downstairs." Demon turned around and left the room with him in tow.

Jackie closed the bathroom door and started the shower. A wave of sadness moved through her body so powerfully that she had to sit down on the edge of the tub. *My poor baby. My sweet, innocent boy. Why him?* As tears streamed down her cheeks, she put her hand over her heart. *I have to stay strong for Wyatt. It has to be all about him now*, she told herself.

After Jackie showered, she texted Sarah: "Wyatt stopped peeing, need to move quicker on transplant."

Sarah texted right back: "OK. Call Mary. I'll work on my end."

Jackie called the pediatric nephrologist's office and got Wyatt an appointment for that morning, then called Mary.

"Hi, Mary, this is Jackie, Wyatt's mom. Is this a good time?"

"Sure. I have about ten minutes before we start rounds. Everything okay?"

"Wyatt stopped making urine for the first time last night, and he has a headache today, so I'm bringing him in to see our peds nephrologist this morning. I just wanted to update you on his condition and check to see if you need anything else from us to move his transplant forward." Jackie could feel her pulse quickening as she spoke.

"We did present his case at selection, with Sarah as the donor for the paired exchange, and it looks like that's a go. I just need to confirm with Dr. Bower; he'll be on rounds, so I can ask him then," Mary said.

"Great, Mary. Thanks so much. We'll be in the city, so if you need us to stop by for any last-minute tests just give me a call on my cell. You have the number, right?"

"I sure do, Jackie. I'm so glad you all decided to have Wyatt's transplant here; he's the sweetest kid, and you know we'll take extra-special care of him. I'll get back to you after rounds. Tell Wyatt I hope he feels better soon."

After Jackie hung up, she decided it was best to let Laura know about Wyatt's condition. She knew Laura would be in her morning meeting at the medical examiner's office, where they would be dividing up all the new autopsies to be done for the day, so Jackie sent her a simple text: "Wyatt stopped making urine, has headache. Taking him to peds nephrologist now. Will keep you posted." Jackie left off the emoji heart and kiss she used when ending a text to Laura.

Grandma waved goodbye to Jackie and Wyatt from the front door, and Jackie rolled down her car window. "It'll be a great day for you to catch up on your soap operas. We won't be home for dinner, so go ahead without us." Jackie gave her a pretend smile and pulled out of the driveway.

• • •

As Jackie had predicted, the kind pediatric nephrologist prescribed a pill that would help Wyatt get rid of some water and suggested some over-the-counter liquid Tylenol for his headache. He bent down to Wyatt's level and said, "You're gonna feel better real soon, my friend. Now, I need to talk to your mom for a minute, so please go back to the waiting room. She'll be right out."

"Okay if I play with the Legos, Mom?"

"Sure thing, buddy," Jackie said.

After Wyatt had left, the doctor closed the door of the exam room and said, "I think we may have to schedule Wyatt for a temporary dialysis access. I know you and Laura didn't want to go down this path, but the water pill isn't going to work that long, and I also need him to start on some medication for his blood pressure, which is really elevated. There's very little, if any, kidney function left, and unless his transplant is scheduled within the next couple weeks, we're going to have to dialyze him. I can tell just by looking at him that he's anemic, so a blood transfusion isn't out of the question. We're getting in rough waters here, Jackie. I'm sorry." He put his hand on her shoulder as she stared at the floor and shook her head.

"It just went so fast, but I hear what you're saying. I spoke with Mary at the transplant institute this morning. She's calling me today about a transplant date." She felt a wave of nausea rising in her stomach and grimaced.

"You have to take care of yourself, too," the doctor said, watching her. "Have you eaten today?"

"I knew I forgot something. I just hate to eat or drink in front of my boy, so I only had coffee," she admitted.

"Jackie, he's going to need you to be strong for him, so promise me you'll take better care of yourself."

"You're right. You don't need to be worrying about me. I'll get the prescriptions filled and take him to get his blood drawn after lunch."

"I'll call you as soon as I get the lab results. Keep an eye on his blood pressure, and keep me posted on how much urine he makes. As soon as you find out the transplant date, let me know that, too. There's a great transplant pediatric nephrologist, Dr. Bryant, on the transplant team. I'll send over Wyatt's medical records; just sign a release form before you leave today."

"You're the best. Thanks for seeing us on such short notice." Jackie leaned in and hugged him.

"I'm here for you. That Wyatt is the best kid. He'll get through this. Just remember, he'll take his cues from you and Laura. If you keep it together and stay calm in front of him, he'll think it will all be all right. If you need to lose it, just do it behind closed doors. It's amazing how resilient kids are. Trust me, I've seen them bounce back from much worse." The doctor opened the exam room door and escorted Jackie to the waiting room filled with parents and kids. Wyatt was intently engaged with the Legos.

Jackie and Wyatt were having a snack at a diner near the doctor's office when Jackie's cell phone rang. "This is Jackie."

"Hi, Jackie. This is Mary. Do you have some time to talk?"

"Sure. I'm with Wyatt. I'll step outside for a minute," Jackie responded, and looked over at Wyatt. "I'll be right outside while you finish your sandwich. I can see you from the sidewalk." Jackie pointed to the big window that framed the diner.

His mouth full of food, Wyatt gave her a thumbs-up.

Once Jackie was outside, she resumed her call. "Thanks for calling me back, Mary. I'm hoping you have good news."

"I do have good news. We have a transplant date for you and your paired-exchange match for two weeks from today. We spoke with the other donor and recipient after rounds today, and they've completed all their testing and are also anxious to get this behind them. How's that sound?" Mary asked.

"Perfect!" Jackie exhaled deeply. "Have you spoken to Sarah?"

"Sarah is with a detective from Miami right now, but as soon as she's finished, we'll confirm with her. Her workup is complete, so if everyone stays healthy between now and the next couple weeks, it's a go. I did get a chance to review Wyatt's records that your nephrologist sent over, and Dr. Bryant is hoping you and Wyatt can stop by the pediatric clinic this afternoon. He'd like to meet Wyatt and talk to you as well. Would that work for you?" Mary paused.

"We can come over after we finish lunch. I haven't gotten Wyatt's blood drawn yet. Do you want me to get that done before or after?" Jackie could see Wyatt was almost finished eating.

"Wait until you see Dr. Bryant. He may order a few more tests; that way, Wyatt will only have to get stuck once. The pediatric clinic is on the second floor. I'll meet you there in about an hour," Mary said.

"Okay. Also, will you please be sure to give Dr. Bryant a heads-up that Laura and I do not Wyatt to get an access or go on dialysis before the transplant, if at all possible?" Jackie asked. She remembered what she learned in nursing school about access surgery. They placed a piece of Gore-Tex in the arm that connected the artery to a vein, to allow for long-term dialysis. It looked like a thick piece of rope was under the skin, and it only got uglier over time. . . . *I'm not going there*, she stopped herself.

"We can discuss all that when you get here, but yes, I'll share your request with him. See you soon."

Jackie hung up, walked back into the diner, and paid the bill. As she drove Wyatt to the medical center, she looked over at him, noticing how tired he looked, and said, "Good news, buddy. We have a date for your transplant. You'll be feeling back to yourself in no time." Jackie smiled.

"Will it hurt, Momma?" Wyatt asked.

"Let's ask Mary. She knows all about this, and she can't wait to see you again."

"I really like Mary, Momma. I hope I can play that video game again. That was fun," Wyatt said, and closed his eyes.

Jackie watched his long lashes flutter until his eyes stayed shut. "Take a little rest, buddy. We'll be there in a bit."

Chapter 25

Sarah checked her email on her phone while she waited for Campos to finish her interview with Ned. Then her cell rang. It was Mary. "Hello, Mary. How are things going?"

"Good news: We have a transplant date for Wyatt and the other paired exchange, and Dr. Bower is on board with your being the donor, as long as you understand that the other pair is high-profile and you'll never know who your kidney is going to go into. Does that work?" Mary asked.

"Dr. Bower made it crystal clear to me that this 'high profile' recipient of my donor kidney will always be held confidential. As long as their living kidney donor is the best match for Wyatt, I don't care who they are or what they do, let's go with that date." Sarah looked up to see Ned approaching her.

"Jackie and Wyatt are on their way over to our pediatric clinic to meet with Dr. Bryant, so if you have time to swing by to say hello, I know they'd love to see you," Mary said.

"Sounds great. I'm heading into my meeting with the Miami detective, so will you ask Jackie to call me when they're done with their appointment?" Sarah stood up.

"Will do, Sarah. Bye for now."

After Sarah hung up, Ned gave her an odd smirk. "Detective Campos is ready for you, Sarah. Hope everything goes well. She's nice."

My boyfriends would give me that type of smirk, but Ned? Yuck, she thought.

"I can't see why it wouldn't go well, Ned. You didn't tell her I killed Kayla, did you? That was supposed to stay between us." Sarah laughed.

Ned chuckled. "Don't worry. I kept our secret." He winked at her and mimicked zipping his lips.

Sarah walked into the small conference room where Campos was sitting. "Hi, Sarah. How are you doing today? Will you close the door behind you?"

"Sure." Sarah obliged and sat down in front of Campos.

"I hope this is going to be short. I'm sure you know by now that I didn't kill Kayla."

Campos's face was serious as she answered, "Sarah, I've learned a lot more about Kayla and am hoping you can add more details."

"That's why I'm here, Detective. What would you like to know that I haven't already told you?" Sarah crossed her legs and sat back in her chair.

"I know that this program has had a revolving door of managers and that you've been here only a little over a year. Correct?"

"Correct. This is a hard bunch to manage. Very independent crew, for sure."

"During the time you did manage Kayla, did you ever have any direct altercations with her?" Campos glanced down at her notes, then back up at Sarah.

"As I told you before, I tried to steer clear of her when I could, but there were a few times when I needed to bring her into my office for uncalled-for behavior. Let's just say she didn't take feedback too well." Sarah paused.

"Can you tell me how she reacted to you, exactly?"

"She called me a stupid bitch, an incompetent supervisor who had no right to reprimand her or criticize her work. She said I was nothing but a fly-by-night manager and was sure I'd be gone in less than a year. I think those were the highlights. Several more choice swear words, and then she stormed out of my office."

"How did that make you feel? Did you discipline her? Write her up?" Campos asked.

"I did write her up, and she refused to sign the paperwork, so I alerted our human resources department, and they recommended she get some counseling, which she refused." Sarah sighed.

"Did you get angry with her, yell back at her? If someone said those things to me, I'd sure want to set them straight, especially if I was their supervisor." Campos kept pushing.

"I'm not going to lie—I *was* pissed, but I had gotten some coaching from our HR department on how to deal with Kayla. I wasn't the first manager who had this type of interaction with her. I told her I was going to send the disciplinary note to HR and that they would ensure it was in her file, along with a note that she refused to sign it. That's all I could do. Then she tore up the note and told me to go fuck myself." Sarah's heart rate increased just from recalling the heated interaction.

Campos made some notes and then looked back up at Sarah. "It's amazing that they let Kayla stay here for so long, given the way she behaved. I understand there's no love lost between her and Ned."

"She hated Ned, was vile to him. I put her on a three-day suspension for how she treated him at our staff meeting. They sent the assistant director of HR to give her the news and then walked her to the parking lot. She knew better than to lash out at them." Sarah checked her phone—no call from Jackie yet.

"Do you have any additional thoughts on Ned's relationship with Kayla that you'd like to share?" Campos asked.

"He gets along very well with all the staff. I believe it was Kayla, not Ned, who was at fault," Sarah answered.

"Ned seems to have a sweet spot for you, Sarah. Have you noticed that?" Campos kept her gaze on Sarah.

Sarah felt her cheeks flush. "I think Ned was just grateful I was able to stand up to Kayla, nothing more."

"Did Ned ever ask you out or give you any reason to think he was fond of you?"

Sarah shook her head. "Ned never asked me out, and I never even gave him a second thought in terms of any work romance. I don't date people I work with—never have, never will. Not a good idea."

"Did Ned ever give you any gifts or write you any notes or emails indicating his interest in you?" Campos wouldn't let up on this line of questioning.

Sarah thought for a few minutes. "He did bring by a gift after I made Kayla apologize to him, but I told him he needed to take it back. I don't take gifts for doing my job."

"What was the gift?"

Sarah paused. "It was a necklace."

"From where?"

"Tiffany," Sarah muttered.

"Whoa, there's nothing cheap from that store. He must be making quite a salary to be able to afford something from there. I'd say Ned is very fond of you, Sarah."

"Detective, I think you're reading into this way more than is there. Ned took back the necklace without incident. He's a kind and harmless man," Sarah said.

"I think Ned needs a vacation. If you don't mind my saying so, I met with him today, and he looks beyond exhausted."

"I agree with you, but he won't take one. He's a workaholic. He's lost vacation time on the books because it timed out. I appreciate your mentioning it, though, I'll suggest it to him again," Sarah said.

Campos reviewed her notes and looked up at Sarah. "Couple more things; then I'll let you go. Would you be able to give me information on a different next of kin for Kayla, other than her grandmother?"

"I was just reviewing her HR file and found a telephone number with no name attached that I already shared with you. Is the grandmother doing okay?" Sarah asked.

"Grandmothers can be fragile as they age. Ned mentioned you may be able to sit with me as I review all the files from Kayla's computer. When would be a good time to do that?" Campos asked.

Sarah swallowed. *Shit, I sure hope Ned cleared those files on the managers and doctors.*

"I can't do it today; will you be here tomorrow?" Sarah's cell rang, and as "Born to Be Wild" started to play, Sarah looked at Campos and caught her grinning. "It's my friend Jackie. I think you and Handsome had a call with her while she was in Miami."

Before Campos could respond, Sarah answered, "Hi, Jack, you here?"

"Sure am. Wyatt and I are on our way up to your clinic. Your assistant told us you were with the Miami detective. I'd love to meet her, and Wyatt needs a big hug from his Aunt Sarah. It's been a long day. The little guy's been through a lot," Jackie said.

"Okay, I think I'm done with Detective Campos so I'll meet you in the clinic waiting area." Sarah looked over to Campos for visual permission to leave, and she nodded in the affirmative.

Sarah ended the call. "How about we review the files tomorrow?"

Campos stood up. "That'll work. Say, about noon? I have some early-morning meetings with a few surgeons and a Dr. Fowler. Do you know him?"

"He's the consulting psychiatrist for our living donors. I met with him this week, since I'm going to be part of Jackie's son's paired-exchange transplant in a couple weeks here in San Francisco, and he cleared me for takeoff. Lovely man. We're lucky to have him."

"I'm not sure what a paired exchange is. It sounds complicated," Campos said.

"A paired exchange is when a recipient has a possible living kidney donor but the donor doesn't match them, and another recipient has the same situation with their donor. You swap donors, and each patient gets a transplant, but not from their original donor. What's really cool is that sometimes we have a chain of these types of cases. We've done eighteen kidney transplants by swapping living-donor kidneys across the country."

Campos nodded. "Wow, that is so cool. Thanks for spelling it out for me."

"Sure. Some smart dad who couldn't donate to his daughter came up with the idea and even created software that we use nationally to set up these kinds of transplants," Sarah added.

"Well, good luck. I'm going to review my notes and then head out. Thanks for your cooperation, Sarah." Campos held out her hand, and Sarah shook it.

When Sarah went into the waiting area, Wyatt yelled, "Aunt Sarah!" She went to him and gave him a big hug. "Hey, pal! It's great to see you."

Sarah looked over at Jackie; her eyes were red and swollen. "Hey, toots," Sarah said, and put her arm around her friend while she continued holding on to Wyatt with the other one.

Jackie said, "Let's sit for a moment and decide where we want to go for dinner. Our buddy has been poked and put on some new medicines, and—"

Before Jackie could finish, Wyatt yelled, "I peed, a lot—like, a bucketful, Aunt Sarah!"

Sarah and Jackie both laughed as several other folks in the waiting room looked over and chuckled.

"Big news today. Do you want to tell Aunt Sarah, or do you want me to?" Jackie combed Wyatt's hair back with her fingers. Some color had returned to his cheeks, and his energy had increased since he'd taken his water pill and headache medicine.

"I'll tell her, Momma." He jumped off Sarah's lap. "I'm having a transplant in two weeks—just two weeks, Aunt Sarah!"

Sarah put up her hand, and Wyatt high-fived her. "That's the best news I've heard in a long time." Sarah looked over and saw Detective Campos walking through the door that led to the waiting area. Sarah gestured for her to come over and stood up.

"Jackie, meet Detective Campos, Officer Handsome's partner." Sarah smirked.

Jackie stood up. "Anyone who's a friend of Handsome's is a friend of mine. Nice to meet you in person. Have you solved the case yet?"

Campos looked over at Sarah and raised an eyebrow. "We've got a real jokester here."

Wyatt looked up at Campos. "And I'm Wyatt." He put his small hand out to shake Campos's.

Campos put her briefcase down and stooped down to look at him. "Nice to meet you, Wyatt. I think you know my work partner." Campos glanced up at Sarah and Jackie. "Officer Handsome."

"He was going to marry my Aunt Sarah. He's a nice man. I like him—"

"Well, not actually, Wyatt, but we were close friends," Sarah interjected, and then explained to Campos, "Handsome came out to Jackie's house with me last year, and we played with Wyatt one afternoon while Jackie's broken leg was healing. You know he's great with kids."

"I do know he loves his nephews. They're lucky to have him."

"Well, we're heading out for some dinner," Jackie said. "So nice to meet you, Detective Campos. I really do wish you the best on solving this Kayla case. Sorry I couldn't be more help when I was in Miami."

"Thanks," Campos said. "We're getting closer every day. Looks like you have your hands full right now anyway; best to let law enforcement do their job."

"I couldn't agree more," Sarah quickly added. "I'll see you tomorrow to review Kayla's computer files; then I guess you'll be off to Miami."

Campos picked up her briefcase. "That's the plan. It was so nice to meet you, Wyatt, and good luck with your transplant. I'm sure you'll do great, strong young man that you are. Nice to meet you in person, Jackie."

Just as Campos was about to leave, Jackie said, "Uh, Detective? I wasn't going to say anything, and I'm not even sure it's important, but I think it's best that I share something Zuzu told me when we were together in Miami."

Campos turned and faced Jackie. "You never know what's going to be important as cases evolve. What did Zuzu tell you?"

"You know Zuzu didn't know I was connected to anything or anybody related to this case; she just thought I was a friend of Biker Bob, which I am. I told her I was in Miami with my wife and son for a transplant evaluation, which I was." Jackie was stumbling over her words a bit.

Campos watched Jackie as Sarah and Wyatt stood by. "Okay."

"Zuzu said the night Kayla met her maker, so to speak"— Jackie glanced down towards Wyatt—"Kayla had told her that she had to go meet a man from her work at her grandmother's house, and that Kayla was visibly nervous about it," Jackie blurted out.

"Did Zuzu say anything else about the man, why he was at her grandmother's house?" Campos asked.

"No, Zuzu didn't say anything else, and I didn't want to ask too many questions and blow my cover," Jackie said.

Sarah rolled her eyes. "'Blow your cover'? Seriously, Jack?"

"Who helped solve the case last year? Who?" Jackie looked smugly at Sarah.

"We have bigger fish to fry here." Sarah glanced toward Wyatt.

"I know that. That's why I came clean here. Give me some credit. After everything settles down, who knows? I may want to go to school and become a private investigator, or maybe even a detective. I think I have some untapped talent. Just saying." Jackie smiled at Sarah.

It was good to see a smile on her best friend's face for the first time in a while. "Yeah, you'd be the female version of Columbo for sure." Sarah laughed, then looked over at Campos, who was deep in thought and seemingly hadn't heard the banter between her and Jackie.

Campos snapped back to attention. "Thanks for sharing this, Jackie. It's important. I won't keep you all any longer. If I need to get in touch with you, I'm sure Sarah has your number."

"She sure does. Sarah can find me day and night. I'll be hanging with my best buddy here." Jackie rubbed the top of Wyatt's head.

Chapter 26

Campos stopped at the corner market near her Airbnb and bought a six-pack of Anchor Steam beer, a pre-made sandwich, and a bag of potato chips. Once she was inside, she changed out of her suit and put on sweatpants and a hoodie. *It gets so cold here in the evening*, she thought, as she opened a beer and called Strong.

He answered right away. "Hey. You having fun out there?"

"I just saw your buddy Jackie and her son, Wyatt; he's a cute kid. He said he thought you and Sarah were going to get married—imagine that." Campos couldn't resist busting his chops before she gave him the download of her day.

"You're a real comedian, Campos. How's Wyatt doing, anyway? Poor guy." Strong asked.

"He doesn't look very healthy, but Sarah's apparently going to be a donor for this thing they call a paired exchange. I don't pretend to know a lot about it, but it looks like Wyatt's got a transplant in his future right here in San Francisco, so I guess Miami is off the table." Campos took a slug of her beer.

"That makes better sense anyway, since they live there. So, spill it—how did it go today?" Strong asked.

"As I was leaving the clinic at the end of the day, Jackie shared something extremely important. She said that Zuzu told her Kayla was on her way to her grandmother's house to meet a man from work the night she was killed."

"Work, as in from San Francisco?" Strong asked.

"Yes, and Zuzu said that Kayla was nervous when she left. I'll need you to verify this with Zuzu."

Strong sighed. "I just saw Zuzu and got nothing. Guess it's time for yet another visit to Wilton Manors."

"You can always just call her. If Zuzu confirms this, then I'm starting to think our killer may be from San Francisco, not Miami," Campos said.

"It *would* make better sense, since the only people Kayla knew in Miami were her grandmother, who we know is dead, and Zuzu. This sounds like a solid lead," Strong said.

Campos continued, "I had a very interesting interview with Ned Bisone, who has a sweet spot for Sarah. He bought her a Tiffany necklace for protecting him from Kayla. Mind you, Ned didn't say a thing—I had to pull it out of Sarah." Campos opened up her briefcase and pulled out her files.

"Where does a low-level IT guy get the money to buy a necklace from Tiffany? I cross the street when I see that store; I can't afford to even walk in front of it," Strong said.

"According to Sarah, he never takes any vacations—he lives, eats, and sleeps his job—so, while I'm not sure I'd eliminate him from the suspect list, he's not my top contender. It also seems Sarah was not the first manager to call Kayla out on the carpet for her caustic behavior. Kayla even got a three-day suspension." Campos paused.

"That had to be embarrassing, Kayla must have had some deep-seated emotional problems. I'm wondering if she was seeing a shrink so we can get a clearer picture of her; that might lead us to her killer," Strong suggested.

"I'm not sure we could ever get access to those records—patient confidentiality and all. I'm meeting with Dr. Fowler, a psychiatrist on the living-donor team, tomorrow. Bower said Kayla kept her own counsel but that she did connect with Fowler from time to time, so maybe he can shed some light on her behavior."

Strong chimed in, "This Kayla sounds like a real harsh bitch. I'm guessing there are a lot of her co-workers who are truly relieved she's gone. But killing her in Miami is a stretch. I'm starting to wonder if there was something else going on with her—money problems; drug problems we haven't uncovered yet. 'I hate your fucking guts at work' isn't a very strong motive, or we'd have lots more murders." Strong laughed.

Campos took a break between bites of her sandwich to ask, "Any news on Kayla's Miami bank account or Grandma's cause of death?"

"Grandma died alone at home in her sleep—no suspicious behavior, so there was no autopsy," Strong said.

"Who found her?" Campos asked.

"A social agency did wellness checks on seniors in that area on a regular basis, and Grandma was on their radar. The agency called in the morning, and there was no answer. Later that afternoon, they sent someone over to knock on the door, and no one answered, so they called the police to make a welfare check. No answer, no movement in the house, so they broke down the door and found her. The agency had Kayla's number on file, since she was the one who arranged the wellness visits, and they called her. Apparently, she flew down to make funeral arrangements. I did speak with the health aide who had the grandma's case, and she said the lady was a real sweetheart but had bad congestive heart failure, so she lived a quiet life and didn't go out much, except to the doctor when Kayla came down to take her," Strong summarized.

"Any obit?" Campos asked.

"Yup, just a minute. I made a copy so I could add it to our files, I'll read it to you: 'Lucy Thomas, eighty-three, passed away peacefully Tuesday, June 6, 2014, at her home in Lake City, Florida. She was survived by her granddaughter, Kayla Newman, a nurse in San Francisco. Donations can be made to Living Hope Recovery Center. No services.'

"I called the Living Hope Recovery Center and spoke with the manager. She said she didn't know any Lucy Thomas. I asked her if she got any donations in her name about a year and a half ago. She checked. Seems some anonymous donor sent a cashier's check for five thousand dollars, in memory of Lucy. No name or address to send a thank-you," Strong finished.

"That's odd. The more we learn, the less we know," Campos said.

"Don't get all down in the mouth. I was able to confirm that Kayla actually worked at this clinic before she moved to San Francisco, although I'm not sure that will lead us anywhere. I'm guessing that's why she put them in the obit," Strong added.

"That may be a blind alley. Any luck getting access to Kayla's bank account?"

"I'm almost there. The bank manager is going to call me back. On another note, I did confirm that Granny's house is in Kayla's name from the public records department; it's been paid off for over five years," Strong said.

"Since we're sewing up the details in Florida, I'm thinking we need to dig deeper here in San Francisco. I could really use your help with interviewing a couple of these surgeons. Maybe you can take a look at Ned; it'd be interesting to hear your perspective. What do you think about coming out here and helping me depose these people?" Campos asked.

"I don't know if the chief would like us both being out of town right now, but, thankfully, he's fully distracted by some movie-star murder case in South Beach, so I think we're off his radar temporarily. It's not a bad idea; we could knock off the interviews faster together and maybe get this solved. Do you have a hunch about which surgeon it could be?" Strong asked.

"It's a hard call. When I had my one-on-one with Spencer—and he was a flaming asshole, he seemed too obvious. And I'm pretty sure Bower didn't do it—he seems to be Kayla's biggest fan—but who the hell knows? I'll be meeting the surgeons who were at the Miami transplant conference. I'll also be meeting with Dr. Fowler, the psychiatrist. Maybe I'll get something from him," Campos said.

"I'll call Zuzu and see if she'll confirm Jackie's comment about a man from work meeting Kayla at her grandmother's house; then I can hop on a plane out there and we can double-team those elusive surgeons. Sound like a plan?" Strong asked.

"Sounds good. I think Wyatt's transplant is going to be in two weeks. I hope we can wrap this up before all of that. Anyway, I'm heading to bed now. I have a five a.m. meeting with Dr. Wood tomorrow."

"Get some shut-eye. I'll ring Zuzu and see if she's up for a quick conversation, and who knows—I may see you sooner, rather than later," Strong said.

While Campos got ready for bed, she thought about all the people she had interviewed and chuckled as she recalled her meeting with Jackie. *That woman is a real character. I can only imagine what kind of trouble she and Sarah get in when they're on vacation.*

Chapter 27

After a long day of doctors and lab tests, Jackie decided to avoid commuter traffic by taking Wyatt to Sarah's house and letting him take a nap before they headed home. Sarah would meet them there after work. As Jackie unlocked the door to Sarah's apartment, she looked down at Wyatt. "You look like you could use a little nap."

"I'm not tired, Momma. Can I jump on Aunt Sarah's bed?"

"Go for it." Jackie followed him through the small, tidy living room and into Sarah's bedroom, where he took off his shoes and hopped onto the bed. Sarah's puffy down comforter made for a perfect landing pad. Jackie watched him jump a few times and then lay his head down on a pillow. "I love this bed; it feels like I'm floating on a cloud."

Jackie rested her head on the pillow next to his and said, "It sure does. If we close our eyes, we can pretend we're floating together." She gently closed his eyelids and moved closer, rubbing her nose against his. "I love you so much. You were very brave today."

Wyatt's breath began to slow, and he mumbled, "I love you, too, Momma."

After he fell asleep, Jackie sat and watched him rest, reflecting on what both the pediatric nephrologists had mentioned about putting an access in Wyatt's arm.

They're not going to do that to my little boy; they can always do a temporary access if he really needs it, she thought.

When Jackie heard the door to the apartment open, she walked out quietly, closing the bedroom door behind her.

Sarah was putting her purse and briefcase down on the living room table. "Hey, Jack, how's our guy doing?"

"Sound asleep after a few jumps. He loves your bed." Jackie noticed the dark circles under Sarah's eyes. "You look spent, my friend. Everything going okay at work?"

"This investigation is taking up lots of my time, and the docs are complaining about it and asking me why I haven't hired a new coordinator yet." Sarah let out a sigh. "But I'm fine. How are *you* doing, Jack?"

"As well as I can. Staying strong for my buddy. Can't even think about my marriage right now. Freaking out a little about what will happen if Wyatt needs to have an access put in." Jackie sat down on Sarah's couch and put her hands over her face and started to cry. "It's just too much."

Sarah sat next to her and rubbed her back. "We'll get through this. I'm here for you. I know it sucks big-time. Two more weeks, Jack—just two more weeks." She grabbed a few tissues from the box on the end table and gave them to Jackie.

Jackie wiped her tears, blew her nose, and then put her head down on Sarah's shoulder. "I don't think I could get through this without you."

"Don't even think about that. We can do this." Sarah rubbed her friend's head.

Jackie slowly sat up. "Yes, we can, and when all is back to whatever fucking normal looks like, it's going to be vacation time."

Sarah got up and walked into the kitchen. "That's right. Let's talk about that, our big reward for putting up with all this bullshit. You want something cold to drink?"

"How about a root beer? I'm the designated driver, so I need to keep my wits about me."

Sarah pulled a bottle out of the fridge, put ice in two glasses, and filled them. She handed Jackie her glass and said, "Here's to better times."

"Cheers," Jackie said, taking a long drink of the liquid and then letting out a loud belch. "Excuse me."

Sarah laughed. "Glad to see you've still got your belching skills; they sure came in handy when we were drinking beer down on Rush Street in Chicago."

"We won so many pitchers of beer with those skills. They didn't know how talented I was, challenging me to a beer-chugging-and-burping contest."

"It was a good thing you won, because we never had enough money to buy more than a pitcher," Sarah said.

Jackie's cell phone rang, playing the sound of the Wicked Witch of the West riding on her bicycle from *The Wizard of Oz*. It was Laura. As Sarah laughed, Jackie explained, "Changed the ringtone. Couldn't have picked a better song."

"Hi, Laura. Just a minute," Jackie answered, and then looked at Sarah.

"I'll go grab us some sandwiches and a few appropriate snacks for Wyatt," Sarah said as she grabbed her purse and then headed for the door.

"Sounds great. Get some chips, too."

Sarah left the apartment, and Jackie put Laura on speaker.

"Where are you and Wyatt? I called Mom, and she said you're not going to be home for dinner."

"We're at Sarah's. He's taking a nap, and Sarah and I are going to have dinner. I plan on driving home after the traffic dies down."

"Can you fill me on how Wyatt's day went? Sounds like we need to step up his kidney management."

"That's what happened today. The doctor started him on a diuretic, he started peeing, I gave him something for his headache, he got some labs drawn, and we should know about the results tomorrow." Every time Jackie talked to Laura, her jaw tensed and she got a knot in her stomach.

"We have a date for the transplant in two weeks," she added. "Everything is moving along. But we may have to consider a dialysis access, depending on the lab results." Jackie fell silent, along with Laura, who she knew was as aware as she was what that would look like. *God, I hope we won't have to go there,* she thought.

After a long pause, Jackie said, "I'll be home around eight-thirty. You enjoy dinner with your mom. It would be nice if she didn't mention anything else about my weight. She was very rude to me this morning."

Jackie ended the call and sighed, reminding herself, *I need to put this anger toward Laura in a box until Wyatt's healthy.*

Sarah came back with their sandwiches and said, "Dinnertime. Looks like your call with Laura didn't go well, judging by the look on your face."

"How about you take 'Laura is a big fucking asshole?' for five hundred?" Jackie walked over to the kitchen table and sat down. Sarah plated the sandwiches she had bought and set one in front of Jackie.

"And the question is, 'Why did Laura pick this time to cheat on you?'" Sarah replied.

"You win, Ms. Golden. Let's eat."

Just as they dug into their food, Sarah's cell phone rang. Without looking at the caller, she turned off the ringer, but then her beeper went off in her purse. She got up and retrieved it, then said, "It's Bower. He put a 911 in the message; I've never gotten that from him before. Uh-oh. It's a group message: all the docs, the executive director, and me. I should take this."

Sarah called Dr. Bower and walked into the living room to listen. Jackie heard her say, "Oh no! I'll be there in ten minutes."

"What happened?" Jackie asked.

"We had a patient death. I need to go to the hospital. You and Wyatt stay as long as you need to, I left some snacks for him on the kitchen counter." Sarah grabbed her keys and gave Jackie a hug. "Take care of yourself, Jack. I'll call you when I know more."

Sarah left, and Jackie looked at her dinner. She had no appetite. She wrapped up the rest of the sandwich and cleared the table just as Wyatt peeked his head out the bedroom door.

"Momma, I went pee again."

Jackie smiled. "Good news! How's your headache?"

"I don't have a headache anymore, and I'm kinda hungry. Is Aunt Sarah coming home soon?" Wyatt walked over to the kitchen.

"She was here and had to go back to work, honey, but she brought you some snacks." Jackie handed him cheese sticks and crackers, Low Salt marked on the labels.

Wyatt peeled back the cheese wrapper and took a bite with a cracker. "Yum. Can we go home to see Mom and Grandma?"

"You bet. Just let me finish putting these groceries in the fridge."

Jackie cleaned up the kitchen and smoothed out the comforter on Sarah's bed, and they left the apartment. Traffic was clear, and they got home to San Rafael in twenty minutes. "I'm going to go and tell Grandma I peed," Wyatt said, as he got out of the car.

"She'll be so happy for you. I'll be in in just a minute." Jackie looked around for Laura's car but didn't see it. *Maybe they went out for dinner, and I can get upstairs before they come back*, she thought.

When Jackie walked through the door, Grandma was sitting on the couch with her arm around Wyatt.

"Where's Laura?" Jackie asked.

"She called and said she had a late work meeting tonight and an early-morning meeting, so she's decided to stay in the city. My girl, she works too hard. I don't know how she keeps these crazy hours without getting sick."

Jackie glanced away. When she looked back, Grandma was giving Wyatt a hug. "It's so good to have my Wyatt back home."

Chapter 28

Sarah stepped off the elevator and walked along the transplant floor amid stillness and quiet—a huge contrast with the usual sound of beeping call buttons and hallway chatter, and an indication that something bad had happened.

She walked into the designated conference room and found Dr. Bower and four other surgeons talking. Bart Lincoln, executive director of the hospital, was sitting at the end of the long conference table. *I didn't know he could find his way to the actual transplant floor; all he cares about is the number of transplants and profit margins here,* she thought.

"Hi, Sarah. Thanks for getting here so quickly. I took the liberty of pulling up the plan we developed should a living donor die, although, I must say, I didn't think we'd ever need it." Dr. Bower turned toward the screen at the front of the room. Everyone in the room, faces drawn, looked at it intently.

Sarah sat down and pulled out a pen and the folder from her office containing the same plan. Her heart was racing. This was all new to her, and she hung on Dr. Bower's every word.

Dr. Bower continued, "We will have to notify the United Network of Organ Sharing in Richmond, Virginia, of the death. Dr. Wood, take care of that."

"I'll call UNOS now." Dr. Wood stood up and walked outside the conference room.

Dr. Bower scrolled through the document on the screen and continued, "We'll have to voluntarily shut down our living-donor kidney program until we're cleared."

In the midst of taking notes, Sarah glanced up and said, "I've got a list of all the cases scheduled this month and next; we can discuss them with the living-donor team tomorrow."

"How long do you think the program will be shut down?" asked Bart.

"I'm guessing we're looking at six weeks at best, before all is completed and we're back up and running," Dr. Bower responded.

"Six weeks!" Bart exclaimed.

His internal calculator must be having a fucking seizure, Sarah thought.

Dr. Bower redirected the conversation: "Dr. Lester, who did the donor nephrectomy, is speaking with the family of the donor now. We'll review the entire clinical case when he gets here to try to understand what happened. It was a thirty-five-year-old man with a family, and his older sister was the recipient. I transplanted the kidney; it worked immediately."

A female attorney whom Sarah recognized from the Kayla investigation sat forward. "We need to contain the story and report the facts to the appropriate regulatory bodies."

"I called our local CMS office, since Medicare pays for kidney transplants. They'll be out within seven days," Kathy from the hospital quality control department said. "I'll keep you all informed."

"Looks like we'll be up to our asses with survey teams. Meanwhile, can we still do our deceased-donor kidney transplants?" Bart asked.

Dr. Bower glanced around the table. "We'll continue to do all the other transplants we do every day: deceased-donor kidney transplants; living- and deceased-donor liver transplants; pancreas and islet cell transplants. As sad as it is to have a living donor die, I want to remind you that this has never happened in the history of our program. We have some of the best outcomes in the country, and that will continue. As always, our patients' safety is our highest priority."

Dr. Bower finished reviewing the plan with the team. By the time Sarah checked her watch, it was close to 11:00 p.m.

"I want to thank everyone for coming back in after a long day. Let's plan to meet back here tomorrow morning at six thirty for an update. Thanks again for all your teamwork. Sarah, can you stay afterward?" Dr. Bower stood up, and the group filtered out. Sarah heard cell phones ringing and beepers going off and thought, *Organ offer calls never stop, and patients are still waiting for their lifesaving transplants.*

Dr. Bower sat down next to her. "How are you doing, Sarah? Not what you signed up for, right?"

"I'm overwhelmed, but I can handle this. I'll call a meeting with the kidney transplant team first thing in the morning to provide an update. I feel bad for the donor family. I know we tell them there's always a risk of death, as with any surgery, but these are extremely healthy people we work up to ensure there are no clinical, psychological, or social issues that would preclude their being donors. They get the best physical of their lives. I should know—I went through the whole workup. Our team is thorough to a fault."

She couldn't help but think, *And this sure makes the reality of my becoming a donor scarier. If it can happen to the man who died, it can happen to me.*

Dr. Bower said, "We do have a real A-Team. We'll review the case and see if we missed anything. At the end of the day, we're all human. Don't think I've forgotten about Wyatt's case as this whole thing plays out."

"I'm embarrassed to say that it's the first thing I thought of when I got the news. Jackie and Wyatt were at my apartment when you called. How do you think we should deal with their case?" Sarah asked.

"Well, the good news is that I called my high-profile case, the one you're a donor for, and discussed a change of plans: a different transplant program that's actually a little closer for them. I wanted to run the idea by you first, and then we can decide on the best approach to communicate with Jackie and Laura."

Sarah watched Dr. Bower closely. How he was able to maintain such a calm demeanor in the midst of all this pressure was beyond her. "I can't imagine anyone else is going to be as good as you and our team," she said, "but it looks like that option is off the table if we're going to get Wyatt transplanted as soon as possible."

"I spoke with Dr. Santos in Miami, and he's willing to run your paired exchange by his team. If they agree, they may be able to squeeze your case into their already overbooked OR schedule as early as next week or the week after that, at the latest. They trust our workup process but want to review Wyatt's workup and your donor workup. I know this is a lot right now, but I think it's what's best for Wyatt if it works out."

Sarah felt her eyes widen. "Miami? I don't know. I have to get everyone on board for CMS and UNOS surveyors, I still have this ongoing Kayla investigation, and I haven't replaced her yet." Sarah's stomach tightened. *This isn't just "a lot"—it's too much. I really don't know if I can handle all this at once.*

"You look pale, Sarah. Are you okay?"

"Not really. I need to get some water. I'll be right back." Sarah went to the ice machine at the nurses' station, pushed the lever, caught a handful of ice and put it behind her neck. "Calm down. You'll be okay. Breathe," She said aloud to herself. She took a deep breath as she let the ice trickle down her neck and onto the back collar of her white lab coat. She filled a cup with water and returned to the conference room.

"I'm better, thanks." She sat next to Dr. Bower, who was typing something into his phone.

"Would you be willing to go to Miami for your donor surgery?" he asked.

"Oh, well, I guess if we need to get this done in Miami, then I'll wrap my head around it. I can fly my grandmother there to take care of me. How soon can I fly afterward? Miami is not my favorite place, as you know." Sarah sighed. *Fucking Miami. Why can't I get away from there?*

"Assuming Dr. Santos and his donor team approve all the workups, they'll be the ones who decide when you can fly home. I'm guessing they'll let you leave after a couple weeks if everything goes well," Dr. Bower said.

Suck it up, Golden. It's more about Wyatt than you, Sarah thought. Out loud, she said, "All right. Miami, here I come. Will you call Jackie and Laura, then?"

"Why don't you run it up the flagpole with Jackie? I can make a follow-up call if they're receptive. They've already met Dr. Santos and have seen the institute's outcomes, so that should be helpful in their decision making. How does that sound?" Dr. Bower asked, as he yawned.

"I'm happy to talk to Jackie, but who will take over all my tasks here? I know preparing for the survey is a ton of work. I can get things started, but then I'll be out of commission for six weeks after the donor surgery." Sarah blinked slowly, fatigue knocking.

"It's about time for Bart to roll up his sleeves and come down into the trenches with the rest of us. I'll speak with him and let him know it's not an option, especially since I know he's probably having heart palpitations about the cost of preparing for the surveys and the loss of revenue from the canceled cases. That should motivate the old boy." Dr. Bower chuckled.

Sarah choked out a laugh. "Sounds like we have a plan, then. I'll call Jackie tonight and see you first thing in the morning."

"Go home and get some rest, and I'll do the same. We're going to have some long days ahead, but I know you can handle them. I'm so glad you're part of our team, Sarah. I mean it."

"Thanks for your confidence. I'll do my level best—you can count on that. Good night, Dr. Bower." Sarah replied, as they both stood.

"Remember, transplant is a team sport, and we've got a great team rooting for you. Good night," Dr. Bower said, as he walked down the hallway and Sarah went the opposite direction.

When Sarah got home, she called Jackie.

"Must be bad news if you're calling me this late," Jackie said when she picked up.

"Let's say you'll be seeing Biker Bob sooner than you thought you would, and I guess the silver lining is that we'll both get to have one those amazing cheeseburgers together."

"Tell me everything."

"I will, but first, how are you doing?"

"Surprise, Laura stayed in the city tonight. Her mother feels so bad she has to work so hard, it makes me want to puke. The good news is that Wyatt is peeing and feeling better, he was looking for you when he woke up. What's all this talk about my buddy Biker Bob? I don't see any travel in my immediate future—not until Wyatt's well on the road to recovery."

"Well that road to recovery just went east, my friend. It looks like the Miami International Transplant Institute is going to be the quickest way for our Wyatt to get transplanted," Sarah said.

"What?"

"Yeah. The reason I had to rush off was that one of our living donors died unexpectedly. We have to shut down the living kidney donor part of our program immediately. I can't really share any more than that."

"Holy shit, that had to freak you out," Jackie said.

"It absolutely did scare me, but I want you to know that I *will* be the donor for Wyatt's paired exchange. I'm not backing out," Sarah reassured her.

"I would understand if you needed to withdraw," Jackie said.

"Not gonna happen. If there was any way we could do it in San Francisco, I'd love it, but Miami has a very capable team. We need to get Wyatt transplanted so we don't have to deal with the dialysis cloud hovering over him."

"Talk about a wake-up call, I'll be up for a while but you need to get some rest, I can't imagine all the work ahead of you before we leave for Miami. If I could reach through the phone and give you the biggest hug ever, I would. I love you so much my friend." With that Jackie hung up.

Chapter 29

Campos got to the surgery office at 4:45 a.m. The door was locked, so she waited out in the hallway and thought about the day's itinerary. She needed to review Kayla's computer files with Ned Bisone or Sarah; that would take a chunk of time. Given the new information that Jackie had shared via Zuzu, Campos would also need to interview each of the surgeons who had been in Miami when Kayla was killed—Wood, Edwards, and Lester—to ascertain whether one of them was the killer. *Strong had better find a way to get out here and help me*, she thought.

She heard footsteps and looked up to see a tall, thin, blond man in scrubs coming around the corner, his eyes half-open. "Dr. Lester?"

"That's me."

"I'm Detective Campos, from Miami. I'm supposed to meet with you at five."

"Shit. I don't have time for this, especially today. Sorry." He opened the door and went directly toward the kitchen. Campos followed him.

Lester started a pot of coffee and walked past Campos to his office, which was one in a line of five. Campos saw Dr. Bower's office door open, his desk piled high with files and papers. Lester's beeper went off, and she heard him talking on the phone. She sat down in the waiting area of the suite. The smell of Lester's freshly brewed coffee wafted through the air; she really needed a cup but didn't want to help herself.

Her phone rang, and she picked up. "Campos here."

"Detective Campos, this is Sarah Golden."

"Hi, Sarah. I'm glad you called, I'm going to interview Dr. Lester, and then I'll need to sit down with you or Ned to review Kayla's computer files. Where should I meet you to do that?"

"Detective, we had a very serious incident at our program yesterday: We lost a living kidney donor. Our entire team will be in meetings, surgeries, or clinics today. I'm sorry, but we won't be able to meet with you for the next couple days. We're going to have to temporarily close our living kidney donor program."

"I'm so sorry. I can't imagine what everyone is going through," Campos said. Just then, she got another call. It was Strong. "Can I call you back, Sarah? I need to figure out my next steps."

"Sure, but I won't be available after six thirty this morning. Talk to you later."

Campos accepted Strong's call. "Hey."

"'Hey'? I busted my ass to get out here to help you. How about a 'Great to hear from you, Partner'?"

"You want me to have the Blue Angels fly over and escort you to the transplant institute, too?" Campos quipped.

"Now you're talking. Anyway, it's pretty early for you to sound so stressed. What's going on?" Strong asked.

"Actually," Campos said, "there've been some unfortunate developments since we last spoke—things are completely out of our control. Sarah just called me and told me a living kidney donor died yesterday. It's a big deal. They have to close that part of the program while they're running the rest of show. Not good."

"That sucks! I'm sorry to hear it. But there must be some work we can do in the meantime—can we get access to Kayla's computer files? We wouldn't be in anyone's way."

"I'll call Sarah back and ask her if we can meet with Ned about that. Maybe he can help us. I feel bad bothering the team, but we still have a murder to solve," Campos said.

"That sounds like a reasonable request. Before I left, I was able to connect with Zuzu, and she confirmed that Kayla did tell her she had to meet a guy from work at her grandmother's house the night she was killed. Maybe tomorrow we can get those surgeons all lined up and play Good Cop, Bad Cop. I'll take a cab and call you when I get to the transplant institute. Shouldn't be much traffic this early," Strong said.

"Great idea. I'm glad you're here, Strong. It will be good to get another set of eyes on this. See you soon."

As soon as Campos hung up, she called Sarah back. *I wonder if Sarah will be as happy to see my partner as I'll be*, she thought.

"Sarah Golden."

"Hi, Sarah. Detective Campos again."

"Hi, Detective."

"Would it be possible for Ned to show me Kayla's files? I'm guessing it may take at least half a day to review everything."

"Sure. Text Ned; he should be able to find you a cubicle where you can review the files. Space is always at a premium, so if he can't find anything else, you're welcome to use my office. I'll be in meetings all day," Sarah said.

"Your office may work better, since there'll be two of us looking through the files with Ned."

"Two of you?" Sarah asked.

"Detective Strong just landed at SFO. He's here to help me finish the interviews. He's much better than I am at finding anything suspicious in computer files; he's a whiz at that kind of stuff."

Campos thought she heard Sarah let out a brief sigh. *Well, that answers my question—no doubt there are sparks flying between those two, but I can't tell whether they'll be good ones or bad ones when they see each other.*

"Do you have Ned's number?" Sarah asked.

"No. If you could text it to my cell, I'd appreciate it. We'll stay out of everyone's way until this afternoon, but I'll need to talk to you later. We still need to meet with the surgeons who were in Miami," Campos added.

"I can't make any promises about that right now, but I'll send you Ned's number. Why don't you try my cell after you're done with Kayla's files? I should know more about surgeon availability then. If I were you, I'd stay out of their way right now; they haven't had much sleep, and this donor death is bringing all kinds of regulators to our front door—not to mention, our transplant program never stops."

"I hear you. I'm really sorry your program is going through this."

"Thanks. I appreciate that," Sarah said, then hung up.

Campos made her way to the coffee shop on the first floor of the hospital and called Ned.

"Hi, Ned, it's Detective Campos. I hope I didn't wake you up."

"Oh, no, I've been up since five; I'm already at the hospital. We had an incident yesterday that's going to require lots of shared documents and ongoing communication between select members of our team, so I set up a listserv to make sure everyone gets all the necessary email updates," Ned said.

"That sounds like an efficient way to organize things. The reason I'm calling is that my partner from the Miami PD,

Detective Strong, will be at the institute shortly, and we need to review all the files from Kayla's computer. I spoke with Sarah, and she said we could use her office and that you may be able to get us set up."

"Yes, I just got the go-ahead from her. Is your partner here, too?" Ned asked.

"He's coming from SFO. He should be here in about forty-five minutes if there's no traffic."

"Why don't you page me when he gets here, and I'll come meet you both and take you to Sarah's office?" Ned offered.

"That would be great. Thanks."

"No problem. That will be the easy part of my day. I'll go ahead and get Kayla's files opened and ready on Sarah's computer so you can dig right in when he gets here. I did have to remove all the patient records from her files, for security reasons. We don't want any privacy breaches in the midst of everything else that's going on. Poor Sarah—she's going to be so busy until this whole situation is resolved."

"I know. Sounds like she has a full plate and then some. I'll call you as soon as my partner gets here, Ned," Campos said.

"Sounds like a plan."

After she ended the call, Campos headed out for a quick breakfast. Just as she was finishing, Strong texted her to say he was at the hospital. After Campos sent Ned a text telling him that her partner had arrived, she walked back to the lobby and spotted Strong sitting there, reading a magazine with his legs crossed, looking relaxed.

"Good morning, Detective Strong. Welcome to the San Francisco Global Transplant Institute."

He glanced at Campos and stood up. "Thanks, Campos. I've been here a few times with my ex—uh, Sarah. I don't think these people ever take a break."

Campos looked around and saw Ned walking toward them from just a few feet away. "You two ready to stare at a computer screen?" he asked.

"We can't wait. Ned, this is Detective Strong. Ned is the IT guy extraordinaire; the place couldn't run without him," Campos said.

"That's not really true. I just make sure all the technology works so the team can spend more time with the patients. No one wants to be in front of those computers any more than they have to. Did I overhear you say you had an ex-girlfriend named Sarah who works here?" Ned asked.

Strong raised an eyebrow. "You might have."

"Is it Sarah Golden?" Ned asked.

"I don't really share personal information like that," Strong replied.

Campos noticed Ned squint strangely at Strong, but he quickly recovered and then motioned them to follow him.

"Sarah has offered us her office so we won't be in anyone's way," Campos said. They followed Ned onto the elevator and then to Sarah's office. Ned fetched a key from the administrative assistant and let them in. "Why don't you wait in the hall until I pull up the files and arrange the chairs so you can be as comfortable as possible?" he asked.

After he had everything ready for the detectives, Ned ushered them into Sarah's office. There was a small table with two chairs in one corner and Sarah's desk positioned against the opposite wall.

As all three of them stood in front of the computer, Ned began to orient them using the mouse. "Here are the folders Kayla had on her desktop: one labeled 'Grandma,' one 'Managers,' and the rest are filled with work notes from meetings and conferences she attended. Detective Campos, as I mentioned earlier, I scrubbed them of patient names and patient-related information, so if you see large areas blocked out, that's why."

"Sounds easy enough, Ned. Thanks for setting this all up for us. We'll get to work, and if we need you, I'm guessing Campos has your number," Strong said.

"I do. Thanks, Ned. Good luck today," Campos said.

"Call or text if you need me, but I may be slow to respond," Ned said.

Campos watched Strong casually survey Sarah's office as they both took their seats in front of the computer. Campos pointed to a photo of Sarah with Wyatt on the wall above: "That must have been taken a while ago—he looks so healthy there. Now I can see how sick he's gotten."

"Good thing he's getting a transplant, poor kid." Strong said. "Anyway"—he pulled a folded piece of paper out of his sport coat pocket and handed it to Campos—"I made a list of words to search in the documents so we can expedite this process."

"You came prepared. I would never have thought of this," Campos started to read the list out loud. "Grandma, grandmother, Zuzu, Florida, opioids, drugs, blackmail . . . Wow, I wouldn't have thought of blackmail."

"It's a start. Once we begin the search and read what's around the words, we'll likely find other terms to look for, too. Let's open Grandma's folder and see what she's got in there. Maybe we'll get lucky."

Campos opened the folder and typed "opioids" into the "Search Document" box. The screen lit up with all the yellow-highlighted matches; "opioids" was sprinkled throughout the files. Campos looked at Strong. "Maybe Grandma liked her some oxy."

As they scanned the files, they noticed a couple of typed words, but more numbers.

2010: Owe $30,000 on Grandma's mortgage. Need to sell $5K in opioids.

2011: Owe $25K. Need to sell $5K in drugs in opioids—put excess $ in X account.

2012: Grandma diagnosed with cancer. Owe $20K. Need to pay off house.

2013: Paid off mortgage, gave Grandma the deed. Best day of my life.

"Kayla was a drug dealer? Remember how, when I questioned the surgeons, one of them admitted he had prescribed her some Oxycontin? I believe Sarah told me that Kayla had all the surgeons' DEA numbers, which is the number you need to order narcotics, in addition to her own. What year did her grandmother die?" Campos asked, as she made notes in her Kayla file.

"She died in June 2014," Strong replied.

Campos kept skimming the grandmother's file. Following a summary of her debt, which was minimal, there was an entry about Kayla taking her grandmother on a cruise in December 2013:

Cruise for two, first class: $30K. Sales great, six dealers, nontraceable. $60K into Grandma's savings account. $10K/year x 5 years = $50K. Sprinkle between my account, Grandma's, and X's.

"I wonder who X is. She must have had someone helping her. And where was she getting all the drugs to sell?" Campos asked.

"I spoke to the guy who's head of Narcotics in Miami, and he said that folks were shipping them via UPS all over the world back then, and still are. If Kayla had a reliable source using her cover as a nurse practitioner, who knows? She could have sent them labeled as antirejection drugs. No one messes with those patients," Strong said.

"How did you come up with that idea?" Campos asked.

"There's a big business in mail-order drugs; they're cheaper, and insurance pays for them. My sister gets her blood pressure drugs delivered like clockwork every ninety days. It's common practice. I'm guessing antirejection drugs can be mail ordered, too. When Sarah and I were going out, she told me some people travel to wherever the shortest wait times are in the United States, get transplanted, and then come back home for local follow-up afterward." Strong shared.

"You don't think her transplant patients were taking them, do you? That would mess up their transplant, wouldn't it?" Campos asked.

"I doubt any transplant patient in their right mind would jeopardize their outcome. They probably didn't have anything to do with it, but it would be a logical cover, since she's in the business," Strong said.

Campos kept scrolling through the document and found some more entries about how much X was getting, along with bank account summaries. "We have to get access to Kayla's bank account so we can see whether she was socking away cash, too. Looks like her grandmother had some money when she died. Were you able to get access to the grandmother's account?" Campos asked.

"I didn't think she'd have an open account, since she's been dead for over a year and a half, but I'll call the local bank. I should be hearing back about Kayla's accounts any day now; she has accounts in Florida and California. Let me sort this document for X and see if she assigned them a name." Strong entered a capital X in the search box, and several yellow-highlighted results showed up throughout the document with no name, only dollar amounts, attached to the letter.

As she reviewed those sums, Campos said, "Well, X is definitely in on this if the amount she allocated to them is correct."

Strong had been jotting down all the numbers as Campos scrolled through the file. He finished his calculations and looked up at Campos. "X has over two hundred and fifty thousand dollars, according to my math. All these numbers don't really add up; we also can't assume that Kayla entered everything in this file." Strong searched the rest of the words, but nothing came up under "Zuzu" or "blackmail." "Drugs" did appear, and was connected to the ledger balances.

"Let's look at this next one, 'Manager Blackmail.'" Campos opened the file, which dated back fifteen years, starting in 2001 and ending in 2016. Kayla had entered the managers' names and start and end dates.

"They really chew through managers; looks like there was a new one every two to three years," Campos said, as she read the names in chronological order. There were notes under each name, along with status reports indicating when Kayla had reported the manager to Dr. Bower or HR, depending on what she had on them. "Who has time for this shit? This program is so busy, and Kayla was a workhorse on top of her drug deals and documentation. She was one seriously whacked person," Campos added.

"She's no dummy. She knew if she could keep the manager revolving door moving, no one would have time to take a closer look at her activity. What we do know is that she went to Florida at least four times a year, which was probably where she ran the drugs from. She had to have a partner who was organized, if these dollar numbers are correct; that's a lot of inventory to track and money to account for," Strong said.

Campos scrolled down to the last manager, Sarah Golden, and read some of the notes Kayla had written: "Bower thinks Sarah is real smart—will fix that when insurance company visits and she has no numbers to report. Works from home too much, Miami cop boyfriend in town, comes in late, let HR know she's lying on her time card, dumb friend Jackie picks her up early and they go drinking, doesn't know what she's doing, spread rumors about her sleeping with surgeons to other coordinators. I'll fix her ass for good for embarrassing me in front of the staff and suspending me for three days."

Campos stopped and looked over at Strong. "Wow, she's one twisted sister." His lips were pursed, and his eyebrows were furrowed. "You okay?" Campos asked.

"I wonder what Kayla meant by 'fix her ass for good.' If she had that kind of money, she could easily have hired someone to hurt Sarah, or worse," he said, casting his eyes downward.

"Let's close this manager file out and see what else we have here." Campos closed out all the files Ned had opened and noticed a separate folder on Sarah's desktop. "Look what we have here: a folder labeled 'Surgeon Fuckups and Indiscretions.' This should have some goodies in it. Maybe we can figure out if any of these are X."

"Maybe so," Strong said.

"But before we start on this file, why don't I go get us some coffee and snacks?" Campos offered. "You can look at the notes I've taken so far and see if I got everything; you were scrolling pretty fast."

"Sounds like a great idea," Strong replied.

Chapter 30

"Miami!" Jackie said aloud to herself after she hung up with Sarah. The bedside clock read 12:30 a.m., and she was wide awake, working out all the details in her head. Sarah had briefly explained to her about the living-kidney-donor program shutting down and that Dr. Bower had contacted Dr. Santos about doing their paired exchange at the Miami International Transplant Institute.

Jackie decided to call Laura, and it went straight to voicemail, so she paged her with their agreed-upon 911 urgent-message alert.

Several minutes later, Laura called. "What's wrong? Is Wyatt all right?"

"Wherever you are, I need you to come home now. There's a change of plans, and we have to take Wyatt to Miami for his transplant. I'll give you the rest of the story when you get home." Jackie hung up, went downstairs, poured herself some rum, and brought it back up to the bedroom. Wyatt and his grandmother were fast asleep.

I better start looking at airfares, keep my mind off Laura. I hope she wasn't with what's her name, she thought, positioning herself on the bed with her laptop.

Laura's firm tap on her shoulder awoke Jackie from a sound sleep. She glanced at the bedroom clock. It was almost 2:30 a.m. now.

"What's up with Wyatt getting his transplant in Miami? What the hell is going on?" Laura walked around to the bathroom, leaving the door open while she undressed and put on her pajamas.

Jackie decided not to even ask Laura where she'd been for the past two hours. "San Francisco has to close their living-donor program because of a living-donor death. Bower already called Santos in Miami and the other paired-exchange couple; everyone is fine with going there for their transplant. We really don't have much of a choice if we want to get Wyatt transplanted as soon as possible, and we need that to happen."

Jackie went into the bathroom and closed the door, undressed, and came back just as Laura was getting settled in bed.

"That's really bad, losing a living donor; those people are the healthiest of the healthy. Do you know what the person died from?" Laura asked.

"That's none of our business. Sarah is a professional and would never share confidential patient information. We need to discuss our travel plans, and you'll need to arrange time off immediately. I think we should have your mom stay here while we're gone." Jackie deliberately kept her tone flat.

"When is the transplant date?" Laura got up and took her calendar out of her briefcase.

Jackie opened her computer, where she had kept a running log on Wyatt's health and lab tests. "Miami has two dates open next week: Tuesday and Thursday, I think we should take Tuesday." Jackie reviewed the list of things they needed to do before they left. Sarah had given her some details and then sent her several handouts spelling out how to prepare Wyatt for the surgery.

"Today's Friday. We don't have much time," Laura said.

"We don't have a choice here. We're extremely lucky Bower took care of all these details for us. I was very upset when your mother told me you were planning to stay in the city." Jackie eyes were starting to close, the fatigue was taking over.

"I'm sorry, Jack. I should have called you myself. I worked until midnight and have to be back in at six this morning. I was just sleeping in the city, I told you I'd stop seeing Jennifer and I have." Laura replied.

"It's hard to trust you right now. I feel like I'm carrying Wyatt's entire illness on my back, and I need you to show up and help me—and, more importantly, be there for him. We need you home every night, Laura."

"I promise I'll be home from now on. Right now, I really need to go to bed. I can hardly stand; I'm exhausted."

"Me too. Mary will be calling first thing in the morning to review everything." Jackie turned off her bedside light.

"I have a meeting at six in the morning. I'll go in and sign over my cases and arrange for time away. Goodnight." Laura got into bed and turned her light off.

• • •

Jackie's cell phone ring woke her out of a sound sleep at 6:30 a.m. "Hello?" she mumbled.

"Jackie, sorry to wake you up. It's Mary. You want to grab a cup of coffee and call me back?"

"Yeah, great idea. I'll call you back in about ten minutes." Jackie got up, saw Laura was long gone, grabbed her robe, and went downstairs. Once she had brewed coffee, she sat down at the kitchen table and returned Mary's call.

"I can't imagine what you and your team must be going through if any of the other parents are as freaked out as I am," Jackie said.

"You're the first case we're arranging out of town. Thankfully, Dr. Bower knows the Miami folks and you took Wyatt there already, so your case is much easier than some of our others. How are you and Laura doing with this change of plans?" Mary asked.

"We're okay. Things are a little tense since we need to get our travel plans handled and Laura has to take off work at the last minute. They're not going to be happy, but Wyatt's our top priority."

"I spoke with Sarah briefly this morning, and she told me she sent you some handouts to review. I'm sure they'll have their own protocols in Miami. I did call my counterpart Scott—I think you remember him?" Mary paused.

"Yes, he was great with Wyatt. We don't love him as much as we love you, but Wyatt was comfortable with him for sure. I was thinking we should fly out on Sunday for a Tuesday transplant. Do you think that's enough time for Wyatt to acclimate?" Jackie got up and poured herself another cup of coffee.

"I think you should call Scott after we hang up. He'll be the one to coordinate things going forward. I did send him the updated labs Wyatt had drawn, and I need to tell you, they do not look good. Our pediatric nephrologist reviewed them this morning, and if Wyatt were getting transplanted here, we'd advise a temporary dialysis access pre-transplant. I'm not sure what the Miami folks will recommend."

Jackie let out a sigh. "I kind of figured they wouldn't be great. The good news is that the water pill is working well. I'm guessing his output was over a thousand milliliters yesterday. And his headache responded to the Tylenol. Anyway, you know we'll do whatever the team thinks is in his best interest."

"I need to get to a meeting now. Sarah's running it; she's been here since five this morning. If you need anything while you're in Miami, just call, but you're in great hands there. Tell Wyatt he's my super hero, we'll do his follow-up care here once he's been given clearance to fly home," Mary said.

"I'm sure he'll be happy to hear that. Take care, and I hope we are both on the other end of this soon," Jackie said.

Jackie finished her coffee, called Scott, and left him a voicemail. Then she went upstairs to check on Wyatt, who was still asleep. When she saw no signs of movement in Grandma's room, she took a shower.

As Jackie was getting dressed, her cell rang with a call from a Miami area code. "Hello."

"Hi, is this Jackie? It's Scott, from the Miami International Transplant Institute."

"Hi, Scott, yes, it's me. How are you doing? Looks like we'll be seeing you real soon. We're hoping that Tuesday spot is still available."

"The Tuesday spot is yours. I spoke with Mary, and she said she discussed how Wyatt's case would happen. Our programs are very similar. I'd recommend you fly in on Saturday so Wyatt has time to relax with you and Laura on Sunday. Wyatt's case will be the first one on the schedule Tuesday morning, followed by the other paired exchange in the afternoon. I believe your friend Sarah Golden is the living kidney donor for that case."

"Yes, Sarah will be the living donor for the other recipient," Jackie said.

"Our social worker made a reservation for your family at our housing down the street. Our pediatric nephrologist will want to meet with you and your wife on Sunday to discuss whether Wyatt will need to be dialyzed before his transplant. They have his recent lab results. I'm sure Mary talked to you about them," Scott said.

"She did."

"We'll have you bring Wyatt to the hospital Sunday to get his pre-op labs done, and he'll meet with Anesthesiology. We'll know more after we review those results."

"I understand, Scott. I'd better get going on these flight arrangements. Will you be there on Sunday?" Jackie had a burning pit in her stomach.

"I sure will. Please tell Wyatt I can't wait to see him again, and that he's going to sail through this. I mean that, Jackie—we do over fifty pediatric kidney transplants a year. I sent you my cell number. Any questions, please call me. See you soon."

After Scott ended the call, Jackie's eyes filled with tears. *I think it's best he goes to school so I can figure out all the arrangements. He needs to be around his friends*, she thought, as she tiptoed into Wyatt's room across the hall. She sat on the end of his bed and watched his sweet face while he slept.

Eventually, she touched his arm and said, "Hey, buddy. Time to get up for school."

Wyatt's long eyelashes slowly fluttered open, and he blinked a few times. "Okay, Momma. I have to pee."

Jackie smiled. "Great way to start the day! Get dressed for school; I'll be waiting for you downstairs."

Laura's mom was sitting at the kitchen table in her robe, drinking a cup of coffee, when Jackie entered. "Big change of plans, Wyatt is having his transplant in Miami. The three of us are flying out tomorrow. We're hoping you can hold down the home front. I can share all the details after I drop off Wyatt."

Grandma put her coffee cup down and looked up at Jackie, "I'm here to help Jackie. Please know that."

"I appreciate that, I really do. I'm going to talk to Wyatt's teacher and then I'll be home." Jackie realized she only had so much energy, and she needed to use it on Wyatt and trying to save her marriage, not fighting with Laura's mom.

Chapter 31

Sarah was studying her notes, waiting for her third meeting of the day to start, when someone put a hand lightly on her shoulder. She looked up to see Ned smiling down at her. "Hi, Sarah. How are you holding up?"

"Doing the best I can, Ned. Lots of spinning plates. Thanks for all your help."

"I wanted to let you know I put the two detectives in your office, and they're looking at Kayla's files. I think they'll be busy most of the day," he reported.

Shit! Sarah realized. *I left Kayla's folder on the surgeons on my desktop; if they see what's in that file, they could use it to accuse any number of our doctors of wanting Kayla dead.*

She stood up abruptly. "I have to go. I forgot something in my office. Tell them to start without me," she said.

She bolted out of the meeting room and ran up the stairs up to her office, her pulse racing. She pulled out her keys and charged in—and there was Handsome, sitting at her computer.

As he stood up and faced her, she realized she had stopped breathing. "I forgot you were going to be here," she gasped.

"Sarah. Are you okay?" Handsome asked. He pulled his chair out and gestured for her to sit down.

"I'm fine, I'm fine," she said, slumping in the seat and focusing on taking deep breaths. When her heart rate finally calmed, she took a long look at him. *How is it possible that he's gotten even better-looking since we broke up?* she wondered, feeling her stomach flip the same way it had when she had first met him in Miami more than a year earlier.

"Are you sure you're okay? You're sweating." Handsome put his hand on Sarah's forehead, and she felt her lady parts tingle at his touch. *That's just great*, she thought.

She kept her tone as even as possible as she answered, "Things are insane here. I'm sure Campos gave you the latest news about our donor death. Anyway, I just came in here because I have to get a folder off my computer and get to my next meeting."

She rolled her chair up to her computer and took a thumb drive out of her lab coat pocket. *Stay focused, Sarah, stay focused*, she commanded herself. She dragged Kayla's surgeons folder off her computer desktop and onto the thumb drive and ejected it. She stood up and looked into Handsome's eyes. "Sorry to be so rude, but it's chaotic today, and I've got a room full of people waiting for me."

Handsome opened her office door. "I understand. I'll be around if you want to give me a call. Same number. Take it easy, Sarah."

"Will do." Sarah grabbed her keys and walked quickly back to the meeting with Dr. Bower and the living-donor team. The room was full; the coordinators had their files spread out, and Dr. Bower was discussing a case. He glanced up at her. "Hi, Sarah. We're on the fourth living-donor case."

"Sorry I'm late." She opened her file and found the correct case. She stared at the spreadsheet, but her mind was still reeling about Handsome. *I really thought I was over him*, she reflected. *Guess not.*

Sitting back in her chair, she let out a deep sigh. A few heads turned her way and then back to their papers. She replayed their brief encounter. Staring into his deep brown eyes, she'd had to fight the urge to grab him and kiss him passionately—and, even worse, she knew he'd felt the same way. The feeling of his strong arms hugging her was exactly what she needed right now to combat all the stress she was under.

"Sarah, were you able to contact the OR this morning?" Dr. Bower asked, pulling her back into the room.

"Yes. They want us to send them a complete list of names and medical record numbers so they can take the cases off their schedule," she replied, then added, "Remember, we have a kidney transplant staff meeting now. I'd appreciate it if everyone goes directly there so we can start on time. It will only be thirty minutes."

Some of the coordinators groaned as they shuffled out. Sarah overheard one comment, "I don't know how we're supposed to get our work done when we have all these meetings."

Sarah collected her papers and put them in her briefcase. Dr. Bower walked over to her and said, "I know you can handle the staff meeting. Let me know how it goes."

"No problem," Sarah responded.

• • •

Sarah's heart beat rapidly as she stood at the podium in the transplant auditorium. She looked out at all the members of the kidney transplant team; more than sixty pairs of eyes were stared right back at her.

"Good morning. Thank you all for coming to this meeting. I'll keep it quick, as I know you all have a lot of work waiting for you." She took a sip of her coffee and tried to take a deep breath.

"As some of you have heard, we had a living-donor death yesterday. I know it's very difficult to process, and we're conducting an extensive case review with Dr. Bower and his surgical team. Per UNOS requirements, we have to temporarily shut down our living-kidney-donor program, until an outside team comes to review this case and submits its findings." Sarah looked down at her notes and swallowed.

Amid groans from the audience, she went on, "I know it's not going to be fun, but hopefully this will be over in a timely manner." Beepers were starting to go off, and Sarah could see people getting restless.

"Any questions?" she asked.

A coordinator in the front row put her hand up. "Do we know what the donor died from? What if someone asks us about what happened? What about all the living-donor cases that are already scheduled?"

Sarah responded, "We don't have an answer about why the donor died. There will be an autopsy today. If anyone asks, tell them an investigation is under way. All media questions will go through Media Relations. Our living-donor team just met, and we will be offering our patients and their donors local options, since we have several fine transplant programs right here in the Bay Area."

Another coordinator called out, "Do you have any updates on Kayla? I noticed there are two detectives here from Miami now, and, if I may say so, the man is off-the-charts handsome."

The group all chuckled, which eased the tension in the room. Sarah smiled and said, "We're making progress on that. The detectives from Miami are here to conduct some final interviews and will be heading back home soon. Since it's an active investigation, they can't really share their findings with us. If any of you do have information you'd like to share with them, please let me know."

Bart Lincoln, the executive director, entered the auditorium and approached the podium. "Bart will be working with me to facilitate all the necessary meetings. I know you'll all give him your support," Sarah said.

Bart walked up the steps to the stage, stood next to Sarah, and spoke into the microphone. "I really appreciate everyone's cooperation. Before we know it, this whole thing will be behind us. Right, Sarah?"

Sarah nodded. "Bart will be taking over my role, starting tomorrow, as I'll be going out of town to become a donor as part of a paired-exchange transplant in Miami." The living-donor team already knew about her being a donor, and she suspected the word had made its way to the rest of the team through the rumor mill. Still, her announcement elicited some audible "wows."

"You will all get a brief email summary of what I spoke about today. The rest of our transplant activities will continue, business as usual," she said.

"Remember to stay calm and not overreact," Bart offered.

Sarah concluded the meeting, and the staff slowly left the auditorium, talking among themselves. Bart turned to Sarah and said, "We should discuss all the details, to be sure I'm up to speed. Bad timing on all of this. I had a golf tournament in Monterey that I had to cancel."

Sarah wanted to spit in his face. "You can't really plan these types of things, Bart. Sorry about the golf tournament. I created a file for you with all the documents you'll need. I also emailed them to you this morning." She handed him a folder.

"You're the best. So glad you're on board for all of this. Have you made any progress in replacing Kayla? I know the surgeons are getting anxious about securing a new hire."

Are you fucking kidding me? Nope, I've just been sitting around with my finger up my ass. She suppressed the urge to glare at him as she said, "I do have some final applicants, but the surgeons can't really see them right now. If you have time today to swing by my office and introduce yourself to the Miami detectives, they're reviewing Kayla's computer desktop files."

"I'll see what I can do. See you later at our meeting with the media folks. So far, the press hasn't gotten wind of the donor death, but it's just a matter of time," Bart said, and left Sarah standing alone in the auditorium.

Sarah pulled the Ativan out of her lab coat pocket; she'd put it in there before she left for work, she just didn't think she'd need it so early in the day. She swallowed the pill without water. *This is too much pressure: work, then Handsome shows up, and Bart is being a clueless dick. Not to mention the donor death looming in my thoughts. I just need to get through today*, she thought.

Chapter 32

Campos rounded the corner to Sarah's office and found Strong standing and staring at a photo of Sarah and Wyatt, his hands in his pockets. She cleared her throat. "Uh, I've got coffee and fresh cookies." As she held out a cup to him, he slowly turned toward her with a puzzled expression.

"You've got that 'I'm trying to solve something' look on your face. I've seen it before." Campos sat down and started in on a cookie.

"I just had an impromptu visit from Sarah," he said, still standing, as he took a gulp of his coffee.

"How'd that go?"

"She's under a ton of stress. She wasn't exactly elated to see me. She just said she'd forgotten a file on her desktop. She put it on her thumb drive and rushed out." Strong perched on the edge of the small table in Sarah's office.

"Yeah, well, she's got so much going on, I'm not surprised she was in a hurry. Speaking of being busy, were you able to look at my notes and start on Kayla's surgeons file . . . What'd she label it, 'Fuckups and Indiscretions'?"

"That's the file Sarah took off her desktop. There's probably some juicy stuff in there that could help us better understand Kayla's relationships with all the surgeons," Strong said.

"I'm sure you're right. Let's review what we've learned so far and look at the rest of her files, and then I'll text Ned to see if he can get it for us," Campos suggested.

"Sounds like a plan."

They reviewed Kayla's other files, with patient files, names, and clinical information deleted or blacked out; Campos made some notes, but nothing important.

Strong pulled out his cell phone and said, "Uh-oh, I had my ringer silenced and Kayla's bank just finally called me back; I recognize the number. I'll put it on speaker so we can both listen." Strong accessed his voicemail and started the message.

"This is Mr. Charles from Miami Community Bank. You called about accessing accounts for three customers: Kayla Newman, her grandmother Lucy Thomas, and a Zuzu Perez. I've gotten the proper clearances to discuss the balances in each account. Please return my call when you can. Thanks."

Campos raised an eyebrow at Strong. "This will be interesting, given the hefty figures we found in Kayla's file on her grandmother."

Strong hit the call-back number on his cell, and when Mr. Charles answered, Strong said, "Hello, this is Detective Strong with the Miami Police Department, and I'm here with my partner, Detective Campos. May I put you on speaker so we can both hear what you have to say?"

"That would be fine."

Strong hit the SPEAKER button and said, "Okay, we're ready, Mr. Charles. What can you tell us?"

"I have information on all three of the customers. Kayla was the primary signatory for the account belonging to her grandmother, Lucy Thomas. Funds from both these accounts were closed out several weeks ago—"

Strong interrupted, "Do you have a date and the total amount that was in each of the accounts when they were closed out?"

"They were closed a week and a half ago on Saturday, at nine twenty in the morning. Kayla's account had five hundred thousand dollars in it, and Lucy Thomas's had three hundred and fifty thousand dollars," Mr. Charles said.

"Help me here, Mr. Charles—can this type of transaction be done over the phone, or does it require a personal visit to the bank?" Campos asked.

"It can be done over the phone, as long as all the security questions are answered perfectly. When this amount of money is involved, we require the account owner or their signatory to answer a long list of questions. My records show that Kayla was the person who closed these accounts and that she answered all of our questions correctly."

"That's the Saturday she was murdered," Campos said, as she checked Kayla's file.

"Murdered?" Mr. Charles replied in a low voice.

"Yes, she was murdered, and we're actively investigating her case, so this bank information is extremely important."

"How about Zuzu Perez?" Strong asked.

"Zuzu Perez has one thousand and sixty four dollars in her account. She's overdrawn this account several times, although I don't know whether that's relevant to your investigation," Mr. Charles said.

"Can you tell me the largest deposit Perez has made in the last couple years?" Strong asked.

The sound of computer key clicks came through the speaker. "Yes, just a minute. The largest deposit she made was for six hundred dollars, a year and a half ago; it was a check from a motorcycle shop in Miami. All the other deposits are smaller, ranging from fifty to two hundred dollars."

"Thanks, Mr. Charles. You've been most helpful. Would you be able to send me hard copies of Kayla's and Lucy's account statements and balances at the time they were closed?" Strong asked.

"I can do that. Would you like them mailed to the precinct address you have on your formal bank request?"

"That would be great. Thanks again," Strong said.

After he hung up, he and Campos looked at each other in silence for a few minutes. Campos finally said, "I think whoever murdered Kayla made her close out those accounts before they killed her, or maybe she closed them out because she was planning to leave town permanently."

"Two strong possibilities. We know Kayla and X were running drugs out of Grandma's house, and clearly, it was lucrative. I think we should ask the local PD to continue to keep a close eye on Grandma's house and knock on the neighbors' doors again to see if they can get some descriptions of whoever was going in and out of there," Campos said.

"They tried after they found Kayla's body, and no one would answer their door, but it's worth another try. Someone must have seen something. And money had to be part of the motive, given the timing of the withdrawal and Kayla's death. Hopefully, one of the three surgeons who were in Miami will be a strong lead or even the killer," Strong said.

"Once we've narrowed down our suspects, we can check their bank accounts, too," Campos said.

While Campos added the new information from Mr. Charles to her existing notes, Strong said, "I'll page Ned to see if he can reinstall that surgeon file Sarah took off her computer. How about you go see if there's any way we can interview at least one of the three surgeons who were in Miami?"

"Good idea. I'll go visit my assistant friend."

Campos left Strong in Sarah's office and headed to the surgery office. The waiting area was full of people, some sitting, some standing, as she approached the frazzled assistant, who was answering one call after another, taking messages. She waved and gave him her best smile. "I can see you're very busy. I just have a quick question."

He stood up as he was talking on the phone and put his hand over the receiver. "I need you to wait; please give me five minutes," he begged.

Campos stepped away and found a small wall between two of the offices. None of the other people even noticed she was there. She overheard several staff swearing, and several women intently studying papers attached to their clipboards. A door opened at the end of the hallway, and surgeons poured out and went directly into their offices, not one making eye contact.

The last surgeon to come out was Dr. Bower, followed by Sarah. She looked directly into Campos's eyes, made a slashing gesture under her chin with her hand, and mouthed, *Not a good time!*

Dr. Bower walked past Campos, and he and Sarah went into his office and closed the door.

Campos's cell rang, and she stepped outside the surgery suite. "What's up, Strong?"

"Some IT guy just called and told me Ned had to leave town to take care of his sick mother. The guy said we'd have to ask Sarah for the file; he doesn't know what we're talking about."

"Things aren't going so well here, either. I'll see you in a few," Campos said.

Chapter 33

It was almost eight o'clock on Friday morning when Wyatt came downstairs for breakfast. After she talked to Scott, Jackie had slipped out to the local bakery and gotten a fresh apple strudel and a few donuts. "Donuts!" Wyatt declared, and started to eat one before he was even fully sitting at the kitchen table. "Grandma, are you going to have one?" he asked.

"No, honey. Grandma's just waking up and having her coffee first." She turned toward Jackie and said, "I think I heard Laura this morning. I thought she was going to stay in the city last night."

"She needed to come home with the turn of events in Wyatt's transplant," Jackie said carefully, then added, "Guess what, buddy? It looks like we're going to Florida for your transplant after all. Remember when we went to see those nice people? You really liked Scott."

"I like Mary a lot, too, and Aunt Sarah is there. Why can't I stay here for my transplant, Momma?"

"Well, Aunt Sarah's program had some problems, so we're all going to go to Florida together for your transplant— you, me, Mom, *and* Aunt Sarah."

"Is Grandma coming, too?" Wyatt asked.

"No, she's going to stay here for now. We'll see how you do, and maybe you can fly home earlier to see her," Jackie replied. "Now, let's get you to school. I'm going to talk to your teachers about some homework we can take with us on our trip."

"Okay. Momma, I'm thirsty," Wyatt said, as he pushed back from the table.

Jackie poured him half a cup of milk. "Here you go, and here's your new water pill. Did you pee a lot this morning?"

"Not as much as yesterday. Boy, that was a lot."

"Do you have a headache, son?"

"Nope. I'll go brush my teeth, and then we can go to school. Wait until my friends hear I get to go to Florida again!"

As Wyatt started up the stairs, Laura's mom looked over at Jackie. "This is a sudden change of plans. What's really happening?"

"I'll give you the update when I get back from dropping him off."

When Wyatt came back downstairs, Jackie hustled him into her SUV and drove him to school. As she walked Wyatt to his classroom, several of his friends came up to greet him, and they all went off to play until the school bell rang. Jackie could see Wyatt lagging way behind the boys; he was usually the fastest.

Jackie knocked on Wyatt's classroom door. His teacher was writing on the whiteboard. "Come on in," she said.

"Hi, Mrs. Duerk. Do you have a few minutes before class starts?"

"Just a few. When that bell rings, you know those kids come charging in. How's Wyatt?"

"His kidney failure has gotten worse, so we're taking him to Miami tomorrow for a living-donor kidney transplant. I wanted him to have a normal day at school before we head out," Jackie said.

"Wyatt has been a real trooper; he's a special little boy. I'm sure he'll feel so much better after his transplant. If there's anything I can do to support him or you and Laura, just let me know," Mrs. Duerk said.

"We really appreciate your support. I was hoping you could put together a homework packet that we can take to Miami so he doesn't get behind," Jackie said.

"Let's see—today is Friday. I can have it ready when you pick him up after school today. Will that be all right?"

"Thanks. That would be great. How's he been doing at school?" Jackie asked.

"Wyatt is doing very well. Actually, I'm not worried about him falling behind; he's one of my best students. Some of his artwork is a little concerning, though. I can show you what he drew in class last week."

Jackie trailed her to Wyatt's desk, where Mrs. Duerk pulled out his art folder and handed Jackie a few of his drawings. Jackie studied the childlike image of a woman in a house on one side of the paper and a woman on the opposite side of paper, with an orange bridge between them. Wyatt had drawn himself in front of the house, waving at the bridge. The other drawings had the same theme. Jackie's stomach sank.

"It's been stressful with Wyatt getting sicker and my wife working long hours in the city. He hasn't said a word, but then, he's eight, so he wouldn't. I really appreciate your showing me these drawings. I'm going to take a quick photo of those with my phone." Jackie took the pictures and handed Mrs. Duerk the papers. She put them in Wyatt's desk just as the bell rang.

"Brace yourself—here come my kids." Mrs. Duerk and Jackie watched as all the children came flying in, threw their backpacks into their cubbies, and went to their seats, amid loud laughter and lively conversation.

Wyatt was goofing around with his best friend, Michael, and didn't even notice that Jackie was in the classroom.

Mrs. Duerk addressed her students: "We have a special guest today: Wyatt's mom is here. Maybe she'd like to lead us in the Pledge of Allegiance and our morning song, 'You're a Grand Old Flag.'"

Jackie chuckled. "It would be my honor." Wyatt looked over and smiled as she put her hand over her heart and began the pledge.

Jackie left after her performance was over, leaving Wyatt content with his teacher and friends. But then she remembered his artwork and frowned. *How could our problems not affect him? He's always been a sensitive kid*, she thought, as she drove home.

Laura's mom was dressed and watching the morning news in the living room when Jackie arrived. "Laura called and said she's making all the necessary work arrangements to be gone. She'll let us know when she's heading home, so we can have a family dinner together."

"That sounds like a great idea." Jackie walked into the kitchen, poured herself a cup of coffee, and went into the living room. She sat down in a chair across from the couch, where Laura's mother was sitting, and said, "I think we need to talk."

Laura's mom turned off the TV and smiled at her. "I agree. In fact, I think it's long overdue."

"I'm not going to fight with you; there are more important issues for us to discuss. It's no secret that you and I aren't close, but I will do my best to get along with you and hope you can do the same with me," Jackie proposed.

"That sounds fair."

"Wyatt is getting sicker, as you know, and we need to get him transplanted as soon as possible, so we need to go to Miami tomorrow. There was a clinical problem at the San Francisco program, which is why we're going to Miami. Laura and I discussed this and decided that it would be best if just the three of us go to Florida. We're hoping you can stay until we get home and maybe even a little longer." Jackie paused.

"Laura did mention that when she called, that won't be a problem. I know there's tension between you and Laura. I've felt it since I got here." Laura's mom said.

"Did she also mention that she's been cheating on me?" Jackie blurted out. She could see the sadness come across Laura's mom's face.

"I would hate to see your family break up, Jackie. You've both done an excellent job raising Wyatt, he's truly a happy well-adjusted child."

Jackie looked over at her, "Thank you for saying that, we both love that little boy so much. I'm sorry, I shouldn't take out my anger on you, it's not your fault."

"I'll try harder to be more supportive of you. I can see all this stress is taking its toll on you." Laura's mom stood up and put her hand on Jackie's shoulder.

"Thank you, I'll take all the support I can get right now, I'm glad we had our talk." Jackie sighed as she stood up and gave her a little hug. "I'm going to finalize our travel plans and start getting Wyatt's things packed. I'll be heading to the store afterward. If you have a grocery list, I can pick things up for dinner."

Once Jackie was upstairs, she pulled out several suitcases, one for each of them, and started to pack some of Wyatt's things. *I wish I could talk to Sarah right now, but she's got her hands full,* Jackie thought. *I'll just text her.*

She sent Sarah a quick message: "Know you're crazy busy, but we're flying out tomorrow. I can make your flight arrangements for you. Okay?"

A few minutes later, Sarah texted her back: "It's a cluster-fuck here. Regulators up my ass, pissed surgeons . . . oh, and Handsome is in my office with Campos. Be great if you could make my flight plans. Miss you and need you!" She ended with a heart and a screaming-face emoji.

Jackie texted back six screaming-face emojis and a thumbs-up. *What shitty luck for her to have to see Handsome now for the first time since their breakup. I bet Sarah's heart melted when she laid eyes on him. No way she doesn't still have feelings for him.*

Jackie got online and booked the least expensive direct flights she could find. She downloaded and printed all the files Scott had sent, and set them aside to read later. When she headed back downstairs, she stopped by the kitchen, "Do you have a shopping list?"

"Yes, I wrote down some snack items you can carry on the plane and while you're at the hospital. " Laura's mom handed her the list.

"Great idea. I'm going to get some lunch, shop, and then pick up Wyatt. If you think of anything else, text or call."

While Jackie drove, she decided to call her old friend Liz, who was a therapist, to see if she could get some advice about how to handle this toxic situation with Laura.

"Hey, girl. Long time no hear. How the hell are you?" Liz asked.

"I'm sorry to be calling you when I'm in crisis, but I need your help," Jackie responded.

"Listen, I know what it's like to be married with a kid— life gets fast and real blurry sometimes. Is everyone all right?"

"Not really. Wyatt's sick and needs a new kidney, Laura is cheating on me, her mother is living with us right now, and we're heading to Miami tomorrow for Wyatt's transplant."

"Holy shit! What do you need? Do you want me to wear my therapist hat or my friend hat?" Liz asked.

Jackie pulled her car into the grocery store parking lot and said, "Therapist please."

After she gave Liz the whole story about her life with Laura and Wyatt's health, Liz said, "I'm sorry to hear all this, Jackie. Things are really chaotic, and Wyatt's drawings tell me he's picking up on the tension, big-time. I coach many parents whose kids are sick and whose marriage is going south at the same time, and here's what I tell them. You and Laura need to put all your differences aside for now. Your common ground is Wyatt. You both love him and only want what's best for him. Right?"

"Right."

"Keep your focus on that and only that; don't talk about or mention anything else. Recall that love you both felt when Wyatt was born. It was pure, and you were both beyond mesmerized by that little baby. Get in touch with that; do a little emotional time travel. If you need to pull out his baby pictures and put them in the common areas of your home, do it. Take some to Miami, too. Can you do that?" Liz asked.

"Absolutely. Great idea. I love those newborn pictures."

"Good. Now can I take off my therapist hat and put on my friend hat?" Liz asked.

"Go for it."

"Fuck Laura! I'm so mad at her for hurting you! She's got her head so far up her ass, she doesn't know if she's coming or going. Listen, I have a client coming in, so I have to let you go. Let me know if you need anything. I'm here for you, Jack. When you're back from Miami, call me and let's have dinner. Love you."

"Thanks, Liz. You're a lifesaver. Love you, too," Jackie said.

Before Jackie went into the grocery store, she pulled up the photos she had taken of Wyatt's artwork and texted them to Laura, along with a message: "I know we're furious with each other, but let's set aside our differences. Our love for Wyatt is our common ground, and while he's sick, nothing else matters. Please call me. I promise not to talk about anything else. Your Mom and I had a good talk, we're getting along."

Jackie waited for a reply; she could see by the three small dots on her phone that Laura had gotten the text and was responding. She stared at the screen, waiting and waiting, until finally Laura replied: "K, I'll call you now & WOW on Mom front."

Chapter 34

S arah stared at her alarm and groaned, "What day is this?" *I can't remember ever feeling quite this tired before*, she thought, as she moved her legs over to the side of her bed and walked toward the bathroom. As she glanced at her bedside chair, she saw her suitcase, fully packed, less her toiletries.

"Today's the day, Golden. Who would have thought donating a kidney would feel like a vacation?" she said, as she looked at herself in the mirror over the sink. The person staring back at her had dark circles and bags under her eyes and blotchy skin. "I'll sleep on the plane; maybe that will help."

After she showered and dried off, she examined her body in the long mirror on the back of the bathroom door. *Next time I look in this mirror, I'll have a few small scars, one less kidney, but my Wyatt will be a healthy boy again*, she thought with a heartfelt smile.

She took an Uber to SFO at 5:00 a.m. Bart was supposed to call her in an hour so she could bring him up to speed on the last couple of days. As she stood in line for security, she felt two small arms wrapping around her waist. "Surprise!" Wyatt exclaimed.

Sarah turned around, picked him up, and gave him a warm hug. "How is my favorite boy in the whole wide world?"

Wyatt nuzzled his head under her neck. "I'm tired."

Sarah patted his back, just as she had done when he was a baby, and he nestled into her body and wrapped his long, thin legs around her. She glanced up and saw Jackie and Laura standing there. "You two look pretty good so early in the morning. What's your secret?"

"We decided to stay at the hotel near the airport, order room service, and take their shuttle to the airport," Laura said, as she rubbed Wyatt's back.

Sarah looked past Laura at Jackie and raised her eyebrows. Jackie reciprocated with a smile. *They must have worked something out*, Sarah thought, and let out a sigh. "It's so good to see you, Jack—hell of way to plan a getaway," she said, as she put Wyatt down so they could all walk through the TSA scanners.

Just as she was picking up her carry-on from the conveyer belt, Sarah's cell phone rang.

"This is Bart. I need to find a quiet place to talk, so feel free to board without me if I'm not finished." Sarah started to walk away as she answered, "Good morning, Bart."

"You're wide awake," Bart replied.

"I'm already at the airport. My plane departs in less than an hour. I'm going to Miami," Sarah reminded him.

"Oh, that's right, you're part of the paired exchange for your friends' son. Good for you, Sarah," Bart responded.

*I only told him a million time*s, she thought, as she scouted the area and found a gate with no people near it.

"I know it's been a hectic couple days with the team," Bart continued, "and I appreciate all the work you've done to prepare for the on-site survey before you leave. I got all the emails you sent late last night; it looks like we're as ready as we can be for the regulators."

Sarah sat down and pulled out her work folder. "I think everyone is good to go, and Dr. Bower is doing an amazing job leading the effort. We got the autopsy report on the living donor. A pulmonary embolism was what caused his respiratory arrest. It happened when he was in the bathroom, so, sadly, he wasn't discovered until his nurse made her rounds."

"Do we know why it took so long to realize he had passed out in the bathroom?" Bart asked.

"Because there was no reason to check on him frequently anymore. He was doing great, up walking in the halls, eating . . . They were even planning on discharging him that afternoon. His morning vitals were perfect, surgery went off without a hitch, no way to see this coming. The team reviewed his entire workup and OR notes—not one clinical clue. I feel so bad for his family. Our social worker did a stellar job with them, though, so be sure you thank her personally. I know she'd appreciate it."

"Will do. Your notes are very thorough."

"There's a lead living-donor coordinator in charge of rescheduling all the living-donor cases, and the team can handle everything. If they need anything else, they'll contact Dr. Bower," Sarah added.

"How many cases did we have to cancel?" Bart asked.

"We're having the other local transplant programs perform the living-donor nephrectomies and then ship the kidneys over to us so that we can still transplant them. It's just like if we were to get a deceased kidney shipped in from another procurement agency. There's a total of twenty cases over the next month and a half. Hopefully, we'll be back up and running by then."

"Well, at least we get do the actual transplants, so we won't be losing all that revenue," Bart said.

Sarah sighed quietly. *Oh, please. Give it a rest, Bart! You and I both know the medical center makes a ton of money from our transplant program.*

"Were you able to meet the two detectives from Miami?" Sarah asked.

"Yeah, we had a quick sit-down late yesterday afternoon; they were nice enough, although the woman seems a little pushy. They'll be interviewing the surgeons today and hope to leave tomorrow if all goes well. Talk about adding insult to injury—first, Kayla's dead; then our donor dies and the regulators descend on us. It's certainly not a great time for you to be leaving. Good thing it's for an important cause," Bart said.

"Remember, we were supposed to have our paired exchange done here. Who could have predicted all this would happen?" Sarah said, resisting the desire to add, *You're such a dickwad, no wonder all the managers leave. If it's not Kayla pushing them out, it's you, Bart.*

"Say, did you give Ned time off? The detectives were trying to get ahold of him, and he hasn't responded," Bart said.

"I didn't see any requests in the HR system when I approved everyone's time sheets yesterday. But, come to think of it, I haven't seen him around the last couple days. He got our listserv up right after the donor died, and that was the last I saw him. He needs a vacation, that's for sure." Sarah paused, then said, "My flight is about to start boarding, Bart. Do you have any other questions? I'm going to be offline once I get to the Miami transplant program."

"I can't think of anything, but what's the latest I can call you?" Bart asked.

"Today is Saturday. I'm turning my cell off Sunday morning. I have to get some pre-op bloodwork done and have some downtime before surgery on Tuesday."

"I don't think I'll need you. I'm sure Bower can help me if I need something. How many weeks will you be off?" Bart asked.

"They usually like donors to take four to six weeks off, but I probably won't take that long. I'll let you know when I'm back in town. I'm not leaving the country, Bart—don't worry."

"I hope everything goes well and that you're back on deck soon. You take care and travel safely," Bart said.

"Thanks. Good luck." Sarah ended the call, grabbed her carry-on, and headed to the gate just in time to make the boarding cutoff.

She walked by Jackie and Laura's row. Wyatt was in between them, already sleeping. Sarah said, "I'm going to try to take a nap, too. See you in Miami."

Once the plane took off, Sarah reclined her seat, put on her eye mask, and fell sound asleep. She was dreaming about making love to Handsome on her desk at work, when she felt a strong push on her arm. Sarah lifted her mask and opened one eye to see Jackie standing over her.

"Come on, Golden, I let you sleep most of the flight, but we only have half an hour before we start to descend, and I need to know what happened when you saw Handsome in your office. This is the only private time we're going to get until we're back in SF. Spill it!" Jackie demanded.

Sarah moved from her aisle seat to the empty middle seat in her row so that Jackie could sit down next to her.

Jackie handed her a tissue. "You may want to wipe the drool off your mouth before you start to talk."

"You are such an asshole." Sarah chuckled and wiped her mouth.

"So? What happened?" Jackie pushed.

"I have missed you so much." Sarah leaned over and gave her friend a long hug.

"The quick, *Readers' Digest* version of us, while you're waking up, is that Laura, her mom, and I have a truce—nothing but Wyatt love vibes and support until we're back home.

I talked to Liz, and she gave me great advice. It's all good for now," Jackie said.

"I knew something had shifted when I saw you both. Good for you for putting on your big-girl panties and bonus points for her mom, keeping the peace, that's my girl. Anyway, I have to tell you, when I saw Handsome in my office, it took every ounce of energy not to grab him, throw him down, and screw his brains out. Our chemistry was so intense, anyone within a ten-mile radius could have felt it. I'm glad his partner wasn't there; when he touched me, I thought I was going to have an orgasm on the spot. If that donor hadn't died and things weren't so crazy, we would definitely have had wild sex back at my apartment. . . ." Sarah paused and took a sip of water.

"So the love passion is still piping hot, huh, Golden?" Jackie teased.

"Steaming, girlfriend."

Jackie laughed. "I knew it. I think you should have nailed him right there in your office. Could have been your last chance."

"You're probably right. So, what's going on with you and Laura for real?" Sarah asked.

"Liz really helped me get focused. After that, I called Laura. We had a long talk and decided to put our outside worlds on pause and just be with Wyatt. Her mom is staying at our house for now, and we had a Kumbaya moment too. I did call my doctor to get something for anxiety, which I'll take if I need it. Laura told her new girlfriend that we needed family time and that she wouldn't be in contact with her for a while. I think that's the best we can do right now. We're keeping our world small: Wyatt, his transplant team, you, and her mom."

"Well, I'm all yours now, for real. Bart can handle the work front and put out any fires there. I think I'm going to need to sleep a lot before surgery," Sarah said.

"How about we have dinner tonight after everyone gets settled, and then you can have some time tomorrow to veg?" Jackie suggested.

"Sounds good to me."

The captain's voice came over the loudspeaker, inviting passengers to get up and use the facilities before their descent.

Sarah logged on to the plane's Wi-Fi and checked her work email. There was one message from Ned, saying that his mother had taken ill and that he needed to leave town; he said he would log in to his time sheet and submit a formal leave request. She responded that she hoped his mother would be okay and that she was on her way to Miami and would be offline. She responded to several important emails from Dr. Bower and then saw one from Detective Strong, with the subject line "Kayla's surgeons folder." Sarah's heart quickened and she held her breath as she read it:

> *Sarah, we need access to Kayla's surgeon's folder that you removed from your desktop when Detective Campos and I were in your office. This could be considered withholding evidence in a murder investigation, which is a chargeable offense. Will you please send us the folder? If not, we'll need to issue a formal subpoena directly to Dr. Bower in your absence.*

Sarah stared at the email for a few minutes. She was secretly hoping Handsome would have written something like, "I can't stop thinking about you since I saw you in your office. We were meant to be together. I miss you; I miss us." She let out a sad sigh and then re-read his actual note. *This is the last thing*

Dr. Bower needs right now. I haven't even read everything in that folder myself. I'll have to look it over when I get to my hotel.

Sarah typed her response, "I miss your touch, your smile, our long mornings naked under the covers. No one has ever made love to me like you." Then deleted it and sent him the file.

Chapter 35

Campos met Strong at 7:00 a.m. in the lobby of the transplant institute. "Good morning, Detective," she greeted him.

"I thought we'd get some coffee at the hospital café and review our schedule for the day," Strong suggested.

"Sounds good."

As they walked, Strong added, "I have some good news for you: I got Kayla's surgeons file from Sarah. I hated using the withholding evidence threat—but it worked." Campos glanced over at Strong, his mouth was turned down, she could see he was visibly sad about his contact with Sarah, Campos chose not to say anything.

"I have a feeling there's some incriminating information we can use when we interview our surgeons this afternoon," Campos said.

"What's our lineup?" Strong asked.

"I was able to get fifteen minutes per surgeon, starting at noon. We start with Edwards. She was very nice when I met with the group. Then we have Lester and Wood. I didn't schedule Spencer, since I already interviewed him, and unless there's something damaging about him in Kayla's file, I don't think he did it. Then we keep rolling through the rest."

"I'm hoping we find an X associated with one of those names in Kayla's file. I'm not sure where else to look if we don't," Strong said.

They bought coffee to go and headed directly back to Sarah's office, where the assistant let them in and turned on Sarah's computer.

Strong accessed his emails through the Internet and downloaded the folder Sarah had sent him. The detectives stared at the screen as Strong scrolled through each surgeon's name. Campos added the new information to a spreadsheet she had started at the beginning of the investigation.

"And I thought the characters from *Grey's Anatomy* were fictional. Kayla was minding everyone's business—that's clear," Campos said.

They had reviewed six of the surgeons when they opened Wood's file.

"Holy shit, this is one busy doctor," Campos said, as she took notes. "He had sex with three coordinators and four administrative assistants, according to Kayla. And, looky here, she gave him a X."

"Bingo. This is the first X in this file. Hold on—let me do a document check for X; I should have started with that."

Strong's search produced an X under the names of two other surgeons, Spencer and Bower.

"Just a minute. Let me get out the DEA numbers Kayla had listed in that other file we reviewed. It may be a dead end, but you never know." Campos looked at her spreadsheet; six of the ten surgeons had DEA numbers listed.

"Where are you going with this?" Strong asked.

"I'm curious to see whether Kayla was using these X surgeons' DEA numbers to order narcotics legally," Campos asked.

"We'll certainly ask them when we meet with them this afternoon," Strong said.

"Let's review everything we know and think we know." Campos pulled out all her notes.

Strong started, "We've gotten confirmation that there are large amounts of money in both Kayla's and her grandmother's bank accounts, and that those accounts were closed out on the same day Kayla was murdered. Per Kayla's notes, she was moving drugs. We have no proof of where those deals were being made, but it's safe to say it was likely out of Grandma's house, and who knows where else."

"Correct. We don't know if X was directly involved, but they were receiving some payment. We know from Kayla's notes that she was ready to stop dealing, and then someone from work met her at Grandma's house the night she was murdered. We don't know if it was X, but hopefully we can figure out if X is one of the surgeons, and, if not, maybe they know who it is," Campos said.

"I think it's safe to eliminate Zuzu and Sarah as suspects. Do you agree?" Strong asked.

"I do. They did find another set of prints at Grandma's house, but whoever they belong to is not in the database. That rules out Zuzu; since she spent time in prison, her prints are in the system. While it's clear that Sarah and Kayla didn't get along, I don't see any evidence that points to Sarah. So, who do we have left?" Campos asked.

"We've got no one. Wouldn't our pals back at the precinct be laughing their asses off if they knew?" Strong said.

"We're really going to have to press these surgeons this afternoon. I think we have to use what we found out from Kayla's folder and push hard. We only have fifteen minutes per surgeon, so these are going to be intense interviews," Campos said.

"Too bad Ned is gone. I was hoping to interview him myself," Strong said.

Strong's cell rang. "Strong here." He paused and then said, "Can I put you on speaker, Melissa?" He looked over at Campos, "It's Melissa from our precinct."

He put his phone between him and Campos and said, "Okay, hi, Melissa. Thanks for calling us back. I know I left you a message with a lot of questions."

"You sure did, and that's why it's taken me a while to get back to you, but no worries—your questions are actually helping us figure out a few odd things that have been going on," Melissa answered.

"I know you're short on time, so I'll get right to it. The address you gave me, of some grandmother . . . well, it seems we've been seeing some unusually high drug traffic in her neighborhood over the past three years. Mostly opioids and some heroin. Before that, we busted people for crack, weed, and hallucinogens. The crazy thing is, the snitches we use said that the prices for opioids are cheaper in this neighborhood than anywhere else in the Miami area. Same drug, but lower-priced, which tells us whoever was selling needed to get rid of the stuff fast."

"Were your snitches able to give you an ID on anyone coming and going from the house?" Strong asked.

"Thanks for sending me that woman's picture; they were able to ID her for sure: Kayla Newman," Melissa answered.

"That's correct. Anyone else?" Campos asked.

"They said there was some white dude with sunglasses, but I guess he always wore a hoodie and baggy sweatpants—not unusual for this area, but not helpful, either."

"Is there any way to get ahold of the opioids they were dealing to see if they were pharmaceutical quality?" Campos asked.

"That won't be easy—I don't want to blow my snitches' cover—but I'll see if it's possible. Even if I can do it, there's so much of this shit on the street, it's really tough to tell. It's coming in from all over the place—Mexico and overseas. It's not hard to duplicate the formula. That's why we have such an epidemic—it's cheap and addictive and gets folks really high quickly; then they take too much, and *adios.*"

"Thanks for your help, Melissa. If you hear anything else, please let us know," Strong said.

"Will do. The thing that's weird about this particular house is that they weren't really dealing out of it. I don't think they were storing the opioids there, either. I spoke to the forensic team that did the on-site investigation after they found Kayla's body, and they said there were no traces of drugs anywhere in or outside the house. The only place they found anything was in that poor girl's stomach and blood. I wish I could be more helpful, but we'll keep an eye on the area, and if anyone shows up, we'll be in contact," Melissa said.

"Thanks again," Campos replied, and they hung up. She shook her head in frustration, "I wonder if the hoodie guy is the same dude that Kayla was nervous about meeting?"

"Who the hell knows. We still got a whole lot of nothing." Strong said and let out an audible sigh.

Chapter 36

Jackie and Laura kept the weekend quiet, visiting the Miami International Transplant Institute for Wyatt's pre-op blood tests, meeting with Scott, and dining out with Sarah. They spent the rest of the time snuggling with Wyatt on the couch, watching funny movies. On Monday morning, they walked with Wyatt to the pediatric floor, where Scott met them. "How are you feeling today, Wyatt?" he asked after he greeted them.

"I'm pretty tired, but my moms say once I get my new kidney, I'll feel better."

"You will have lots more energy once you get your new kidney; in fact, it's going to be hard to slow you down. In the meantime, let me show you where your room is and get you settled."

Scott led them down the corridor, past various kids walking with their parents, IV poles in tow. As Jackie watched her son take in all the hallway traffic, a few tears welled up in her eyes. She wiped them away and swallowed. Laura put her arm around Jackie and gently rubbed her back as they continued.

They went into Wyatt's room; the walls were painted a cheery yellow, and there was a smaller bed with two chairs on either side. "These chairs pull out into single beds for your moms," Scott said. "I'll be back in a few minutes with your nurse."

"Thank you," Jackie said.

"Of course."

Once Scott had left, Jackie took Wyatt's hand while Laura combed his hair back with her fingers. "We're going to be with you all the way, sweetheart," Laura said, as she helped him into his hospital gown.

"When can I see Aunt Sarah?" Wyatt asked.

"She donates her kidney right after your surgery honey. We'll go see her first thing tomorrow morning. She'll be so excited to see you." Laura responded.

Just as Wyatt hopped into bed, there was a knock on the door, and Scott and a nurse walked in. "Wyatt, this is Kim. She's going to be your nurse today and tomorrow."

"Hi, Wyatt. I'm going to make sure we take extra-special care of you. These must be your moms." Kim looked over at Laura and Jackie, who were standing by the window.

"Yup," Wyatt responded.

A group of doctors came into the room, led by Dr. Santos. He shook Jackie's and Laura's hands, saying, "Welcome to our transplant program. I hope your trip was uneventful and your accommodations are comfortable."

"We're so grateful that you were able to take our case on such short notice, Dr. Santos. We can't thank you enough," Jackie added.

"I'm glad it all worked out. I just spoke with Dr. Bower this morning, and he sends his best to your whole family." Dr. Santos turned toward Wyatt and sat at the end of his bed.

"You look like you're ready, Wyatt. Do you have any questions for me or the team?"

"Can I drink whatever I want after I get my new kidney?" Wyatt asked.

"You sure can, as long as your moms approve."

Dr. Santos looked toward Laura and Jackie. "How about you, moms—any questions for us?"

"How long will his surgery last, and how long will he be in recovery?" Laura asked.

"I'll let my transplant fellow Dr. Ketel answer that." Dr. Santos looked over at a young woman standing with the team.

"Wyatt will be our first case in the morning; we'll call for him between six thirty and seven. You can both come into the pre-op area and be with him until he goes into the operating room. We'll put the kidney in the lower right abdominal area." Dr. Ketel pointed to the lower right quadrant of her own abdomen, then continued, "Once we hook the new kidney to Wyatt's blood supply, we'll likely see it make urine right away. That's a very exciting time for everyone in the operating room."

"Is my new kidney going to last me a long time?" Wyatt asked.

"We sure hope so, but you'll need to take good care of it and take your medications so your body doesn't reject it. Some kidneys last a very long time, Wyatt," Dr. Ketel answered. "Your operation shouldn't take more than two hours. Dr. Santos is performing it, and he's an expert; he's done thousands of transplants," she added, glancing over at Dr. Santos.

"You're pretty. Will you be helping Dr. Santos?" Wyatt asked. Everyone chuckled, and Dr. Ketel's cheeks turned red.

"I will be assisting Dr. Santos. He's my teacher, and this is how I learn to become a transplant surgeon," Dr. Ketel said.

"Now, if that answers all your questions, can we borrow your moms for a minute?" Dr. Santos asked Wyatt.

"Sure."

The team filed out, and Laura and Jackie followed. Wyatt's nurse, Kim, stayed with him. Dr. Santos and Dr. Ketel led Jackie and Laura into a conference room near the nurses' station, where they all took seats around a small conference table.

"How are you both doing, truly? I know this can be a scary time for parents," Dr. Santos said.

"I'm not going to lie to you—I'm freaking out," Jackie said.

"I'm in the same boat," Laura added.

When Jackie looked over at Laura and saw that she was tearing up, Jackie started to cry herself.

"Didn't see that coming," Jackie sniffled.

"I think Wyatt is going to do well. His anatomy is normal, so his case will likely go quickly, and he's getting a very healthy kidney, so we have no reason to think it won't last a long time. I am concerned about his blood levels going into surgery, though. They're pretty high, and I'm seriously considering putting in a port to dialyze him tonight," Dr. Santos said.

Jackie let out a deep sigh. "We were really hoping to avoid that whole thing, Dr. Santos."

"I understand. I did speak with Dr. Bower about this, and we're on the same page," Dr. Santos answered.

"How about if Wyatt's new kidney opens up right away, and you give him a diuretic to bring his numbers down immediately post-op—maybe then he wouldn't need a port or dialysis?" Laura suggested.

"That could work. But if we run into any issues in the OR, and we don't see copious amounts of urine, I'm going to need your signed consent for the port before he goes to the OR in the morning," Dr. Santos replied.

"Sounds fair," Jackie said.

"Dr. Ketel will have you sign those now." Dr. Santos stood up. "I'll see you both in the pre-op area tomorrow morning."

Jackie stood up and gave him a hug. "Thanks so much."

"Yes, truly," Laura said, standing to shake his hand.

"Thank *you* for trusting us with your son's care. Even though you're both medical professionals, when it comes to your own flesh and blood, it's still scary and emotional. Our team is here for you; if you need anything, just ask." Dr. Santos left the room to join the rest of his team waiting to continue rounds.

Dr. Ketel pulled out the consent forms, one for the transplant and another for the port, and reviewed all the possible complications that might occur with each operation. Jackie and Laura reviewed the documents and then signed them.

"Do you have any other questions?" Dr. Ketel asked.

"Will you be doing the second paired-exchange transplant, too? My best friend, Sarah Golden, is the living donor," Jackie said.

"Yes, the same donor team and recipient team will be doing both cases," Dr. Ketel answered. "Anything else?"

Jackie looked over at Laura, who shook her head. "I think we're as good as two moms can be at this point," Jackie said.

Dr. Ketel put all the consent forms inside her folder and stood up. When Jackie and Laura rose, she gave each woman a hug. "Hugs are good for the soul," she said.

"They sure are," Laura said.

"You can stay in here for as long as you need to," Dr. Ketel offered.

"Thanks," Jackie said.

After Dr. Ketel left, Jackie wrapped her arms around Laura, held her close, and started to sob.

Laura pulled back just enough to cup Jackie's face with her palms and gently kiss her lips. "We'll get through this, honey."

Jackie nodded and let out a big, shuddering sigh. "No matter how mad I've been at you, I'm so glad we're here together, Laura. There's just no way I could ever go through this without you."

Early Tuesday morning, Jackie and Laura followed Wyatt up to the pre-op area and watched as they inserted his IV.

"That didn't even hurt," Wyatt told the nurse.

"That's 'cause I'm an expert. Ready for your fancy cap?" she asked.

Wyatt gave her a thumbs-up, and she put a thin green mesh cap on his head to cover all his light brown hair.

The nurse unlocked the gurney he was lying on and told him, "Say goodbye to your moms; we're going for a ride."

Jackie leaned in and kissed Wyatt's forehead, and Laura followed suit. "See you soon, my brave boy," Laura said.

"Bye, Moms." Wyatt grinned.

Both women took one last look at their son, and then Laura put her arm around Jackie and led her out toward the waiting room. Jackie's eyes flooded with tears as she tried not to think of all the things that could go wrong.

Chapter 37

Sarah was looking out her hospital window when she heard a familiar voice behind her: "One down, one to go, Golden. How's my BFF this morning?"

Sarah turned around and saw Jackie walking toward her. "I'm ready—all systems go. Saw the team early this morning, signed my consents, pre-op labs are stellar."

Jackie hugged her friend. "Our boy is getting his new kidney right now. He was so brave, Sarah. You would have been so proud of him."

"I *am* so proud of him, and also of you and Laura. How are you doing?" Sarah sat down in the chair next to the window.

"I started blubbering like a baby after we signed all the consents, and Dr. Ketel left the room. I held on to Laura for dear life and sobbed in her arms. I didn't expect to be this emotional," Jackie said.

"You've been through the wringer, honey. Your marriage, Wyatt's illness, and then flying across the country last-minute— that's called stress with a capital *S*," Sarah said.

"You're right. I just didn't give myself permission to think about any of it, much less process it emotionally. As a nurse, you know all the things that can go wrong . . . tried not to think about that." Jackie sighed.

"Where's Laura?" Sarah asked.

"She's holding down the fort in the OR waiting area. They'll come out and let us know as soon as they finish. I told her I wanted to come see you and wish you luck. Dr. Santos thinks Wyatt will sail through—his normal anatomy and the healthy kidney from the "high profile" recipients' donor. You're my hero donating your kidney to someone you'll never know."

"As long as Wyatt gets a healthy kidney, I don't care who they give my kidney to, he's going to sail through this. Did you hear anything about his donor?" Sarah asked.

"Not a word, just that Wyatt's getting a very healthy kidney. Santos did make us sign a consent for a port just in case he needs emergency dialysis. I will be so glad when this day is done," Jackie said. "Anything I can do for you before I head back to Laura?"

"Nah, I'm good. Enjoying the peace and quiet—relaxing, believe it or not. They'll call you when I'm in recovery."

"Sounds good. I'll be back to see you just as soon as I can," Jackie said, hugging Sarah again.

"I'll be fine—but we are going out for one hell of a night on the town when this is all behind us, Jack."

"On me," Jackie said.

About an hour later, Sarah's nurse came in. "They just called to bring you up; an OR tech will be down in a few minutes to take you to pre-op. You all ready?"

"Ready, willing, and able," Sarah replied. Her nurse took her vitals and entered them into the bedside computer. "I'll be here when you get back, Sarah. You'll do great." She left the room.

A few seconds later, Sarah heard a knock. When she called out, "Yes?" Handsome walked into the room, holding a brightly colored floral arrangement.

"This is a surprise," she stammered. *When did I see him last? Friday before I flew here? That feels like months ago.*

"I finished what I needed to do in San Francisco, and I just had to come and wish you good luck," he said. As he extended the bouquet toward her, she gaped at him for a moment, feeling her pulse quickening.

"They're beautiful. Thank you. And it's really nice to see you." Sarah placed the flowers on her bedside table and reached up to give him a hug.

"I figured you could use a friendly face before you go under the knife. I'm guessing Jackie and Laura are waiting to hear how Wyatt does."

"They are. I'm so touched that you remembered all this." Sarah put her hand over her heart.

Another knock at the door announced the OR tech. "Ms. Golden?"

"That's me," Sarah responded.

"Looks like you're able to get on the gurney by yourself," he said, as he rolled it into her room.

"Healthy as a horse," she said, as she hopped on.

"Mind if I walk you to the elevator?" Handsome asked.

"I'd love an escort," Sarah answered.

The OR tech rolled her down the hall and pushed the elevator button. A few seconds later, the doors opened. "After you," he said.

"A kiss for good luck?" Handsome offered.

"Why not?"

Handsome bent over, put his hand behind her neck and gave Sarah a long farewell kiss, until the elevator door started to buzz.

"See you soon, Golden. I'm proud of what you're doing," he said as the elevator doors closed.

Sarah gave him a big smile and waved. Her lips tingled from his kiss, and her heart was fluttering.

"What a send-off," the OR tech said, smiling.

"No kidding. Doesn't get any better than that." Sarah sighed.

He wheeled her into the pre-op area, where they started an IV, and the living-donor surgeon came by to check on her. "Everything looks good. We'll be bringing you to the OR in about thirty minutes. Need anything?"

"Nope, but thanks."

"See you soon." The doctor exited, and the pre-op nurse gave her a drip of something to relax.

Sarah dozed off but was awakened by a loud voice over the hospital speaker: "Code blue, OR 3. Code blue, OR 3. Code blue, OR . . ."

Chapter 38

It was early Tuesday morning when Campos went to meet with Inspector Davidson at the SFPD precinct. "Back for more fun, Detective?" Davidson asked, as she led Campos to her small office.

"I think we're finally making some progress. This case has really been hard to work," Campos replied.

"Please sit down. Sorry my office is so messy. Coffee?" Davidson offered.

"That would be great. Black," Campos said and looked around the cluttered space. Tall piles filled each corner, and the top of her desk was barely visible.

Davidson walked back in and handed Campos a cup. "Admiring my filing system? When I said I was buried in paperwork, I meant it."

"No shit," Campos said.

"Bring me up to speed and let me know what I can do for you," Davidson said.

"My partner, Strong, flew out and helped me finish interviewing the transplant surgeons, but he had to leave yesterday. We were able to obtain some computer files that Kayla kept on the surgeons she worked with. She titled it 'Surgeon Fuckups and Indiscretions,' and it was a gold mine. It really helped us pressure a couple of surgeons; she was blackmailing one of them, and we were able to get him to talk."

"Which one was it?"

"Dr. Wood. Seems he's married with four kids but also likes to play the field. He's slept with several of the nurses and assistants."

"Nothing illegal about that, unless you're Catholic—then you'll burn in hell."

"Well, he must have been Catholic, because he was willing to do anything Kayla wanted him to do, as long as she didn't tell his wife. Kayla made Dr. Wood write prescriptions for opioids as well, using transplant patients' names as covers. The patients never got these drugs, but no one ever checked. Seems she had quite a scam going on. Wood claimed he didn't know anything about records or spreadsheets. I asked him. He just admitted that Kayla was blackmailing him and said if she put a prescription in front of him to sign, he signed it," Campos said.

"How did you leave things with him?" Davidson asked.

"I told him he was to stay in San Francisco. I don't think he's a flight risk. We don't have hard evidence or a witness, so I don't think we can charge him yet. I let him know that I would be working with you to open an investigation into his behavior. I notified Bower and the medical center's legal department. I also asked Bower to get us a summary of all the surgeons' narcotics-ordering history a while ago, but his team had a living kidney donor die recently, so it's insane there right now. I'm not sure how soon I'll get that paperwork from his staff," Campos said.

"I'm sure the medical center wants to keep this drug scandal out of the public eye. Can't make any promises on that, but it's great leverage to increase everyone's cooperation," Davidson said.

"Exactly. But we still don't have a solid suspect, and we're hoping someone knows something they haven't shared yet. Lots of pieces are falling into place: drugs, money, blackmail. There's certainly motive, given everything we read in Kayla's files on the surgeons and managers. . . ."

"You think it could be Wood?" Davidson asked.

"He was in Miami at a transplant conference with two other surgeons when Kayla was murdered but said he has solid alibis. My partner is checking those out. Wood said we should contact his attorney for further questioning; he's lawyering up," Campos answered.

"Did you talk to the other managers in Kayla's file?"

"My partner spoke to all of them. They were all relieved to get out of the department and not have to manage Kayla. They're all working in different departments at the medical center and say it's much less stressful."

"I'll call Dr. Wood's attorney and request a meeting with him and Dr. Wood, to see if I can shake anything else out of him. Any other staff or surgeons you interviewed who you think may be involved?" Davidson asked.

"Not really. I did meet with their IT guy, Ned Bisone, a couple times, but all I really got from him was how overworked he was and that Kayla tortured him—and I could tell he has a crush on Sarah. Not much to go on there. You may want to take another pass at the coordinators who had to work closely with Kayla," Campos suggested.

"I can do that. It does sound like you've covered all the bases, but, since we don't have actual records of the patients' names that were used, or a witness who can confirm that Kayla sold the drugs, we may be at a standstill with this case," Davidson said.

"I know. It's so frustrating, and my chief is going to have my head if I can't close this one. I'm flying home today.

I appreciate anything you can do. Maybe we'll catch a break. I feel like we're so close." Campos stood up, leaned over, and shook Davidson's hand.

"Speaking of your boss, he called my boss and asked how the case was coming. My boss left me a message this morning. I haven't gotten back to him yet, but our bosses are apparently buddies from long ago. I'm scheduled to meet with him this afternoon. I let him know we're making progress, so that should buy us some time. I know how you feel, Campos—you work so hard, and then the case goes cold. We have to prove everything with hard evidence. Did you get access to Kayla's cell phone? Any messages?" Davidson asked, as she walked Campos out.

"Good question. From what I remember, they didn't find a cell phone at the scene, but I'll circle back to the team. Wouldn't that be a break?"

"Just thinking of any way you can get access to her messages on her cell or work phone. There might be something that glues some of these pieces together," Davidson said.

"I did check her work voicemail. She had no saved messages and no new ones. I guess everyone uses their cell phone for everything," Campos said.

"Have a safe trip home. If I hear anything else from Dr. Wood or the coordinators, I'll let you know. If I don't get any new leads, I'll have to close out the case on my end. I'll refer Wood to our narcotics department, but without evidence it will get buried."

"Thanks for all your help, Davidson. I really appreciate it. I'll let you know if I get anything new," Campos said.

Chapter 39

Jackie and Laura had both dozed off in the OR patient waiting room, when they heard, "Code blue, OR 3. Code blue, OR 3. Code blue, OR . . ."

Jackie bolted out of her seat and looked at Laura, who was also standing, eyes wide. "It can't be!" Jackie yelled.

Several men in dark suits with listening devices in their ears also stood up and approached the reception desk. Jackie walked over to stand behind them and overheard one say, "I need to check on Connor Mitchell. He's a VIP, here for a kidney transplant."

The desk phone was ringing, and the receptionist held up a finger. "I need to get this, sir. Just a minute." After she hung up, she looked up at the man and said, "I'll need your name to confirm I'm able to share information about his case."

She paused to checked her roster, then continued, "Someone from the team is on their way to his private room. I believe his wife is in there."

The two men turned around and bolted out of the waiting area, and Jackie almost dove over the reception desk. "Please, I'm Wyatt Larson's mom. Can you give me a progress check?"

Laura had come to stand next to Jackie and rubbed her back, saying, "He's okay; he's got to be okay, honey."

Just as the receptionist was picking up the phone, a nurse with a lab coat and an OR head cover walked into the reception area and announced their names: "Jackie Larson and Laura Gallagher?"

"That's us," Jackie said.

"Please come with me. Your son is in the recovery room, asking for you." As they followed her to the elevator they had taken earlier, the nurse said, "I'm Kathy. Your son is doing great. Dr. Santos is in another case right now but said to tell you he'll stop by Wyatt's room later this afternoon. Wyatt's kidney started making urine right away, and it hasn't stopped. We didn't need to put a port in, either. All good news."

"Good news? That's *great* news!" Jackie said, turning to hug Laura.

I don't mean to be nosey, but we did hear a code blue announcement over the hospital intercom. What happened?" Laura asked.

"I can't say—HIPAA compliance," the nurse responded.

"My best friend is part of the paired exchange our son was in. I'm listed as her next of kin. Can you at least check and let me know if she's all right? Please," Jackie pushed.

"I sure can."

"Thank you so much, Kathy," Jackie said.

The elevator doors opened, and within a few seconds, Laura and Jackie were standing on either side of Wyatt's bed. The nurse had just finished checking his vital signs and adjusting his IV.

"He's doing awesome," she said. "I just gave him a little something for discomfort. He's been asking for you both."

Wyatt opened his big eyes and said softly, "Hi, Momma. Hi, Mom. Dr. Ketel said my new kidney is a winner."

Jackie looked at the side of his bed, where a bag that collected all his urine was hooked up to a catheter in his bladder. "I'll say your kidney is a winner, buddy—you're peeing up a storm!"

"How are you feeling, sweetheart?" Laura asked.

"I feel different—a good different. The tube in my penis hurts a little, but Dr. Ketel said they might take it out tonight."

"That's great, buddy. Are you thirsty?" Jackie asked.

"The nurse gave me some ice chips. She said I could have some more if my tummy feels okay," Wyatt said, and then dozed off.

Jackie let out a deep sigh. "He's through the hard part. I'm going to see whether that nurse has an update on Sarah. I can't imagine the code blue was her, but I have to know. You cool to stay with our boy?" Jackie asked.

"I have this. I'll be right next to him when you come back, and honey, I hope Sarah's okay." Laura said.

Jackie noticed she was holding her breath as she walked out to the recovery room desk. Kathy, the nurse who had taken her and Laura up to see Wyatt, spotted her and walked over. "Hi, Jackie. Good timing. I have an update for you, but we need to talk privately." Jackie took a deep breath trying to move the lump that was in her throat.

She led Jackie into a small room near the recovery room, and Jackie sat down and started to cry. "Oh my God! What have I done? I know when they put you in a small room, it's always bad news. She's my best friend."

Kathy reached out and patted Jackie's hand. "Sarah is fine, Jackie. She's okay."

"What?" Jackie looked up and wiped her nose with her hand.

Kathy passed Jackie a box of tissues. After Jackie blew her nose, the nurse continued, "Sarah did not donate her kidney. The recipient she was donating it to had to have some surgical procedures prior to their transplant. The code blue was for the recipient."

"What! I don't understand," Jackie said, her mind spinning. "Wyatt got his kidney from that person's living donor, and Sarah was supposed to give the other person her kidney. What happens now?"

"Sadly, that person will not be getting Sarah's kidney. I'm not allowed to share any more information than that. But I can assure you that Wyatt will keep his kidney. This rarely, if ever, happens," Kathy said.

"Where's Sarah now? Does she know this? Did they already start her surgery when the code blue was called on the recipient?" Jackie asked.

"Sarah was in the pre-op area and had gotten some medication to relax her, but she never made it to the actual OR. She's back in her room now, sleeping. I thought you and I could go down to the transplant floor so you'll be there when I wake her up and give her the news."

"Okay. Just give me a minute," Jackie said.

"I'll wait for you right near the elevator."

Jackie went into the bathroom, threw cold water on her face, and looked in the mirror. "What the fuck?"

She returned to Kathy, who took her to see Laura. Wyatt was still asleep. "Sarah's okay," she told Laura. "She didn't have to donate her kidney, but she doesn't know it yet. I need to go with the nurse to her room and tell her."

Laura smiled and gave Jackie a thumbs-up. Jackie met Kathy at the elevator, and they went down to the transplant floor and walked into Sarah's room.

Sarah was fast asleep when Jackie approached her bedside and put her hand gently on her friend's shoulder. "Hey, Sarah. How are you feeling?"

Sarah's eyes fluttered. "Hey, Jack. How's Wyatt?" she mumbled.

"His kidney is peeing up a storm. Are you okay?" Jackie asked.

"I feel very relaxed. They have some really good drugs here." Sarah's eyes closed again.

"How about a little water? I need you to try to wake up." Jackie put a straw into Sarah's mouth and propped up her head. She took a sip and opened her eyes.

"I feel like I just went to the OR, and it's done already? No, it can't be—I'd be in recovery. What's happening?" Sarah put her hands under her sheets to feel her body. "There are no incisions; I still have both my kidneys. What the hell?" Sarah sat up straight and looked at Jackie, then over her shoulder. "Who's that?"

Jackie turned and saw Kathy standing by the door. "Kathy, meet my best friend, Sarah Golden."

Sarah's eyebrows furrowed. "Is there something wrong with my kidney? I thought everything was good to go."

"Sarah, everything *was* good to go—you're perfectly healthy and were cleared to be a living kidney donor. Unfortunately, the proposed recipient for your kidney needed to have some surgery before we started your kidney recovery, and he's not able to get a transplant right now."

Jackie watched Sarah's eyes flit between her and Kathy's faces as she asked, "But Wyatt got their donor's kidney and is doing fine, right?"

"Exactly," Kathy answered.

"All I knew about the other part of our paired-exchange case was that it was a high-profile case, which, where I work, means it's either a celebrity or a politician," Sarah said, glancing at Kathy.

"I'm really not at liberty to say anything else about this case, except that we won't be recovering your kidney," Kathy said.

"Okay, well, as long Wyatt gets to keep his kidney and it's working, I guess that's that," Sarah said.

"That's correct. I need to get back to the OR now; we're very busy. If you have any other questions, your staff nurse can help you. Take care, both of you," Kathy said.

As soon as Kathy left, Sarah stared at Jackie. "You need to find out who this bigwig is!"

"We heard a code blue announced in the OR, and I thought, *Oh my God, I hope it's not Wyatt or Sarah.* There were a couple suits with earpieces in the waiting room where we were, so whoever it is has some bodyguards. That much, I can tell you," Jackie said.

Sarah's nurse came in and asked, "How are you feeling, Sarah?"

"Confused and healthy. Looks like I'll be taking both my kidneys back to San Francisco."

"I know. We've never had this happen before, but I guess there's a first time for everything. I'm going to take your vitals and order you something to eat, but then you're free to go home."

"Sounds good to me, but no need to order me a meal. I hear there's a great burger place around here, and I'm going to eat a hearty meal there," Sarah said.

"Good decision—you know how hospital food is. I'd be heading for a burger, too, if I were you. But how about you at least have a little snack and some juice, since you haven't eaten since last night?" the nurse offered.

"Good idea," Sarah said.

When the nurse left, Jackie asked, "Are you really going to Biker Bob's hamburger joint?"

"You bet your sweet ass I am. Also, guess who came to see me before I went to the OR?"

"No, he did not. Handsome?"

"See those flowers over there? He brought them, walked

with me when they rolled me to the elevators, and gave me a whopper of a kiss before I headed up. My toes were tingling. I'm going to let him know my surgery got canceled and ask him to come pick me up and take me out for lunch. Can I borrow your phone?" Sarah asked.

Jackie handed Sarah her cell. Sarah called Handsome, briefly explained what had happened, and promised to give him all the details over lunch.

"I'd say you've had a pretty good day overall, my friend," Jackie said. "I think the name of the high-profile person is Connor Mitchell; I overheard the OR receptionist tell the suits before they took off. It's probably an alias—shit, he must have had some really serious complications."

"If it's a real bigwig, we'll probably hear something on the news. Turn on the TV."

Jackie put on CNN, but no breaking-news alerts popped up, so she muted the TV.

The nurse returned with two containers of cranberry juice, some peanut butter cracker packets, and a couple of apples. "Here you go. It's not gourmet, but it should do the trick. You may want a wait a little while before you leave; the Republican leader of the Senate just died here, and the press is all over the place. Actually, once I discharge you, I'd recommend you leave through the ER."

"The Republican leader of the Senate! Holy shit!" Jackie said.

"Was he supposed to get a transplant, per chance?" Sarah said.

"You'll find out soon enough; the CEO will be giving a press conference any minute now, so I'd keep CNN on."

Jackie downed her juice, scarfed down her crackers, and started on her apple. "I forgot to eat today—you know, just a few minor distractions."

"No kidding. You want some of my crackers?" Sarah offered.

"Sure . . . Oh, here we go—breaking news." Jackie turned up the volume on the TV.

A white-haired male announcer said, "We have some very sad news. Senator Connor Mitchell died during a surgical procedure today in preparation for a kidney transplant. Senator Mitchell had been on hemodialysis for over ten years and had exhausted all the locations on his body where he could be dialyzed. He was to be part of a paired-exchange kidney transplant."

As Jackie and Sarah stared at the screen, the announcer displayed pictures of what it looked like to be dialyzed and then explained what a paired exchange was. He continued, "Patient confidentiality rights prevent us from sharing any other details of the case."

Chapter 40

After they finished watching the broadcast, Sarah and Jackie stared at each other, eyes wide and mouths agape. Eventually, Jackie suggested they go see Wyatt.

They found him in his room, sitting up in bed. "Aunt Sarah!" He put his arms out, and she gave him a gentle hug.

"You look so good, Wyatt. How are you feeling?"

"I feel like someone put new batteries inside me," he answered.

Sarah laughed, noticing a sparkle in his eyes that had been gone for some time.

"Mom said you weren't a donor. Are you sad you couldn't help someone else?" he asked.

"I guess it just wasn't meant to be, buddy, but I was ready to help. The important thing is that you got a new kidney and it looks like it's really working." Sarah pointed to the bag full of urine attached to his bed.

His nurse came into the room and said, "I'd better empty that before it overflows. Wyatt, you're doing great. How are you feeling? Any pain?"

"Not really, but I'm thirsty and hungry. Can I have anything I want to eat?"

"You sure can—no more fluid or food restrictions. What can I get you?" she asked.

"A hamburger, french fries, a chocolate milkshake, and Reese's pieces." Sarah looked at Wyatt as he watched his moms' reaction to his last request. They both grinned and Jackie pulled a bag of Reese's pieces out of her pocket and tossed it to Wyatt.

"Seems your Mom knew you liked candy. I believe I can order the rest up for you. Do you want cheese, too?"

"Yes, please. Can I put as much ketchup as I want on my burger?" Wyatt asked.

"As much as you want. I'm going to take your temperature and blood pressure first; then I'll get your lunch." The nurse took his vitals and charted them. "Everything looks great—back to normal. You just let me know if you're feeling any pain or discomfort, Wyatt." She lifted his gown to check his dressing, which was clean and dry.

Sarah watched Jackie and Laura gazing at Wyatt as he opened his candy and started to eat it. They were both wearing sweet grins. "It's amazing how fast they get better," Jackie murmured.

"It really is a gift of life," the nurse replied, and left the room.

"All this talk of food is making me hungry. I need to go meet Handsome so he can take me out for my burger," Sarah said.

"Is that all he's going to take you out for?" Jackie snickered.

"I'm open to dessert afterward," Sarah said, laughing.

"Now we're talking. I want to hear everything," Jackie said.

"Can I get either of you anything?" Sarah asked Laura and Jackie.

"I think we're going to keep it light tonight, but thanks for asking," Laura said.

Sarah left via the emergency room, per the nurse's suggestion. Once she was outside, she saw Handsome's big truck by the curb and walked toward it.

Handsome saw her coming and got out and opened the door for her. "Still a perfect gentleman," she said.

"Always," he replied, as he closed her door and walked around to his. "Where to? You mentioned some hole in the wall I don't know about. I love surprises."

Sarah took out the directions Jackie had written down for her and shared them with Handsome. Fifteen minutes later, they pulled up in front of a shabby-looking shack with a neon OPEN sign out front.

• • •

"This thing is huge!" Handsome said, as he dug into his double cheeseburger. "I had no idea our own Biker Bob had a burger place. Looks like it's mostly a hangout for biker dudes."

Sarah was almost finished with her burger and fries. "Jackie was right—these are amazing, even if you don't have a hangover."

"Speaking of health, you're telling me you were supposed to give your perfect kidney to that arrogant asshole? How could that happen?" Handsome asked.

"The deal all along with Bower was that I could only be part of Wyatt's paired exchange if I didn't pry into who the other pair was. If he caught me snooping, then I was out. He made that crystal clear. I care too much for Wyatt to have jeopardized his transplant. I minded my own business—family first. You would have done the same thing if it were one of your nephews," Sarah explained.

Handsome put down his burger, gazing off into the distance and then back at Sarah. "I guess you're right. I'm not sorry it turned out the way it did, though."

"I'm not, either. It's sad that he ran out of sites for his dialysis—that's really bad. He would have been the oldest transplant patient we ever had in our program; I think he was seventy-two."

"Why did he even end up all the way across the country to get his transplant, when there are so many options on the East Coast?"

"I'm not sure, but I'm guessing he was going to get his transplant when the Senate was in recess and try to keep the whole thing under the radar. It would have looked like he and his family were just on vacation on the West Coast, which is comical, since he hates California and everything we stand for," Sarah said. "Speaking of the West Coast, can you tell me how Kayla's case is coming along?"

"We have lots of solid information but need to string it all together. Campos has worked her ass off, and if we don't get a break pretty soon, we're going to have to declare it a cold case and close it out."

"Does that mean that whoever killed Kayla will get away with it?"

"For now. You can always reopen a case, but you have to have strong evidence." He paused, then went on: "I don't mean to bring up a touchy subject, but I do have to ask you why you removed Kayla's surgeons folder when Campos and I were in your office. It makes me wonder if you're hiding anything else, Sarah."

"Are you serious? I would never withhold information that would help you solve this case," Sarah said.

"But you did. I had to ask you for that file, or you would never have given it to me. I just need to understand why."

"I was being protective of my docs. There was some nasty stuff in there, and who really knows if any of it was true? Just because Kayla wrote it doesn't make it a fact. Yes, some of the surgeons fool around on their wives, and yes, they have made mistakes in the operating room, but that doesn't make them murderers. Kayla was a bad seed, you have to have seen that," Sarah snapped.

"She was crazy, but that's no reason for someone to kill her. . . . Look, I'm sorry—I'm just frustrated. I don't want to waste the little time we have together discussing Kayla's case. Did you say you're flying out in a couple days?"

"I'm leaving Friday morning. I took a few days off. I really needed some downtime before I jump right back into all the chaos. I spoke with Bart, and he's fine, as long as he can leave on his golf trip early Monday morning, which won't be a problem."

Handsome leaned across the table, took Sarah's hand, and looked into her eyes. "Well, good—that gives us a little time to talk."

"What do you want to talk about?" Sarah asked softly, gazing down at their linked fingers.

"I want to talk about the fact that I still have feelings for you, Sarah. And if that kiss we shared before you went to the OR is any indication, I'd say you feel the same about me." Handsome raised his eyebrows.

Sarah gave him a little shrug, feeling her face grow hot. *Just tell him the truth*, she commanded herself. "You know I do," she finally said. "Honestly, I was so happy to see you at my transplant hospital, it took all my strength not to grab you and kiss you right there in my office."

"Well, I'm here now," Handsome said. He half-stood from his seat, took her cheeks in his hands, and gave her a long, passionate kiss.

Sarah closed her eyes and slowly explored his mouth with her tongue, her entire body vibrating. When she came up for air, all she could say was, "Wow." Then she pulled Handsome back toward her, searching for his lips again.

Afterward, they sat in silence for a minute. Sarah could tell by the way he was looking at her that Handsome had something on his mind. She started to jiggle her thigh under the table and pick at her nails. "I guess we should address the elephant in the room, huh?"

"Elephant? You mean us and the electricity between us every time we're near each other?" Handsome clasped his hands and put them on the table. "I don't know about you, but I've never felt this way about anyone before. Is there any way we can make us work?"

"I don't know, but I want it to work, too. How about we enjoy our time together while I'm here and see where that takes us?" Sarah offered.

"I like that idea. I'd also really like to take you out for a nice dinner—followed by a slumber party at my place before you head out. How about Thursday night?"

"I would love that. I'm planning on plowing through my email tomorrow, making a few work calls, and then spending some time with Wyatt at the hospital; then Jackie and I are going out for dinner. Between Wyatt being sick, my crazy job, and her home life, we haven't had any fun in a long time."

"Uh-oh. You and Jackie out alone in Miami—that could be dangerous. I'll alert the local PD." Handsome chuckled. "Thankfully, I don't have to worry about you, now that Sergio and his gang aren't hunting you down."

"I don't think we'll get in too much trouble—Laura's here, and Jackie has Wyatt to look after, so we'll be lucky if we can stay awake until ten. I'm pretty tired. All this activity in one day—I think I'll head back to my hotel and take a nap."

"I'll drop you. Where are you staying?"

"It's a Best Western near the medical center; they gave me a great discount. Free breakfast, too."

"Well, then let's get you settled." They stood up and Handsome put his arm around her shoulder; she felt her whole body relax.

Sarah could tell he was taking the long way back to her hotel, since they had hopped on the freeway on the way to the burger joint. "You know, I still have some wine left from our last visit to Sonoma," Handsome said. "I ordered three cases, but no one drinks wine out here. I'll bring a bottle on Thursday. I've got a great steak place I'd like to share with you. I know you like a good piece of meat."

"I sure do," Sarah said, and couldn't stop herself from looking pointedly down at Handsome's crotch. When she glanced back up at him, he was smiling ear to ear.

Handsome's phone rang, and his car speaker picked up the call. "Hey, Strong, Campos here. I'm flying home in a couple hours, but I just got a weird call from the administrative assistant at the transplant clinic."

"Campos, I have Sarah Golden in the car. Can I call you after I drop her off?" Handsome said.

"Sorry to disturb. Hi, Sarah. Did you change your mind about donating your kidney? Wasn't the transplant supposed to be today?" Campos asked.

"It's a long story. Jackie's son got transplanted, but the second paired exchange was canceled, so I'm heading back to the zoo on Friday. How's my team doing?"

"They're all looking pretty stressed out right now. I feel bad for them," Campos replied.

"I felt bad leaving everyone in the middle of so much chaos. I'm glad I'll be home to pitch in and get them through this disaster."

"Strong, I don't think it will make any difference if Sarah hears what I need to tell you," Campos said.

"Okay, shoot," he said.

"The administrative assistant in the Transplant clinic called me. I gave him my card early on and said he should call me if he thinks of anything about Kayla. He told me that a while ago, he went out for drinks at a bar near the hospital and saw Kayla and Ned there together, laughing it up. He thinks it was the same day that Kayla got in trouble for screaming at Ned in front of the entire staff and thought it was weird that they were having a jolly time the same night."

"That sounds out of sync with everything I saw and heard about the two of them," Sarah said. "I wonder why he chose to tell you that now."

"I mentioned that I was leaving when I stopped by the clinic today and let him know we were still investigating. Maybe he could tell I was a little down in the dumps. I really don't know. What do you think, Sarah?" Campos asked.

"Kayla was always ripping Ned a new one. I even put her on probation for her behavior with him. It's hard to imagine that hate-fest was just for show, but, after everything I've learned about Kayla through all those folders, I'd say anything is possible," Sarah said.

"Where is Ned now?" Campos asked.

"His mother is sick, and he's been out of town, taking care of her. I was actually going to call him this afternoon to see when he's coming back. I've had a ton of emails about IT glitches since he left, and he seems to be the only one who can fix them."

"When you speak with him, will you ask him to give me or Strong a call?" Campos asked.

"Will do," Sarah replied.

"I'll call you when I get back to the precinct, Campos," Strong said.

"Sounds good. Bye."

"I find it hard to believe that Kayla and Ned were yukking it up—he hated her. At least, that's the impression he gave me," Strong said after he hung up.

"Seriously. If they were friends, they both deserve an Oscar," Sarah said.

Handsome pulled up to the Best Western, hopped out, and opened Sarah's door. As she stepped down from the truck, she gave him a hug. "I'll see you Thursday. What time?"

"I'll pick you up at five. I thought we'd stop for fresh oysters first at a small place by the ocean, then head over to the steakhouse."

"Sounds wonderful. Thank you for everything today. I may call you after my nap this afternoon, and if I have some energy, maybe we can even have dinner tonight. Are you free?" *Free to make out again?* she added silently.

"For you, Sarah Golden, I will make the time. Call me when you wake up, and we'll go from there."

"Perfect." As Sarah walked to her room, she looked over her shoulder and saw Handsome waiting until she was safely inside. She gave him a wave, then unlocked her door, took off her clothes, and turned on the shower.

"What a day," she said out loud. *Connor Mitchell almost got one of my kidneys. I guess everyone should get a second chance at life. And Handsome—wow. He and I really need to figure this out. I love him too much to waste this chance*, she thought.

The bathroom was steamed up when she finished her shower, dried herself off, put on her comfortable clothes, and wrapped her hair in a towel. As she walked toward the bed, she came to a dead stop. The silhouette of a tall man wearing a hoodie was standing by the door of her room. "Hi, Sarah."

Sarah gasped; she thought she had dead-bolted the door. "You need to leave, whoever you are." She quickly scanned the immediate area to see if she could grab something to protect herself, but the man lunged toward her, turned her around, and pulled her hands behind her, binding them tightly with a zip tie. Her heart was beating so rapidly, she could hear it. "If it's money you want, my purse is in the dresser drawer. Please take it all," she pleaded.

"I want you, Sarah. I have waited for you for a long time. If you struggle, I'm going to have to hurt you. Please don't make me hurt you. I had to hurt Kayla; I don't want to hurt you, too." His voice sounded vaguely familiar, but before she could place it, he covered her mouth and nose with a rag.

Chapter 41

C ampos was waiting for her plane to leave SFO when she got a call from Davidson. "Campos, you still here?"

"I'm at the airport. What's up?"

"I decided to give Kayla's apartment one more look before we handed it back over to the landlord. After we did our initial inspection, someone else got in there and tore the place apart; it was a shambles. The smell hit us as soon as we opened the door; the stench of rotten something was so bad, I almost barfed. We went into the kitchen, and the fridge and freezer were wide open, food all over the floor. My assistant and I went through everything, and I found a thumb drive inside spoiled meat wrapped in white butcher paper. Whoever trashed the place was in a big hurry and didn't look too closely."

"Were you able to open the thumb drive?" Campos asked, as she paced back and forth.

"It took some doing because it was password protected, but, thankfully, our IT guy cracked the code and opened up the files inside. You're not going to believe this: It has every drug deal, amount, and patient name, and it has Wood's name listed with every prescription he signed," Davidson said.

"Were you able to find any name associated with an X?" Campos asked.

"Not at first, but this is a new kind of spreadsheet, called a pivot table. It's like a 3-D spreadsheet; don't ask me to explain it more than that. We did find several X's connected to what looked like foreign bank accounts, which I'm working on gaining access to. I didn't think Kayla could have created these types of spreadsheets, so I asked our IT guy if he could tell who did, and he was able to do his magic. You'll never guess whose name we found."

"Ned Bisone!" Campos blurted out, so loudly that a few people sitting near her at her gate turned their heads toward her.

"Bingo. And our innocent Ned has an X next to his name connected to a bank account as well," Davidson added.

"I'll grab a cab and meet you back at your precinct. Can you run a background check on him? I'll see you as soon as I can get there. I'll call the medical center and see if I can get his mother's name and address. I think Sarah told me he had to leave suddenly to go see her because she was ill. See you soon."

Campos rushed back through security and hailed a cab. Once inside, she took a deep breath and grinned. "Finally, we get a break," she said.

"Pardon me?" the cab driver said.

"Nothing—I'm just talking to myself." Campos speed-dialed Strong. "Strong, we've got solid evidence on the drug deals, money, and names."

"Slow down—you're talking a mile a minute. What's going on?"

After Campos reiterated everything that Davidson had just shared with her, Strong said, "I just dropped Sarah off a couple hours ago. I can see if she has more information on where Ned's mom lives; it may be quicker than trying to get anything from the medical center. It's good you're there to work this with Davidson—finally, a lucky turn."

"I'll call the medical center anyway; I want to get them to get Ned's desktop computer and see if their IT guys can download his files and get me access to his work voicemail. Let me know as soon as you talk to Sarah. The sooner we can get our hands-on Ned, the faster we can crack this case. I can't tell you how jazzed I am, Strong."

"Good work Detective—and that Davidson has a nose, too. I'll be in touch."

Campos spent the rest of the cab ride on hold with various departments at the medical center—first Legal, then IT, then HR. She finally got a human being after she left urgent messages on everyone's phone. "Legal department. This is Gail. How may I help you?"

"My name is Detective Campos. I've been investigating the murder of one of your employees, Kayla Newman, and I need to gain access to some records immediately."

"May I put you on hold for just a minute?"

"Please, Gail, don't leave me hanging too long," Campos pleaded.

"I promise I won't, but I do have to confirm your name and access; it shouldn't take but a few minutes."

True to her word, Gail was back quickly. "Detective Campos from Miami?"

"Correct."

"I have authority to share the following information with you. Do you have a pen?"

Campos pulled a pen and paper out of her bag. "Yes."

"Here are the names and numbers of the people you need to speak with in HR and IT. You need to tell them Legal has approved your clearance; give them our on-call attorney's name and number if they need to reconfirm."

"No problem," Campos said.

After Gail provided her with the names and cell phone numbers of the directors of IT and HR, as well as those of their assistants, Campos said, "Thanks so much. You've been most helpful."

"Good luck catching the bad guys, Detective," Gail said, as she signed off.

Traffic inched slowly toward San Francisco while Campos called the director of IT.

Chapter 42

Jackie and Laura spent the rest of the afternoon with Wyatt as he recovered from his surgery. Laura was being so supportive, rubbing Jackie's back and fetching lunch and bringing it back, Jackie couldn't help but think, *I'm starting to believe we may be able to save this marriage after all. Who knew?*

At 3:00 in the afternoon, Dr. Santos and his team came in for rounds. Dr. Ketel went right to Wyatt, who was sitting up in a chair, eating crackers. "How are you feeling, Wyatt?" she asked, placing a hand on his head.

"I feel like I drank an energy drink." He smiled at her.

"Well, we put a very powerful battery in you this morning." She looked over at Laura and Jackie and said, "His BUN and creatine levels have dropped dramatically, which tells us the kidney is working quite well."

"Great news," Laura replied.

"I think we'll take his IV and catheter out so he can use the bathroom and walk around without being hooked up to everything," she announced.

"It's just so amazing how quickly things turn around," Jackie said.

"It's one of the best parts of this job—watching the kidney start to work normally and seeing the energy returning to our patients," Dr. Santos said.

"You and your team have had quite a day, Dr. Santos, what with the code blue and making national news, plus a couple transplants for good measure," Jackie said.

"No kidding, and now we're off to transplant a living liver after rounds. Never bored around here," he replied. "Couldn't do it without my team, that's for sure."

As they prepared to depart, Dr. Ketel added, "We'll see how Wyatt does, and if he's feeling well, we'll talk about discharging him to our on-site hotel tomorrow afternoon. It's attached to the hospital, so we can still make rounds there, but it's a bit more comfortable and has accommodations for him and both of you."

"That's a great idea," Laura said.

"He'll come here for his post-transplant classes with the other kids, where he'll learn all about his anti-rejection drugs and all the signs and symptoms of rejection." Dr. Ketel looked over at Wyatt. "You'll need to pass a test before you get discharged, Wyatt, but I can see you're a smart fella, so I think you'll do great."

"I'll do my best," Wyatt said.

"You look a little tired. Maybe we should get you back in bed for a nap—big first day." Dr. Ketel and Laura helped Wyatt navigate his IV and catheter and tucked him into bed, where he dozed off immediately. Dr. Ketel waved and left the room.

Jackie looked over at Laura, who looked as exhausted as Jackie felt. "You want to go back to the hotel and take a nap and I'll keep watch here?"

"Great idea. I didn't sleep too well last night, although I don't think you did either, honey. How was Sarah when you saw her?" Laura asked.

"She was freaked out at first but was happy to leave with both her kidneys, and, most important, she was thrilled that Wyatt got his new kidney. Handsome picked her up; he came to see her before she went to the OR, brought her flowers. Who knows what may happen? We've all been through some intense emotional times. I'm ready for some smooth sailing. How about you?" Jackie asked.

"Yes. Let's slow things down, get our boy back to his new normal, and take stock of what we have. That code blue scared me to death. I couldn't bear to lose Wyatt. But it also made me stop and realize how important you are to me and what an asshole I've been to you." Laura went to Jackie and embraced her.

Jackie buried her head in Laura's neck and mumbled, "I don't want to lose you, Laura. I've never loved anyone more than I love you. I know we can work through this."

"I want to, Jackie. I realize now that I lost track of what was important. I let my job suck every ounce of energy from me, and I never had anything left for you. I've missed so many of Wyatt's moments. Maybe I need to rethink my promotion."

While they were still wrapped in each other's arms, Wyatt's nurse walked in and said, "Sorry to interrupt—you two are such a cute couple. I'm here to take out Wyatt's catheter and IV. Looks like he kept his lunch down."

"He did. He was in the chair until a few minutes ago," Jackie said.

"This should only take a minute, and then I'll let him sleep until dinner."

The nurse nudged Wyatt and let him know what she was going to do. After a few minutes, she said, "All done."

"I didn't feel hardly anything," Wyatt said.

"That's good. Are you having any pain?" the nurse asked.

"Just a little."

"What number is it, if one is no pain and ten is really bad?"

Wyatt hesitated and then responded, "It's two and a half."

"Okay. I'll be back in a little while. You call me if it gets worse." The nurse charted everything and left.

Jackie pulled Wyatt's covers up around him and fixed his pillows. As he dozed off, Jackie returned to Laura and gave her another hug. "You go get some rest, and I'll see you in a couple hours. I love you, Laura. We have a special family."

Laura kissed Jackie on the cheek. "We really do. I'll see you in a little bit; call if you need me for anything."

After Laura left, Jackie put on the TV and found an old episode of *I Love Lucy* for comic relief, until she drifted off to sleep in the chair next to her son.

Chapter 43

Sarah awoke with her chin down on her chest. She felt a metal chair beneath her. Her neck felt stiff, and she couldn't fully lift her head. She attempted to focus by blinking her eyes rapidly, but her vision was blurry. She flexed her fingers and toes and realized that her hands were tied behind her back and each of her ankles was bound to a leg of her chair. She could hear her heart was pounding.

"Where am I?" she asked, but the room was silent. She vaguely remembered having seen the shadow of a man in her hotel room and hearing a familiar voice. *Who was that?* she thought, as she struggled to move.

She tried to move her neck again, one way and then the other, getting a little dizzy from whatever drug she could tell she'd been given. "Help! Help!" she yelled, as loudly as she could, but no one responded. Sarah squinted and looked around the room. The walls were cement, a few high windows seemed closed, and the air felt damp.

"Help!" she screamed again. She kept blinking and bit the inside of her cheek as hard as she could to elicit some feeling. She tasted blood.

She heard a door slam and footsteps coming down a flight of stairs. A man in a hoodie walked in with a tray and placed it on the floor near her. "No use screaming, Sarah. No one's going to hear you."

Sarah squeezed her eyes tightly to see if she could make out who he was, but her vision was still blurry. "Who are you? What do you want?"

"Of course, you can't recognize me with my hoodie on." He took it off and got close to Sarah's face.

Sarah looked into his eyes. "Ned? What are you doing? Are you crazy?"

"Don't call me crazy, Sarah!" He slapped her hard and walked away.

"I'm sorry, I'm sorry, Ned. I'm just so confused. I didn't mean to call you names." *Holy shit, it was Ned all along! Oh my God! He had access to everything in our system. I can't believe this!*

Ned approached Sarah again and said, "I don't think you're in a position to call me anything, Sarah Golden. I saw you kissing your cop boyfriend at lunch. I know everything."

"That was nothing. He doesn't mean anything to me anymore. Can you please loosen these ties around my wrists? They're hurting me. Why are you doing this to me? I didn't do anything to you. Please," Sarah begged.

"That's not going to happen right now. If you're a good girl and drink this entire glass of milk then maybe I can untie you. Can you cooperate with me, Sarah?"

"Okay, Ned. I'll do my best. Where are we?" she asked.

Ned slapped her again. "No more questions."

Sarah's cheek stung. "Okay, no more questions. I'm sorry. But please don't hit me again."

"I won't hit you as long as you do what I tell you to do. I've waited to have you all to myself since I first met you. All those surgeons staring at you, your comedian boyfriend and then your detective boyfriend—you're so popular. They won't be able to help you now." Ned held the tall plastic cup of milk in one hand and walked around behind her and put his lips right in her ear. "I'm in love with you, but you never gave me a chance." He kissed her ear, moved around to her other side, and began to whisper again, "I even bought you an expensive gift from Tiffany, and you didn't get it." He kissed her other ear and moved his tongue around in it. Sarah had to do everything she could not to gag.

"Now, we're going to have a nice, long talk. But first, open your mouth and take a big gulp of this yummy drink I made special for you." Ned squeezed the plastic cup at the top to make it easy to pour the milk into Sarah's mouth. Sarah swallowed as fast as she could but some dripped down her chin. She started to choke, spitting some milk out. She tasted something bitter, and realized, *He's put some kind of drug in this.* "Don't spit any more out Sarah, or I'll just go refill this and we can start all over. Do you want that?" Ned brushed Sarah's hair back, allowing the milk to drip on her clothes. Ned held the cup up to her mouth and poured more of the laced milk down her throat.

"Good girl. Now I'll tell you a story about Kayla and me while we let the magic milk start to work. You thought we hated each other, didn't you? That's what we wanted everyone to believe." Ned sat back and crossed his legs. "I was the brains behind the whole drug deal, not Kayla. She needed to take care of her grandmother, and I wanted to have enough money that I never had to work again. I'm so sick of fixing dumb people's computers and watching them act like they're better than me just because they're doctors or nurses."

"Please, Ned, don't kill me. You know I'm not like those other people at work. And I'm sorry I didn't know you were in love with me, but please don't kill me," Sarah begged.

"I won't kill you; I just want you to relax so we can get to know each other better, after you're nice and comfortable."

Sarah obliged, thinking, *How am I ever going to get out of this?* She slowly studied each inch of the basement, knowing the drugs in the milk would hit her bloodstream soon.

"Everything was working perfectly," Ned continued. "Kayla got the prescriptions signed by Dr. Wood and filled and mailed to her grandmother's house every month; then we started getting the cheap stuff from Mexico and doubled our profits and production. Then Granny died and Kayla wanted to close up shop. She demanded that we close the whole thing down, like she was in charge. She wouldn't listen to reason. She threatened to turn me in, said she had enough evidence for them to put me behind bars for life, so I had to send her on her way. What else could I do?" Ned asked.

"Sounds like you didn't have a choice, Ned," Sarah slurred intentionally, attempting to sound more drugged than she was.

"Sarah, it looks like your medicine is starting to kick in. That's good." Ned leaned over and kissed her forcefully, moving his tongue back and forth in her mouth. Sarah kissed him back, even though the sensation nauseated her.

He backed away. "Wow, no wonder those fellas are after you. . . . You need to finish this last sip of milk; the good stuff is on the bottom." With that Ned held Sarah's nose to be sure she didn't spit the remaining milk out and poured the rest in her mouth. Sarah swallowed then dramatically shook her head so Ned would take his hand off her nose so she could breath. As he removed his hand, she started to cough violently. He sat there calmly waiting for her to stop, throwing the cup down on the floor.

"I hardly talk can and see not, Ned." She slumped over and closed her eyes.

"Sarah." She didn't respond. "Sarah!" He pulled her head up and pried open her eyes, which Sarah purposely rolled back in her head. She faked a few epileptic seizure–like moves with her restrained arms and legs and then collapsed again.

"Sarah, this never happened so fast with the other girls. I'd just drug them, have my fun, and then drop them off at the bar I found them at. . . . Sarah!"

Sarah slowly looked up at Ned and smiled, "Hi, Ned. You how doing?" She puckered up so he'd kiss her again, and he did. She responded with a slow-motion kiss. "Maybe I gave you too much," Ned said.

Sarah smiled again. "Bathroom, go?"

Ned stared at her. "You need to go to the bathroom?"

"Yes, walk, can't," she mumbled.

"I'll help you; then you can lie down upstairs." Ned untied her wrists and ankles, and she slid off the chair and on to the floor. Ned put his arm around her waist and slid it up under her shirt and onto her breast. "Sarah, that feels wonderful. Do you like it?"

Sarah nodded slowly, feeling stomach acid making its way up to her throat. *The drugs are really kicking in now*, she realized.

Ned took his hand off her breast and supported her at the waist as she dragged one foot in front of the other. *Just make it upstairs before your brain gets too cloudy*, she thought.

Ned helped her up the stairs and into the bathroom, pulled down her pants, and put her on the toilet. Waves of dizziness took over and Sarah couldn't hold her head up and started to fall forward off the toilet.

Ned pushed her head back and filled a cup from the sink with cold water, and splashed it in her face. "Wake up!' He demanded.

Sarah started to cry. "Sorry, sorry, sorry," and put her hands over her eyes. She sat up to pull up her pants, and Ned grabbed her by her hair and dragged her from the bathroom into the bedroom, where he threw her on the bed, pulled her arms over her head, and tied them to the bedpost. He draped a bedspread over her and said, "I'm going to let you sleep this off so we can enjoy our first night together. Don't try anything funny. I'll be right outside."

As Sarah heard him close and lock the door behind him, she struggled to fight the heavy fog seeping into her mind and numbing her body, but it was too powerful. The last thing she thought before she lost consciousness was, *I was hoping to escape once I was upstairs, but I can't even feel my legs.*

Chapter 44

Strong called Campos while she was speaking with the director of IT. She let him go to voicemail, but he kept calling. "Thanks for all your help. You've been invaluable. I may need to call you back; will you be available for the next hour?" Campos asked.

"Yes, Detective." He hung up.

Campos called Strong back and asked, "What's wrong?"

"Sarah's missing. I called and called to get Ned's mother's info, and she didn't pick up, so I went over to her hotel and had the manager let me in. She was gone, but her purse, phone, shoes—everything—was still there. It looks like she was abducted. The bedspread was missing." Handsome's voice shook as he spoke.

"We'll find her, Strong. I think we know who the hooded guy is," Campos said calmly, and continued, "I just got off the phone with the IT guys at the medical center and also spoke with the HR director. Apparently, Ned was hospitalized for a psychotic breakdown over five years ago, then discharged on drugs, which I'm guessing he stopped taking."

"I'm going to find that sick fuck and lock him up for good. I can't lose her Campos, she's the love of my life." Strong blurted out.

Campos eye's widened, this was the first time Strong had verbalized what she figured he'd been feeling about Sarah all along. "We'll find her partner, we'll find her. And when we do we've got enough evidence with the information on this new thumb drive to put him away for life ten times over. Just find him. I'll work my end. We had Wood arrested; he's got his attorney working on bail right now. I'll call back the IT director and see if we can put a tracer on Ned's cell phone," Campos said.

"If he's a smart guy, he's likely using burner phones now, but it's worth a try. Keep me posted."

Campos hung up and went into Davidson's office, where their IT forensics guy was still downloading files.

"We're getting an early Christmas here, Campos, and so is our narcotics division," Davidson said.

"Not so fast. I just spoke with Strong. Sarah's missing. She was abducted from her hotel, and I'm sure it was Ned who took her. I need to call IT to see if they can put a tracer on his phone. I called HR and found out Ned was institutionalized for a psychotic breakdown and is likely off his meds, so we've got a real sicko out there. I pray he doesn't kill her. The only saving grace is that he has a real soft spot for her, or at least it looked that way when I interviewed him. I saw how he looked at her," Campos explained.

"Not good news. You call IT, and then I'll brief you on all these files," Davidson said.

Campos called IT, and they said they would put out a tracer and call her as soon as they got a signal. When she walked back into Davidson's office, she said, "Now, tell me about this early Christmas present. I need some good news."

"Not only did Kayla and Ned log every transaction, they also have the names of people they were getting the drugs from in Mexico. There were also a few other sources in the US, as well as overseas. Once our narcotics department follows up on this information, they can trace the source and try to infiltrate it or stop the operation—and hopefully prevent at least a few overdoses and deaths," Davidson said.

"Another small silver lining is that I spoke to one of the coordinators at the transplant institute, and they said these poor donor families of the overdose victims said organ donation was the only positive thing that came out of their loved one's deaths," Campos said.

"Sad but true, unfortunately," Davidson said.

"I'm going to start logging all the evidence we have so far. Okay if I use that desk outside your office for now?" Campos asked.

"Help yourself. They're on vacation."

Campos spent the rest of the afternoon preparing the paperwork for Wood's formal arrest and kept checking her cell phone, hoping to hear from Strong, she had never heard him so upset. Around six, she got a call. "Campos here."

"Med center IT. We got a hit on Ned's phone. Seems he's in Miami, near the airport. I can give you an address."

Campos jotted it down and thanked the caller, then dialed Strong. "I got an address."

"Great. Give it to me," Strong said. "Hopefully, I'll have Sarah the next time I call you. I'll send a squad car there now."

Chapter 45

Jackie helped Wyatt to the bathroom after his nap. "Hot dog! Everything is working great, buddy."

Wyatt looked up at her. "It sure is, Momma. Now I'll be able to write my initials in the snow again when we go to Tahoe."

Jackie let out a laugh. "Ready to take a small walk around the floor?"

"Sure."

She put her hand gently on Wyatt's back and guided him a short way down the hall and then back to his room. "Good job," she said. "How did that feel?"

"A little scary, but not bad," Wyatt said.

Jackie sat down on the edge of his bed and showed him how to place his hand gently over the area where his new kidney was and support it while she helped him lift his legs and get into bed.

Laura came walking into the room a moment later, and Jackie took one look at her face and said, "Wow, you look great! Amazing what a little rest will do."

"Yeah, Mom, those black circles under your eyes are almost gone," Wyatt chimed in.

"Thanks, you guys. Looks like you're doing great, Wyatt; I saw you walking when I was heading this way. Way to go. Give me five." Laura put her hand up, and Wyatt slapped his against it.

Jackie's cell rang, and she excused herself and went out in the hall. "Hello?"

"Hi, Jackie. How's Wyatt?"

"Who is this? I'm sorry, I don't recognize your voice," Jackie said.

"It's Ned Bisone from SF Transplant. I was the one who helped Wyatt with the video games when he was here for his evaluation."

"Oh, Ned, yes, I remember you. How nice of you to call. He's doing great. He's already up walking a little," she said, wondering, *Why is he calling me right now?*

"I don't mean to disturb you, but I have Sarah with me. I know that you know her close friend Detective Strong. If he tries to look for her, I need you to let him know to stop, or Sarah's going to end up like Kayla. Thanks, Jackie, and tell Wyatt hello."

"Hello, Ned?" Jackie almost yelled into the phone.

Laura poked her head out into the hall. "Everything okay?"

"Sarah's life is in grave danger, I need to find Handsome. Can you stay with Wyatt?"

"Oh no!" Laura exclaimed.

"I'll let you know what's going on as soon as I find out." Jackie's heart was beating faster than usual.

"Just check in as soon as you know something, and please be careful." Laura leaned in to give Jackie a kiss.

"Will do." Jackie dialed Handsome and started walking toward the elevator.

"Jackie, how's Wyatt?" he asked.

"Doing great, but I just got the weirdest call from Ned. Can you meet me at the front of the hospital?" Jackie said.

"What did he say?"

"He said he has Sarah, and I'm supposed to tell you not to look for her, or she's going to end up like Kayla. What the fuck!"

"I'll meet you in front of the hospital in ten."

After Strong hung up, Jackie called Sarah's cell and got her voice mail. "Hey, Sarah, it's me. Give me a call. Wyatt's doing great."

Jackie paced back and forth out in front of the hospital, her stomach churning. She called Sarah's hotel room phone and let it ring and ring. "Pick up, Sarah. Pick up."

Handsome pulled up and motioned for Jackie to get in the car. "What is going on?" Jackie yelled.

"It's not good, Jack. I'm gonna give it to you straight." Handsome told Jackie everything he knew.

"How did Ned know you were looking for him?"

"Not sure. He called you, though, so we may be able to trace it. I'm no expert on this shit, but I have a guy from the precinct meeting me near here who is."

Handsome started driving south of the hospital, and several minutes later, they were in the parking lot of a grocery chain. A young man walked over to his car and said, "Detective Strong?"

"That's me. You from our precinct?"

"Yes, I'm John Mills, head of IT forensics."

"Hop in back." Handsome gave Mills the rundown on Ned, his IT experience, and the location in Miami to which the med center had traced Ned's work cell.

"He may have pulled the chip from his phone; he knows it can be traced through that. May I see your phone, ma'am?"

Jackie unlocked her phone and handed it to him.

Then Strong's cell rang. "Strong here . . . Good . . . Okay . . . Yes, this guy has a history of psychotic behavior. He's already threatened to kill her if we try to find her. He *will* kill her if he thinks we're anywhere near him. I'll meet you two blocks away."

Strong ended the call and said, "I think we've located him. They found a rental car parked outside an abandoned house near the airport and confirmed that it was Ned's. We have officers surrounding the house."

"Sounds like you may have found your guy," said Mills. "If you need me to try to trace the call from Jackie's phone, let me know. Good luck." He handed Jackie back her phone and got out of the car.

"Jackie, I think you need to go back to the hospital," Strong said. "I'll call you as soon as I have something."

"I'm not going anywhere. I'm not leaving your side until I see Sarah. It's my fault that she's even here in Miami," Jackie insisted.

"Okay, but you cannot go *anywhere* near the scene. It's too dangerous. He killed Kayla, and he will kill you if you get in his way. Do you understand that?"

"Yes."

Strong parked his car two blocks away from the house where Ned and Sarah were and met with the lead undercover officer. "He knows what I look like," Strong said, "so I'll stay here. He's been dealing drugs and has already killed a woman with an overdose. It's possible that he also gave Sarah an overdose of drugs, so I'll get Medical on standby."

"Sounds like a plan. I'll keep you posted, Detective," the other officer said.

Strong phoned in the request for emergency medical assistance and gave them his location. The team responded quickly, and Strong briefed them on the situation. The medical team stood by waiting to hear from the officers at the house.

Jackie looked over at Handsome's face, it was ashen as he glared at his phone, waiting for it to ring. "What is taking them so long?" Jackie insisted. "It's taking them too long." Each second felt like an hour. Jackie was jumping out of her skin.

Chapter 46

Meanwhile, inside the house, Ned glared down at Sarah. "I'm going to tie your hands a little tighter, just in case you try anything funny."

Ned studied Sarah as he brushed her hair back from her face, "I've waited a long time to get my hands on you, Sarah Golden, and I want to be sure you enjoy it as much as I will." There was no response from her. He was leaning down to kiss her when he heard sounds outside of the house.

Rushing out of the bedroom, he went to the living room window and looked around the front of the house, everything looked quiet, nobody in sight. As he walked down the hall towards the back of the house someone busted open the front door.

"Stop where you are and put your hands up." A male voice declared.

Ned grabbed a stool that was in the hallway, turned around and threw it as hard as he could at the officer's head and ran out the back door. "Fuck you!" he yelled.

As he rounded the side of the house, he saw two officers heading toward him, one was shouting.

"Stop where you are and put your hands in the air, or we'll shoot." Ned turned heels and started to run when a scalding burn in his thigh made him fall.

The officer was pulling Ned's hands behind his back and putting handcuffs on his wrist.

"You have the right to remain silent." The officer said but Ned cranked his neck around and could see a large pool of blood gushing from his thigh on to the sidewalk.

"Call an ambulance, looks like the bullet hit his femoral artery." He heard the officer order.

"What the fuck, I was trying to help Sarah, someone drugged her and left her here to die. You shot the wrong guy, asshole."

"We'll see about that. Where is she?" The officer demanded.

"She's in the upstairs bedroom, I was just about to untie her hands, whoever did this to her is probably long gone, you're wasting time. You got the wrong guy." Ned declared again glancing over his shoulder again the pool of blood was getting bigger. The cop turned him over and tied a tourniquet above the gunshot wound, "That should slow down the bleeding."

"It's too tight." The officer ignored him.

"We found her," another voice screamed from inside of house, "we're starting CPR, no pulse, and she's not breathing."

Ned felt the officer drag him from behind and lean him up against the side of the house, "What'd you give her?"

"I'm telling you, I found her that way." Ned responded. Loud sirens wailed from the front of the house, two paramedics quickly approached, lowered a gurney to the ground, and put Ned on it.

"You're ripping my shoulders out of their sockets. Take these handcuffs off now!" Ned demanded, realizing his voice sounded blurry.

"Looks like he's lost a lot of blood," one paramedic said to the other.

"He'll live." The officer said. "Once you get him to the ambulance, I'll move his handcuffs to the front." They rolled Ned to the front of the house, he saw two ambulances and lots of flashing lights from the numerous squad cars.

Coming through the front door of house were more paramedics pushing a gurney with Sarah's body on it. Ned could see she wasn't moving.

"Is she dead?" he asked.

"Like you care, you sick motherfucker." The officer standing next to him declared.

Chapter 47

Beeping sounds and dings danced around Sarah's head. She was floating, infused with peace. *This is wonderful,* she thought.

The next thing she felt was someone shaking her arm. "Sarah, can you hear me? Blink if you can hear me," a voice said.

She blinked slowly.

"Can you squeeze my hand, Sarah?"

Sarah squeezed the hand.

"Good. Can you open your eyes?"

Sarah tried to open her eyes, but only one complied; the other one was too heavy.

"Hi, Sarah." There was a nurse close to her face. "Welcome back. We thought we had lost you."

Sarah looked at the nurse and moved her hand toward her face, but it was connected to wires and lines.

"You're in intensive care, Sarah. Can you tell me your last name?"

Sarah tried to think of her last name, but nothing came to her. She shook her head slowly.

"Can you say hello?"

Sarah tried to move her mouth but could make only a circle. No sound came out. She went back to her floating cloud. More sounds of beeping and pressure on her arm pulled her back. She slowly opened her one good eye. A short woman was standing over her, touching her cheek. "Hello, my friend."

Sarah smiled, although she had no idea who this person was.

"My name is Jackie. I'm your best friend. Do you remember me?"

Sarah smiled and shook her head no. The woman started to cry and kept patting Sarah's cheeks. Then she left and Sarah went back to sleep.

Sarah felt the head of her bed move up and saw a group of people in white lab coats all around her.

One of the lab-coat people asked her, "Are you Sarah Golden?" Something opened up in her mind. "Yes, I think so," she mumbled.

"Great news, because we've been looking for you for a while. Do you remember what happened to you?"

"Not really." She touched her closed eye; it was swollen shut. "Someone hit me. Ned hit me." Her eyes widened, and she glanced around, as if looking for him. She heard the beeping sound speed up.

"He's not going to hurt you. He's locked up, Sarah. You're safe now," a doctor said.

"We're your medical team, and we're going to be giving you some medications that we hope will help you to start remembering things. You are one strong woman, Sarah Golden."

The lab coats disappeared. A nurse came to check on her and put some medicine into her IV lines. A hot rush of energy shot through her arms and into her head. She shook her head and opened her good eye very wide. "Wow. What was that?" she asked the nurse.

The nurse smiled. "It's your wake-up medicine, Sarah. Nice to see you feeling better. How about a sip of water?"

Sarah smiled. "Please." She took a long sip; it tasted cold and refreshing. The cloudiness started to leave her mind. "How long have I been here?" she asked the nurse.

"It's been almost four days. A lot of people are concerned about you. They'll be so glad to know you're coming around." The nurse gave Sarah more water and kept the head of her bed up. Sarah looked around her room; there were curtains on three sides and a window behind her. She touched her right arm and looked down at it; purple and blue bruises covered it. Her left shoulder was sore. She looked down under the covers and wiggled both her feet and her toes. *They work*, she thought. Her knees were swollen and bruised. She bent each leg, one at a time, and felt some stiffness there, too.

The nurse came back in with more medication. "I can see you're doing an inventory. You got some bad bruises and a cut over your eye, but everything is in working order."

"Thank goodness," she said.

"There's someone who wants to see you. Are you ready for a little company?"

"Yes."

When Jackie walked into the ICU, Sarah sat up taller. "Jackie! It's about time you stopped by."

"I've been here all along. Aren't you a sight for sore eyes, Sarah Golden. I'm so happy you're waking up." Jackie bent over and gently hugged her friend. "Welcome back," she said, and started to cry. "Do you remember anything?"

"Stuff is starting to come back, slowly. I remember Ned kidnapping me . . ." Sarah stopped as a more terrifying possibility entered her mind. "Did he rape me, Jack? You can tell me." She studied her friend's face.

"No, thank goodness. He did tie you to a bed, though," Jackie said.

"He had me downstairs for a while; at least I was able to get him to drag me upstairs. I was afraid he was going to kill me, Jackie."

"We don't have to talk about it now. Let's just get you better, back in shape. Now that we have contact with that crazy noggin of yours, the rest will come."

"How's Wyatt?"

"He's doing so well. You'll be so proud of him. We'll be here a couple more weeks; then it's back to San Francisco."

"Best news ever. And Laura?"

"We're working things out; we have therapy in our immediate future for sure. Everyone needs a good dose of therapy every once in a while, though, right?"

Before Sarah could answer, she looked over Jackie's shoulder and saw Handsome come in. She beamed at him and said, "Hi there."

He approached her bed and kissed her cheek. "Hello, Sarah. Good to see you back on the planet. We thought we might have lost you."

"Good to be back, although floating on those clouds was a trip."

"Problem with those clouds is that we couldn't visit you there, and we missed you."

"I guess that's my cue to leave. I'll come by later." Jackie squeezed Sarah's hand, nodded to Handsome, and made her way out of the room.

Once she was gone, Handsome looked deep into Sarah's eyes, leaned in, and kissed her gently on the lips. "I was so scared you were gone for good, Sarah. It was a close call."

Sarah felt warmth between her legs. *I guess everything really is working properly*, she thought.

Chapter 48

It was several weeks before Sarah could see through both eyes and the bruises disappeared. She decided to take off the time that she would have taken had she donated her kidney, and spend it at Handsome's place. No promises—just togetherness.

Handsome invited Jackie, Laura, Wyatt, and Campos over for a barbecue at his house before Jackie's family flew home.

Sarah was helping Handsome prepare a salad in the kitchen while Campos gave them an update on Ned.

"When Ned tried to escape from the house where he took you, one of the officers shot him in the leg. He's recovering now—in solitary confinement. He's been examined by a psychiatrist and started on medications. He'll be tried for first-degree murder, drug smuggling, kidnapping, assault, and sexual abuse. There may be a few other charges, too, when all is said and done. I'm going to need you to come in and give us a statement when you're ready, Sarah," Campos said.

"I need a little more time. Then I'll be ready to relive that horrible day." Sarah said.

"I understand. Ned also gave us the location of his safety deposit box at the bank; there's over a million dollars in it, and we haven't been able to get access to his account overseas yet. No telling how much money he had," Campos said.

"He's not going to be able to use it where he's going," Handsome said.

"Too bad that money can't be donated to drug-treatment facilities," Sarah suggested.

"That's a great idea, honey. You never know—anything's possible." Handsome put his arm around Sarah and kissed her cheek.

"I'm just so thankful to both of you for all you did to solve this case. To think Ned was under our noses for so long, and I just didn't see it," Sarah said.

"We're just happy you're alive and on the mend, Sarah," Campos said.

Jackie walked into the kitchen with Wyatt following her. "Hey, we're getting hungry. When are you going to start the grill? Wyatt and I are going to get his backpack out of the car. Let me know if there's anything I can help with when I get back."

Sarah heard Jackie open up the front door and then whoop. Sarah walked to the open front door and saw Jackie running across the lawn toward Biker Bob while Wyatt stood at the door, his mouth hanging open. He finally managed to say, "That's a big motorcycle guy, Aunt Sarah. He won't hurt Momma, will he?"

"No, buddy, that's our good friend Biker Bob. You want to meet him?" Sarah asked.

Biker Bob got off his bike, scooped Jackie up in a big hug, and then looked past her at Sarah and Wyatt.

"Special delivery! I heard someone could use a double cheeseburger, so I brought plenty for everyone." He held up two large brown paper bags and handed them to Jackie.

"There's a bottle of your favorite rum in the pack on my bike," he added.

He walked over and looked down at Wyatt. "Is this the amazing Wyatt I've been hearing about?"

Wyatt nodded as he craned his neck to look up at Biker Bob.

"That's me." Wyatt grinned.

"Want to sit on my motorcycle?"

"Can I, Momma? Please?" Wyatt pleaded.

"Sure, why not, but don't get any ideas. No rides—just sitting," Jackie said.

Biker Bob picked up Wyatt gently and put him on his big Harley. Jackie handed Sarah the bag of burgers and took a picture of them.

"Wait'll your friends back home see you with your new friend, Wyatt. You'll be the talk of the school!" Jackie said.

Sarah laughed and put her arm around her best friend, and they walked together back into Handsome's house.

The End

Author's Note

- **1 of 3** Americans are at risk for kidney disease, but don't know it. You can take a one-minute quiz at www.kidney.org to find out if you are at risk.

- 37 million people have chronic kidney disease.

- More than 100,000 people are awaiting a kidney transplant. If you'd like to be an organ donor go to www.donatelife.net

- The National Kidney Foundation (NKF) is a great resource that has amazing programs, like **The Big Ask— The Big Give.** A conversation can save a life. Whether you need a kidney or are considering a living donation.

- NKF also wants everyone to know their **eGFR—** kidney function. Similar to how most folks know their cholesterol numbers.

- Check out the NKF website for these programs. www.kidney.org

Acknowledgments

Writing a book always sounds like such a great idea when you start. Then comes the ebb and flow of inspiration paired with the *What was I thinking?* moments where it's oh-so-easy to quit. That happens about a thousand times. Eventually, with perseverance and lots of support, a book is born. But it doesn't happen in a vacuum.

First, I must thank my writing soulmate sister Betsy Graziani Fasbinder, who held my hand during times of doubt and fear in creating this book. Betsy was always there for me, I'm grateful for her kindness and honesty. She is one-fourth of my valued writing tribe that we call *Bella Quattro*—Beautiful Four—which includes the incomparable memoir guru, Linda Joy Myers and the elegant and eloquent Christie Nelson. Twenty years in the making, *Bella Quattro* is still going strong.

Thank you to Annie Tucker for her partnership through development and copyediting. She coached me with grace and clarity. She encouraged me to set my next book in a restaurant, since I love to feed my characters a lot more than what gets on the printed page.

Thank you to Dr. Laura Brosch, my long-time friend and colleague in transplant, for being my first beta reader and providing me hope and feedback on how to improve my story.

Thank you to Susie Chinisci's keen editing eye and wit, my book is better for having gone under her careful review.

Brooke Warner is the mastermind behind She Writes Press. She and her incomparable team have opened up a critical portal for the stories of women to find their place amongst published books throughout the world. What a force She Writes has become.

Thanks to Susan Diaz, pediatric nurse practitioner, who provided accurate pediatric clinical details while she was finishing her doctorate in Nursing at UCSF and working full time. Thanks to Sandra Weinberg, MSW, who shared her expertise and the clinical perspective she's gathered as the independent donor advocate at UCSF.

Thanks to Karen Lynch for her input on the detective details of the story. Who knew San Francisco has inspectors not detectives?

Thanks to my agent, Kimberly Cameron, for reading the manuscript three times and pushing me to distill the story while adding important details to keep the reader connected. I feel grateful and lucky to have her on my team.

And of course, to my beloved family, I owe huge thanks. I married Mark Schatz because I knew he'd help me to create a family full of love and fun, and that he did. Together we created Gracie and Bennett Schatz, now grown adults, out on their own. I couldn't be a prouder mom, and I'm grateful to call these two not only my kids but my friends.

Lastly, a thank you to Elaine Petrocelli, co-owner of Book Passage bookstore in the San Francisco Bay Area. She and her staff facilitate one of the BEST mystery-writing conferences in the country. It's at these conferences that I've gotten highly professional guidance and inspiration. What a gift she and her team provide to all readers and writers in the Bay Area.

About the Author

Amy S. Peele grew up and went to nursing school in the Chicago area, where she began her transplant nursing career. She later moved to San Francisco in 1985 to follow her transplant career, serving until her retirement in 2014 as Director of Clinical Operations from the renowned program at UCSF, overseeing more than 600 organ transplants annually.

Amy enjoys comedy in every form. She studied improv and graduated from Second City Players Workshop. She loves to swim, teach chair yoga, meditate, and kill the people she doesn't like in the pages of her books. Not to worry, she's a transplant professional so she makes use of all of the organs from her victims. Amy was recently elected to the Novato, California, City Council where she's discovering a new population of folks that may find their way into being her literary victims.

Peele's previous novel, *Cut*, was honored with the 2017 Independent Press Award, The Chanticleer International Book Award 1st in category for Mystery & Mayhem, a Pinnacle Book Achievement Award, and a Finalist designation from the 2017 International Book Awards.

Find out more about the author at amyspeele.com

SELECTED TITLES FROM SHE WRITES PRESS

She Writes Press is an independent publishing company founded to serve women writers everywhere. Visit us at www.shewritespress.com.

Cut by Amy S. Peele, 978-1-63152-184-3. *Can you buy your way up to the top of the waiting list?* In their quest to find out, transplant nurse Sarah Golden and her best friend, Jackie, end up on a sometimes fun, sometimes dangerous roller coaster ride through Miami, San Francisco, and Chicago—one from which they barely escape with their lives.

Glass Shatters by Michelle Meyers. $16.95, 978-1-63152-018-1. Following the mysterious disappearance of his wife and daughter, scientist Charles Lang goes to desperate lengths to escape his past and reinvent himself.

A Girl Like You by Michelle Cox. $16.95, 9781631520167. When the floor matron at the dance hall where Henrietta is working as a taxi dancer turns up murdered, she is persuaded by the aloof Inspector Clive Howard to go undercover to help find the killer—even as they try to withstand their growing attraction for one another.

True Stories at the Smoky View by Jill McCroskey Coupe. $16.95, 978-1-63152-051-8. The lives of a librarian and a ten-year-old boy are changed forever when they become stranded by a blizzard in a Tennessee motel and join forces in a very personal search for justice.

Water On the Moon by Jean P. Moore. $16.95, 978-1-938314-61-2. When her home is destroyed in a freak accident, Lidia Raven, a divorced mother of two, is plunged into a mystery that involves her entire family.